She Came From Socorro

Bob G. Stidham

ISBN-10:0615501028
ISBN-13:978-0615501024

SHE CAME FROM SOCORRO

DEDICATION

It will be my pleasure to dedicate this novel to the person that purchases the First copy of ***She Came From Socorro***. Notify me at bobstidham@yahoo.com and I'll send you a free copy of another of my books.

ACKNOWLEDGMENTS

I have had help from several people in my writing career. I want them to know of my deep appreciation. I will only name two of them. First, to help and encourage my efforts was **Roger Wentzel** (of Snohomish, WA.) Last, but by no means least, **Diane Stidham** contributed to this work. It was she, who named my leading character.

SHE CAME FROM SOCORRO

CHAPTER ONE

The throbbing of the chopper rotors grew in intensity until moonlight disclosed a silvery shape descending into the clearing. A cloud of dust streamed about the area before the blades decreased their speed.

The craft sat motionless for a few moments before two men stepped out, removed a human form from the interior, and deposited it against a nearby boulder. With one last act, they placed a saddlebag beside the body and gently folded the form's arm around the leather object.

"Amigo, we are done here. Let's head for the Cantina."

"Si, two things of importance wait for us only a few hours away."

"Speak for yourself. Only the money is important. Women are more easily found with money in my hand. If my woman was equal to the one we're leaving here; I might consider her important."

As the aircraft's doors swung closed the rotors surged with power. During this entire operation, not a single light was used.

Since the men knew this area well, only aid from a bright moon was needed. The visit was unseen and no prying ears were in hearing range of the helicopter.

Minutes later, the clearing returned to its natural state and the usual night noises began to prevail. The motionless female was the only change to the scene.

She was unaware of the sounds as the night winds brushed gently across her face. The breezes caressed her cheeks with constant rhythm and moved her dark hair outward.

Whenever the wind pressure ceased, her dark hair fell back and rested against her olive skin.

Though a huge New Mexico moon towered overhead, this radiance seemed wasted on the frame of the unconscious young woman. Her body was well proportioned, yet her height seemed above average.

With her back resting against the boulder, she was unaware of the coyote howling from a nearby mound. Except for the coyote and the whispering winds, the little clearing was cloaked in utter silence.

Clad in western type clothing common to the area, her jeans were slowly gathering dust from the eddying winds. The green western style shirt and riding jacket, made of brown suede leather, gave adequate protection to her upper body. The emerald green scarf hung loosely knotted around her neck with its ends protruding from the jacket. Her boots, styled for saddle work, were fashioned of tooled leather. The leather saddlebag was still nested inside her arm.

At that moment, a shooting star streaked silently across the sky in a garish blaze of light.

A noisy diesel locomotive towed a train of freight cars and gave a shrieking call into the night. The faraway sound of the whistle may have awakened the woman, but she stirred awake for whatever reason.

She failed to respond with a normal reaction to a sleep period. Instead, her eyes slowly opened as she roused. Gently, she touched her face with searching fingers. In robot-like movements she explored her legs and arms.

Then she became interested in the area of her heart. This vital body area drew her full attention for several moments until she decided that the pumping action of that organ would not cease. Suddenly, her eyes turned in the direction of her palms.

After spending several seconds in silent examination of her hands, she stood to full height and took a few steps until better balance was established, she returned to the saddlebag. She seemed lost for further direction, as though seeing this object for the first time.

After hoisting the bag to the top of the boulder, she opened the clasp. It was partially filled with objects, but she ignored them and placed her full attention on a contraption affixed to the interior lining. Her unsure fingers found a release catch under the padding and pressed it.

Instantly, the thing came alive with an eerie glow. Low garbled sounds came from a small speaker and were followed by intermittent static. She frowned at the object in dismay. When suddenly the sound increased, she nodded agreement.

"I understand, sir," she voiced aloud.

Probing at the padding, she felt for another control switch and touched it with care.

Out of the bag came a voice soft and far away. After pressing the control again, the voice grew louder and she listened to stern tones.

After a short wait the voice continued, but the woman's eyes did not stray from the device.

He paused for a moment to allow her to absorb his orders.

"Though time could become a factor in your mission, you will learn the ways and actions of a southwestern woman. You were tutored by the finest experts, using the latest available data. You are near the town of Socorro, in the State of New Mexico. You are close to Holloman Air Base and the White Sands Proving Grounds."

He paused again, as though to create suspense. The ploy seemed to work, as the woman stayed spellbound and silent. He spoke again.

"Because these installations are security conscious, it seemed the logical place to stage this mission. If your arrival had alerted one of these installations, they would assume that the other unit was the intruder. This is not your final destination though. You are here to gain a foothold, make friends, and establish an identity. These things you will do in a manner that will draw as little attention as possible."

He paused briefly.

"At the proper time, vital information will be available for you to recall. You have the ability to cope with these people and will prevail. You will know the trading methods of earth and their obsession with a thing they call money. We did not furnish you with money, but we made adjustments. Items in your bag can be traded for money. Guard them wisely, for there will be no replacement."

He paused to allow for her full understanding of his words before explain her upcoming agenda.

"Your priorities are to find housing, food, and clothing. After establishing these basics needs of life, you will obtain a means of transportation known as an automobile. This will allow you to cover more area in your mission. Keep this transmission unit in your possession at all times. If I have sudden need for you, I want you available. I will give no further details of the mission until you have completed this first phase."

"I have many questions," she said haltingly.

"I shall answer three," he said with finality in his voice.

A short pause followed as she pondered his insulting tone. She became somewhat more irate, though she did not understand why.

"Then forget it. I shall ask you none."

"As you wish," he replied hatefully and closed the transmission device.

Unsure of her next proper step, she removed a few of the objects from the saddlebag and placed them atop the boulder. They felt heavy, but they could hardly be examined properly by moonlight. She chose eight flat pieces and placed them in her jacket pocket.

At the edge of the clearing she viewed the night sky and gazed in all directions. With moonlight enhancing her vision, she saw the outlines of nearby rising foothills. From earlier training, she recognized these as the foothills of a small range known as the Los Pinos Mountains. Looking southward, lights shattered the darkness between her and another distant range of mountains. The distance to these lights matched Alexi's estimation of less than two hours walking time. Gazing once more toward the stars, she guessed the time to be four hours till dawn. If she wanted to attract a minimum of attention, her entry into town must wait until the residents were up and about their daily business.

Shivering slightly from the prevailing early morning chill, she buttoned her jacket. She did not need sleep and little need existed for rest. Still, with nothing else to do for four hours, she returned to the clearing and the boulder.

Unable to find a comfortable position in the area of the huge rock, she delayed the idea of sleep. It was time to gather her wits and think about her situation.

This is not happening to me. This is only a dream and I'm sleeping somewhere in safe comfort.

The mournful howl of a coyote jolted her back to reality. She was in the wilds of New Mexico and only God and Alexi knew the reason she was here. She had no memory, but he said she was not from this place. He hinted that she came from another world. If truth lay in that hint, how did she get here? If she had a name, she should know it. If she had a mission to fulfill, someone must have briefed her.

It was as if she had been born at this boulder, as there was no recollection of anything earlier. He said she had been tutored and would know things of importance when the proper time came. If he thought those words gave her courage and strength, he was terribly mistaken.

She tried to envision some circumstance that might endanger her in Socorro. Thoughts swelled from her worried mind. What will these people be like? Will they suspect that I'm from another world? What will I say when they ask my name? Without memory of my past, how can I answer their questions? If I lack confidence, it will be difficult to confront these earth people.

The early morning chill seeped into her bones, though she soon passed into a fitful sleep. Nearby, still wasting his mournful howls, the coyote continued trying to lure a mate to his area. The other sounds of the night went unnoticed as well.

She awoke to warm sunshine. After a few moments of exposure to the sun's heat, she moved to a sitting position and looked about the area. Thirsty and without a canteen, she realized the urgency of moving toward town. Patting her jacket pocket with a light touch, she discovered the objects were still there. Rising, she angled the bag across a shoulder and left the clearing.

Her stomach was growling with hunger pains, her throat was dry with thirst and the rocky terrain was killing her feet. Because saddle boots were not designed for mountain walking, they seemed driven toward giving her a memory that she could never forget.

Many surprises might lie ahead at Socorro, but her present ordeal was nearly over. Having slept late and walking slowly because of her boots, much of the morning was already spent. Nearing the edge of town, she saw several people who were out and busy with chores. Although she had not seen her own image, their limbs looked identical to her own. Perhaps this was the reason she had been selected for this mission.

After a few minutes of walking, she began to notice motels and fast food shops. Amazingly, she recognized these places and their use. A part of her training was beginning to take charge. Alexi had not exaggerated his claim that she was well prepared.

Peering closely as she passed, she was so intent in looking at the business signs that she ignored the people on the street. They gave her only a casual glance and continued on their way. Unsure of what she sought, was there a chance she might not find it? A few seconds later she noticed a storefront that drew all her interest. The letters of *Dugan's Diggings* was formed by a neon sign in the window. With a deep breath, she opened the door and heard the tinkling bell that announced her arrival. An energetic man, seemingly in his early fifties, quickly came to the front and greeted her.

"Good morning. I'm the owner of this shop. May I help you with something?"

A period of silence elapsed before she answered. "I hope so, sir. I had a horrible experience and found myself walking. I only speak of it because I'm now without money. We were on the way to Albuquerque when his personality changed. I can't believe I misjudged him so badly during our meeting in Tucson. He took my purse with cash and credit cards. I'd go to the authorities and report the theft, but I might have to see him again if they catch him. He didn't know I had valuables that my Aunt Clarita bequeathed me. Now, I must part with some of them."

"I'm sorry to hear of your trouble. I'll help you if I can, but you must tell the credit card people that your cards were stolen. Now, let me have a look at your aunt's valuables and I'll see what I can do."

He examined them through a magnifier before carrying them to the scales and weighing them separately. Each of the eight objects weighed the same. With no obvious flaws, the clean lines seemed perfect in every detail.

After entering the total weight on a jot pad, he peered at them through the magnifying glass. They were a perfectly matched set. With a face clearly showing his excitement, he turned to the young woman.

"Your aunt must have been a rich lady. This is some of the finest work I've seen. After examining them closely for flaws, I've found none."

"These were created by a master artist," he added. "But not here in the States. I've studied and can recognize the work of any noted artist in North America. I've seen many good things from Mexico, but not of this quality. These objects must have come from Europe or the mid-eastern sector of the world. Did your aunt travel in any of these regions?"

"Yes, she traveled most of the world. She had few relatives and left four heirs. I got the collection of valuables and the remaining three heirs shared her other assets."

"Have you had these things appraised?"

"No, I've always had employment that kept me in funds."

"Maybe your relatives will help you through this problem and you can hang onto the valuables. If you wish, you can use my phone."

"They won't help me. We didn't get along well and they resent my getting any portion of the will. These people are from Aunt Clarita's husband's side of the family. My aunt took me in and raised me after I was orphaned by a storm that struck near Fort Lauderdale, Florida.

"You're fortunate in coming to my shop. I always conduct business in an honest and open manner. My profits may not be as big as other dealers, but I hold my head high. You'll get a fair deal from me. I won't worry about these objects being stolen, either. When items this precious are stolen, it's put on the wire right away."

With worry in her voice, she questioned him.

"Do we have a problem here? I expected haggling since you agree that they are valuable and I need funds. Why have we suddenly hit a snag?"

"I'm sorry, young lady. I'm a little amazed by your valuables. Another dealer might strike a quick deal, based on your need and his greed, but I won't do that. I honestly don't have enough money to buy these items. I doubt if the whole town of Socorro has enough working capital to buy your objects. This is a small town and wealth is not one of our best-kept secrets."

"I see us with two options," he said carefully. You can choose the one you prefer. I can buy one of your items. With the money, you can afford to wait for other dealers to come here and bid on your valuables. Shipping them to a dealer on consignment is the other option.

"I'm so lacking in experience, I simply can't make this decision. What do you recommend, please?"

"Well, first off, don't make it known that you're a wealthy woman. Public knowledge that you have these expensive items could bring trouble and you've already had some of that. We'll quietly handle the sales here in town. It'll take some my savings to buy just one of your items."

He added quickly.

"I may have it a bit rough until I get a buyer here and turn the sale, but that's the best suggestion that I can offer."

"We've not discussed a price and you expect some hardship until you make a re-sale. You *must* be an honest man. I may have a better plan. Try seeing us as business partners in this venture. Advance money to me that I might establish housing, food, and a down payment on an automobile. I won't need much money until you get a buyer. When you make a deal, we'll split the proceeds sixty five percent for me and thirty five percent for you."

"Your offer will help both of us. This gives me time to have several buyers come here and offer bids for your items if necessary. If we do as you suggest, then we should offer two of the pieces for sale. I won't hold you to the same percentage on the second, as you offered for the one item. That would be unfair to you."

"I made the offer and I stand by it. You are a godsend to me during troubled times. I really appreciate it. If you space out the sales, we'll sell several pieces before we're through. I want to get settled and find some type of employment."

"As I said earlier, this is a small town and except for the mining university, most everything is part time work. It wouldn't be proper for a lady of your means to be working for minimum wages. You saw the motels and fast food shops; they're about the only ones hiring help."

"Albuquerque is my destination. I'll stay until our sale is done. I like this place. I'd love to live here if I could afford it."

"Since we're partners, just call me Sam," he said and extended his hand.

"My name is Katie Ryan. Just call me Katie, if you wish."

"I like the sound of our names as temporary business partners," he hooted. "Look out world Ryan and Dugan are here."

Suddenly, he frowned and looked strangely at Katie. It surprised her and she waited for a clue to his strange action. He walked to the register and pulled out several twenty-dollar bills. With a downcast look, he placed them before her.

"I'm sorry, but I've completely lost my manners and senses. You probably haven't eaten anything in hours and you've been in here for nearly an hour. Go across the street to the diner. They serve a fine breakfast. When you're done, go to the shop two doors down and buy yourself a handbag or purse. If you need other things, get them and tell Thelma to call me."

Without a word she nodded and left the store. She felt hunger, but her main priority was a bathroom. Because of this need, thirst was forgotten.

On entering the diner, her eye caught the rest room sign and she sped in that direction. The first priority was taken care of and then came the lavvy work.

Placing the bag within easy reach, she began removing the trail dust damage to her face. Through lovely green eyes, her image looked back at her from the mirror and she smiled with approval at what she saw.

Though her facial features seemed more attractive than these earth people, her appearance was strikingly similar to theirs. If they saw her in the same light, she had an advantage in this new world.

She sponged the dust from her hairline by using a paper towel. Washing her hands and face generously in the cold Socorro water was very stimulating.

In a window view booth, with the bag safely tucked beside her, she had time to consider what had come to pass. Without even thinking, she fabricated a story that convinced Sam how much she needed his assistance. Aunt Clarita would become her favorite aunt, even though she was deceased.

Surprisingly, she was conversing in nearly the same slang mixed language that prevailed in Socorro. This alone seemed remarkable, but from where did she get this name Katie Ryan? There had been no hesitation when she introduced herself to Sam. How had she known about a down payment requirement for purchasing a car? So many things seemed unexplainable and her memory still refused to extend beyond that boulder in the hills. Lost in thought, Katie gazed ahead at the far wall.

"Miss, your food is here."

"I'm sorry. My mind was far away just now."

As she ate, she began to make plans. Things were working out unbelievably well. Sam would expect her to remain in Socorro until her valuables were sold. This offered an excuse to settle here for a while. Though employment seemed unavailable, having a job was not a priority item now that Sam had moved to help her. Finding a place to live became the next area in which to direct her attention. She did not intend to sleep in the big outdoors again.

Done with her meal and her thoughts, she paid at the register. It was time to buy a few personal things.

Thelma's shop was crammed full of things through which any woman would love to browse. Katie knew what items were needed and began collecting them in serious fashion. She found feminine things and then spent time in the shoe department.

In looking at the assortment of things, she calculated that she would be far short of funds. She located Thelma at the register and deposited her haul atop the counter.

"It looks like you need to call Sam, at Dugan's Diggings. We're working out a deal, but it's still not all put together."

"Whatever Sam says is as good as gold," Thelma laughed.

Picking up the phone, she punched his number from memory and began a lively conversation. In a few minutes, she hung up and turned to Katie.

"He's coming over right away. He told me to give you anything you wanted and he's bringing more money."

Since she chose sport clothing, finding three changes of clothing was not difficult. She would need other articles of clothing later.

It took little time for Sam to pay for her purchases and when they could break away from the bubbly Thelma, the pair walked back across the street to his store.

Sam's wife was at the register when they entered and he made introductions. Rosalie Dugan was an attractive woman. Though not as old as Sam, she had luckily avoided the aging process that often strikes at mid-life.

She wore a mysterious look of intrigue that could have been born of her obvious Indian ancestry. Her olive skin carried a deeper tone than that of Katie, but was somehow similar. Her dark, piercing eyes could draw and hold the attention of anyone that she met. When those mysterious organs of sight were turned toward Katie, they seemed to look through and beyond. The Indian woman seemed to be probing for information as she focused on Katie.

"Sam told me of your plan. I'm grateful for your generous offer. It will make us a little richer, but I sense there is a deeper purpose. Though I'm not known as a suspicious woman, I'll wait to see if this plan is beneficial to all of us. I hope you'll forgive an older woman's doubts."

"There *is* a deeper purpose, Rosalie. I want to settle in Socorro for a while. I have a need to put down new roots somewhere. There's some unhappiness in my past and I need time before I move on."

"I could sense that, but it goes deeper. Now is not the time to delve into things that could be none of my business. If you ever need to confide in someone, just call me," she said knowingly.

"We've taken up enough of her time in personal talk today," Sam said hurriedly. "I have to tally up the balance that she needs for basic essentials."

"I want a small furnished house. If money is available, I'll take anything Rosalie approves."

"Get a motel room for tonight. I'll have a place for you tomorrow. I'll see you at home, Sam."

"I'll make no apologies for Rosalie," he said. "She always speaks her mind and irritates some people, but she is usually close to the mark."

"She's a lovely person. I'd like to spend more time with her, if she's willing."

"We'll see how it goes. To get back to our deal, I called a buyer in Tucson. He'll be here in two days. Unless this buyer makes an offer of ten thousand, we'll send him packing."

"Your items are flawless," he added. "They'll be prized by some of the wealthier people in Phoenix and Tucson."

"I want to take the route that works best in the first stage of our partnership. I'll gladly leave these routine details to you."

"Though you may not stay long in Socorro, we should go to the bank and set up an account. It's hard for a stranger and I'm sure it'd be harder for a lady without identification. I'll introduce you to Fred Wallace. He's an honest man. If you need a car, he can help with that too. His bank finances automobiles for the public."

"You must have been sent by an angel to help in my time of need. I may never be able to repay all these favors."

"Well, you're trying to make me a richer man. That's a good start towards doing me a favor. I'll get the helper and let him watch the store while we're gone."

Fred Wallace was an impressive gentleman. Stylishly handsome, the possession of a powerful aura made the banker an even more magnetic figure.

Taller than Katie, and carrying the weight that often comes with middle age, he peered at her from behind his magnificent desk. Introductions went well and he seemed impressed with her, although Sam opened the conversation.

"Fred, this young lady has seen some trouble and needs help. She owns some very valuable assets, but no ID and no cash. She told me most of the details, but we'll keep them private for now if you don't mind. She'll stay in Socorro for a spell and I'm trying to help her get located. We entered a partnership to liquidate some of her valuables and she needs to open an account."

"Did you just happen to walk into Sam's shop, or did someone refer you to him?"

Fred asked this honest question in a suspicious tone of voice and looked at her closely.

"I just walked in to his place, Mr. Wallace."

"With Sam's backing, I see no problem with the banking requirements. Do you want to fill out an application now, or return it later?"

"We're here and if you have the time, you might help with the details."

"It'll be my pleasure, young lady. I have no appointments waiting."

After completing the form she passed the paper to the banker and waited patiently for him to examine it.

He scanned the form and turned a worried look at her.

"I'm sorry you have no living relatives. You've listed Clarita Cromwell as being deceased. Family life is real big here in New Mexico."

"You also failed to list your Social Security number," he added. "Miss Ryan, a federal requirement insists that you have that number on your form."

"I intend to apply for one," she replied.

"Okay, we'll open the account with a flagged note. Bring the number to me when the feds send you a card. I don't normally run the bank's business in this fashion, but I trust the judgment of Sam. You can't be a serious risk, if he vouches for you."

"I'll show you how much I believe in her. Take five thousand from my savings and credit it to her account," Sam said. "This venture with her could make my old age be a bit easier to accept. Katie, may I show one of the collector pieces to Fred?"

Seeing her nod of assent, he pulled an object from his pocket and handed it across the desk. Fred took the gold piece, examined both sides of the metal object, and then exhaled sharply.

"You're the expert. If you say this piece of good quality gold, then it's a winner. I can see that the quality of design is excellent. May I ask how you acquired this valuable piece?"

"It was given to me by Aunt Clarita Cromwell's will. She accumulated a rather large collection of items during her travels overseas. I suppose she remembered how much I loved her collection. I have no expertise with collections, or their value. I'm lucky that fate lead me to Sam's door."

Fred was deeply impressed by this young woman and her valuable item. Still, he felt a need to voice some old fashioned wisdom toward the pair.

"If this partnership works, you both have been blessed by fate. Some joint ventures fare quite well, but I've seen many of them fail. Drop in tomorrow morning and I'll have bank checks and deposit slips for you. If you need my help with anything else, feel free to give me a call."

"Mr. Wallace, I appreciate your offer very much. I'll likely need your advice in the coming days."

As they walked back to Sam's shop, the talk was of this day and how much had been accomplished. It was the type of conversation that flows between the oldest of friends.

"Let's go inside this luggage shop. In this county, ladies don't enter a motel without luggage."

With her purchases and the saddlebag packed inside the luggage, she eagerly looked forward to the comforts of a motel room. Sam phoned the manager of a nearby motel complex and the man graciously insisted on sending a car to get her.

"Earlier today, I prepared a document that explains our agreement. It shows that I'm in possession of eight of your valuables. The agreement describes the valuables and lists their weight. I also promised to not sell them without your written consent. If you have no objections, I'll keep the items in my safe. If you agree to this, we'll sign it and the deal is done."

He gave her a copy of the signed contract and placed his copy in the cash register. After storing the valuables in his safe, he turned back to face her.

"I'd bet this has been the longest day of your life, young lady."

"I'm totally exhausted. It'll be good to get there and freshen up. You've done huge favors for me today, Sam. I didn't know that people like you still existed."

"I sometimes read people correctly and I believe you're worth any effort I've made on your behalf. In words and actions, you show a huge amount of self-respect."

A car horn's beep stopped the flow of talk and she loaded into the vehicle for a ride to her first opportunity of comfort. She found the motel adequate in every way.

Checking the room with a sharp eye, she moved the bed and hid the saddlebag behind it on the floor. Returning the bed to its former position, she decided the bag was as safe as she could make it for the night. She then explored the bath possibilities.

When morning came and after the amazing glory of the sunrise had passed, she sipped coffee at the manager's office.

With lots of spare time and with the stimulation received from the dark liquid, she concentrated on her situation. She wanted to find answers and set a few goals.

Despite not yet knowing the reason for being sent to this place, she still felt grateful. There was a sense of peace here that was becoming increasingly attractive. This seemed to be a place that would accept you with open arms if you were worthy.

Without memory of a past and hesitant about a future, Katie homed in on the present with a keen sense of enthusiasm.

Concerned about her valuables, she removed the saddlebag from behind the bed. She decided they were not really safe until they were in the bank.

Fred saw her enter the bank and moved swiftly toward her. He wore a look of concern on his face and spoke carefully as he reached her.

"Miss Ryan, is everything all right? I didn't expect you so early."

"Nothing is wrong, Mr. Wallace. I just feel uncomfortable about the safety of this saddlebag. It has the balance of my aunt's valuables inside and should be kept in a safe place. Can you handle this problem for me?"

"Of course we can," he replied. "We only charge a small fee and I'll be happy to assist you."

He gave her a soft cloth bag and a key before leaving her alone.

Under the brightness of the bank's light fixtures, she got her first good look at the items given her for trading purposes. Though admittedly an amateur, the collection seemed exquisite. Slowly, she placed them into the cloth bag. This action took very little time and then she returned to the bank's main area. With saddlebag in hand, she waited for Fred to approach.

"I have some banking items you may need before your personalized ones return from the printer. If you sign this form, we'll deduct the deposit box charge from your account."

Katie was learning the importance of having good friends.

SHE CAME FROM SOCORRO

CHAPTER TWO

In the district's core, she found a small building that housed a Social Security System branch office. Pausing only a moment, she steeled her nerves and went inside. If her odd pattern held true, she would know how to fill out the forms when the time came. The friendly representative at the counter glanced carefully at her completed form and had only one remark.

"You've gone a long time without a job," he said with a smile. "Please advise us when you get a permanent address. General delivery will do for now, but notify us of any address change."

She continued walking through the district with the thought of employment weighing on her mind. With a social security number, she was now legally employable. A much larger worry was the background information that most employers demand. How deep would their search into her schooling and references go? Sam and Fred's references might not satisfy an interviewer, even if she remained in Socorro.

Most people she met during her walk took second looks as they passed. Socorro held much promise as a place to live, but that would have to be cleared with Alexi.

Returning from the town core, she walked toward Sam's shop. She was eager to learn if they had located a place for her to live.

He greeted her with his usual happy face, though busy with a customer. She dawdled about the display shelves in search of an interest until Sam was free. The sight of Rosalie entering from the back room broke her idle thoughts.

"Hello, Katie. I came to the shop to get a message to you. I think you should keep your motel room for a few days. I have the ideal place for you, but it won't be available for a while. One of my friends spent the last few months learning to live among white people. She's done well in that respect, but her heart is back on the reservation. She wants to close her shop temporarily and return to her old life. I think a love interest helped sway her into making that decision. She has a nice little home. You can get the place for a lease arrangement, or through monthly rental. Though your stay in Socorro may be temporary, you can save money over the motel's cost."

"It sounds great to me. I don't mind putting up at the motel while she works things out."

"I'll see you later in the week. I'm going down to Reba's shop now and help her inventory everything for consignment."

With Sam's customer out the door, he turned to Katie with a question.

"I didn't expect to see you before noon. What are you up to today?"

"I walked over this entire town during the morning, Sam. It's one of the friendliest places I've seen. I also rented a safe deposit box from the bank to store the remainder of my valuables."

"That's a wise move and I'll follow your lead unless our buyer comes up with a decent offer."

The next morning, she began working with the saddlebag to remove the transmission device. Padding protected the device against damage. It was small enough to transfer to the larger of her two handbags. Safety pins from a local variety store secured the padded unit to her purse lining.

Later, with the purse strap over her shoulder, she walked leisurely down the sidewalk. Giving little notice to the shop windows as she moved along, Katie proved to be a woman of purpose. The jewelry shop was her destination and a timepiece was her goal.

She dawdled in the store until her choice was made. After adjusting it to her wrist, he set the watch to the correct time of day. Smugly satisfied, she paid for her purchases and left the shop. Aiming her gait in the direction of Sam's shop, she meant to be present during the buyer's visit. She would take no role in the transaction unless asked.

Their expertise with valuables and collectibles needed no input except her final acceptance. Once inside the shop, she heard they were in Sam's office.

"They've been busy for a while now," Steve the helper said.

"It makes no difference to me. I only want to be present if they need me. If I can help with any of your tasks while I'm waiting, just let me know."

"Thanks for offering, but things are pretty slow today."

She browsed patiently until the office door opened.

"I'm glad you came early, Katie. We have a real development here."

Introductions were made and Claude Pepper grew impressed with Katie.

"How very unique this situation gets? To find an exceptional collection owned by an outstanding young lady is extremely rare. Please excuse me if I embarrass you, but I appreciate beauty in all things," Pepper said glibly.

He swiftly added, "I'm sure you have been told and will be told again, that you possess more than your fair share of beauty."

"Honestly, you're the first man in this state to mention my looks. When a compliment is handed out, I'm like most women. I appreciate them if I know they're sincere."

"If I were twenty years younger, I'd take advantage of the fact that the men of this state are either blind or married. I'm sorry to carry on so, but I *am* impressed. I think I ought to get back to the business at hand."

"Katie, he wanted to see the other pieces of the collection and I showed them," Sam said with rising excitement. "Oh shoot, I'm way too excited for this. You lay it out to her, Claude."

"I don't know how long it's been since your aunt came into possession of these pieces, or what amount of money she paid for them, but that has little effect on today's market. They could only be more valuable if their history was known. Sam tells me that you know nothing of their origin."

"My aunt traveled most of the world. She left nothing to indicate the area of their purchase."

"I don't want to buy the two pieces that you are offering. It would be a world class tragedy to divide this collection. Sam says you have more articles in your collection. Are they similar to these eight pieces?"

"Only eight pieces are alike. I'm disappointed that you aren't going to buy our offer?"

"Nonsense, I want to buy all the pieces you have and if there are only eight, then I'll buy the lot. I've made an offer to Sam, but I'll repeat it to you. I'll be happy to make out a check for one hundred and fifty thousand dollars for these eight pieces as an unbroken set."

Where most owners would have danced with pleasure on hearing this news, she was unruffled. Somewhere from within her psyche came an understanding that he was making an honest offer for a very valuable collection. She waited several moments to comprehend this huge sum of money that Pepper was eager to spend. Had Alexi's superiors miscalculated the worth of these trade items?

While she waited and pondered this colossal moment, Pepper looked as if he would burst due to the delay. Sam was trembling with excitement. This deal could help secure a decent retirement for his future.

He saw his share of the original agreement as amounting to a lot of money. This was a nice nest egg for Rosalie, should anything happen to him.

"I told Sam at the beginning, that I knew nothing of the value of these items. I look now for him to voice his approval and I'll abide by his decision."

"Claude's offer is more than I expected," Sam said eagerly. "In the past, he's been very fair with me. I questioned his ability to resell these items for a profit. He assured me that in Phoenix, he'll have no trouble in turning a sale to wealthy people whose only purpose in life seems to be in finding items like these."

"That's the truth. I'll have a showing at one of the better hotels and at least forty people will attend. These items will go that very day and I expect to get a return of ten percent, maybe even more. Your items are very precious, young lady."

"Since she is letting me do the yea or nay thing, this is a done deal," Sam said happily.

"Let's go to your bank and I'll transfer the money to your account. I'm hot to take this collection back to Phoenix."

The conference at Fred Wallace's desk finally ended and after a phone call to Pepper's bank, the obligation of the buyer was over. Claude took his leave, but their business was not quite complete.

Fred eyed them and asked a simple question.

"How does your partnership divide this draft?"

"I'm the major partner," she replied. "Sam gets thirty seven thousand five hundred of the amount."

"Now Katie, our deal was only for two of the items. You really ought to be more careful with your money."

"I told you partnerships don't always work out. Partners always seem to have problems. Already, she is trying to give you more money that you expected. I just don't believe you two, not at all," Fred told them.

"Sam has no voice in this instance, Mr. Wallace. Any further deals we make as a team will be for fifteen percent of sale. During my time of desperation, I really needed someone and he was there. For that reason alone, I will always be grateful."

For two weeks, she lived peacefully in her new place. On this night, the house was quiet and allowed more time to study her situation. She thought of the statements that she made earlier to her new friends.

After all the good things he'd done for her, why had she lied to Sam about being orphaned in Fort Lauderdale?

Gnawing in the corners of her mind was an oddly conceived notion.

It began to grow in size and importance. For hours, she paced and when morning came, she made a small pot of coffee.

Bone tired, physically and mentally, she sipped the coffee and began to relax.

A plan had been born this night. If it survived and grew to her full expectations, she would have roots.

Her training might not have included Fort Lauderdale, but she meant to go there.

When she told Sam about going to Florida, they had their first argument. He was irked about her taking the long trip and wasted no words in telling her of his feelings.

"It's just something that I have to do, Sam. I appreciate your concern, but I think a trip to Florida may solve some problems. I'll only be gone a short while and when I get back, I want to go looking for a job."

"I'll worry until you return. You've become almost like a daughter to me."

"You can't know how much those words mean to me. Take care of yourself and we'll talk more when I return."

The next day, Steven drove her to the Albuquerque airport complex. The vehicle angled to the curb at the departures entrance. He turned her luggage over to a redcap and waved good-bye.

After checking in at the ticket counter, she found a seat and began the wait until departure time. She passed the time by watching others who intended to fly, or were awaiting the arrival of a plane. An air of sadness prevailed in the people passing nearby. Knowing their loved ones were departing for some period of time brought a measure of sorrow.

Selfishly, she wished someone were there to cry for her departure. A few hours later, the sleek jet squealed its tires on impact and settled heavily onto the Miami runway at breakneck speed.

Katie grimaced as the pilot applied the brakes and the jet trembled uneasily while hydraulic pressure was bringing the speed under control.

Just a few moments elapsed and they were at the gate. She dodged a group of people embracing their loved ones and felt that icy chill of loneliness again.

Forcing a smile and squaring her shoulders determinedly, she moved toward the sidewalk and a taxi. She inhaled the fresh air before hailing a passing cab.

"Take me to Fort Lauderdale, please. I want to locate as near the downtown area as I can and still find a good motel."

"I can manage that easy enough. I grew up and went to high school. I know my way around that town like the inside of my cab."

"I want to find the City Hall records building. I need to track down some of my family."

"Just leave it to me, lady. I know a fine motel that's just three blocks from City Hall."

With the talkative cabby under the wheel, the twenty-five mile trip went rather fast. He pointed out many sights along the way. It was a beautiful day and the highway hung alongside the beach most of their route. At their destination, he made another concession to his fare.

"I'll take you by the City Hall first and then drive to your motel. That way you won't have to ask strangers for directions. A lady should be very careful with strangers while in Fort Lauderdale."

Like a giant sleepy kitten, Katie yawned and stretched across the bed.

She was sleeping in late this morning and enjoying it immensely.

It was easy to blame her laziness onto the jet flight, whether true or not. Whatever the reason, it was giving her an opportunity to relax and think.

She rehearsed her plans during the morning's final preparations. Her scheme could definitely work and all she needed was a little luck in the right places. The time she spent now in doing her hair could pay dividends at City Hall.

She knew she was attractive, but enhancing her looks was an added incentive. Satisfied by what she saw in the mirror, she could only hope that others saw her in the same light.

Pretending to study a standard form at City Hall, she waited near the counter until a male clerk was available. As she approached the window, she saw that his nice blue eyes sparked with interest.

"Good morning, Miss. May I help you in some way? It would be my pleasure."

"I certainly hope so. I'm searching for a family named Ryan. They're supposed to be from here, but I have no available addresses."

"Just a moment and I'll bring the PQR book."

Upon his return, he motioned toward a desk and an elderly lady took his spot at the window. Beckoning Katie to a vacant area of the counter, he opened the large volume to the R section.

"Vital Statistics at your service," he said with a smile. "I have to stay with the book, you know."

She gave him her most dazzling smile and the impact nearly knocked him down. If help was available, she would get help.

"I believe I need expert advice. My name is Katie. What may I call you?"

"I'm David Brooks and part of my job is in making sure that the public understands our system. If I can help, just let me know."

"David, let me tell you how important it is that I find these people. There's an inheritance involved and it's a sizable one. I'm authorized to pay a finders fee for information leading to their location dead or alive. The agents of the deceased want very much to settle this estate. All we have to do is find them or discover indisputable proof of their death."

"Well now, do I qualify for that finder's fee? I can do wonders with this system when I'm furnished with an incentive," he said.

"I can qualify anyone that I choose. If you can dig it out of your system, you're the man."

"I'll explain this much to you. Everything is in the computer now. The normal usage of these books is to make quickie checks on people. I can get a printout for every Ryan that was born, lived, or died in the city of Fort Lauderdale. It might consist of a large folder, or a single sheet of paper. I can have this ready in time to take you to lunch. You will buy, I'm sure," he smiled again.

Darn! He has a knockout smile. "Lunch sounds wonderful. I wouldn't dare turn you down?"

"Thanks a lot for considering yourself my hostage" he frowned.

Later, they walked to a Cajun style joint fronting the beach. She decided that David was a charming companion. He held a tan folder in one hand until they reached their table. When they were seated, he opened the folder for her to see. Twenty pages listed the Ryan name at an average of twelve individuals per page and included updates.

"Just to brief you, each Ryan item has pertinent information that reflects addresses, date of birth, date of death and it even gives family connections in some instances," he said helpfully.

Upon arrival of the waiter, they put the folder away. David suggested the Bourbon Chicken dinner and chose white wine. She hopefully agreed with his choice and they resumed their conversation.

"I'm not allowed to take printouts from the Hall without supervisory approval. A job like mine isn't easy to come by. I hope you won't let this go beyond you and me."

"I'll be discreet, David. Who could I possibly tell? I am from so far out of town that I could be from another planet. I'm staying at the Marrioti Inn nearby. I'll give you my room and phone number before you return to work. If there's no proof in this folder, you'll still receive a sizable compensation. You seem to have done your best."

"If you have problems locating any of these Ryan families, make a note. I can easily go back in the computer and check for updates. I may do some follow-up on them later anyway. The credit bureau owes me a few favors."

They grew quiet, as the waiter began delivering their order. The aroma of Cajun food turned her appetite to a high level and she devoured the chicken.

David matched her pace and after finishing the meal they had more wine. She felt satisfied in body and spirit, but her head began aching. Something in her psyche was trying to surface again. What was the cause of so much loneliness and depression?

"I'm sorry, but I must leave as soon as we can get the check. I think I'm developing a wine headache. I really need to get back to the motel."

He signaled to the waiter and the man came immediately with their check in hand. David placed a generous tip on the table and escorted her to the cashier.

"I'll pay this check," he said firmly as she fumbled her purse. "I was joking with you at the Hall. It is a privilege and pleasure to dine with a beautiful lady. I'd love to have a chance to enjoy dinner and candlelight with you before you leave our city."

"What a nice offer, David. I appreciate the thought of dining with you and I'm sure we can make that happen. When you have time, call me at room ten," she said.

They parted on the sidewalk, with each going in different directions. He was hoping to see her again in a more personal fashion. Whereas, Katie was merely thinking that in finding him at the city hall window, she had been extremely fortunate.

Later, the Ryan files were arranged neatly on the circular motel table. A short nap had chased her headache and she was ready for work.

Having formed the framework of a plan back in Socorro, she began to give it more substance.

Since she had lied herself into a corner, she must now build a firmer foundation based on the dates of those lies. She needed to find a female Ryan with the letter K in her given name. She hoped to find someone near her age, but she could make her age agree with theirs. Intuition told her that few background checks would dig deeper than to establish a date of birth and school records.

She scanned the pages that covered her chosen time. Her interest perked quickly when she found an entry listing the address for a Henry and Leona Ryan.

A birth date for Katherine Ryan was listed and it seemed ideally suited.

Surprisingly, there was no further mention of this Ryan family.

Puzzled by the lack of data, she decided that David might have an answer. He had certainly been interested. Surely he would call.

The balance of the afternoon was very boring. She could do nothing without more direction from David. Idly, she opened her purse and removed her checkbook. Though nothing substantial had developed from David's assistance, she intended to reward him. He risked his job for her, though she neither asked nor expected him to go so far. She filled out the check, but excluded the amount and the date.

Something tugged at her mind, but could not quite break free from her mental haze. This was happening with more frequency, but still nothing would surface. Eventually, some clue might come shining through the fog and bring enlightenment.

Twilight was closing in when the phone rang and she jumped as if shot. There were only two possibilities, the motel management or David and she eagerly grabbed the phone.

"This is David speaking. Have I caught you at a bad time?"

"No! You certainly have not. I'm just sitting here, bored out of my mind. I'm very thankful that you called."

"I don't want to be a pest. Still, I'm hoping you might do dinner with me tonight. There are so many things that I want to know about you."

"I'd love having dinner with you, but there is nothing about me that deserves much interest."

"I'd prefer to be the judge of that, my lady. I'll see you at seven, if that works for you."

With elated spirits, she began preparing early. There was a hair salon associated with the inn and she prayed silently for an open slot in their appointment book.

She laid out the nicest sport outfit that she had brought and sighed in dismay.

"Oh God, please don't let him select a fancy place for us."

Later, their date was going splendidly at a nice type of establishment. To prevent a recurrence of headaches, she chose non-alcoholic drinks and he was drinking a rum based selection.

He tried extremely hard to learn of her family, her schooling, and her hometown by means of common conversation.

She skillfully countered his questions by repeating almost the same answer.

"I'm not trying to be a woman of mystery. I've really had a rather boring life."

It was time to stop before his questions became prying.

Their conversation then began to center on the Ryan files.

She pulled the one appropriate sheet from her purse and handed it to him.

"It's too bad there's no recent information on this family. I believe they're the ones that I want."

"This is unreal," he said after scanning the sheet. "I'm surprised that so many years have passed without an update. This is becoming a challenge and I love challenges. It may take the combination of some old fashioned detective work and help from the computer world, but I'll dig into it first thing tomorrow."

She kissed him lightly when they said goodnight. She was appreciative of his assistance and companionship, but she must not lead him on.

This friendly relationship was not going beyond friendly.

She owed him a great deal, but she would pay off with money and their relationship would be ended.

One day soon, she hoped it would be possible to have a meaningful romantic relationship.

Without credit cards and hating the problems of offering an out of state check for goods or services, she'd brought along considerable cash.

She decided to walk down to a nearby strip mall and buy new clothing. By spending hours shopping in the stores and dallying in the deli at lunchtime, she depleted most of the working day.

Like a victorious maiden warrior following a battle with a worthy foe, she returned to the inn with her purchases. It had been a very good day. About seven in the evening, her phone rang sharply.

"May I come over for a short visit? I may have some good news for you."

"Please do, David," she replied hastily. "I can use a little good news. We can order food from room service. Their menu looks promising."

On his arrival, she could see that he had brought more folders. His grin was wider than a mailbox and he was itching to talk.

"Don't say a word until we've ordered our food. I'm very anxious to hear your news, but it can wait another five minutes."

When the food order was placed, she gave him the go-ahead signal and he began his account.

"I turned every file we had and called in every favor that was owed me, but there was nothing. In desperation, I thought of the school system. Every kid must go to school until they're past sixteen. When I called the Superintendent's office, he pulled up his files and faxed me the records on Katherine Ryan. Her last year showed up as a sophomore. She passed her grades that year with exceptional ability, but never returned in the fall. No requests were ever logged for transferring her grades to another school. The superintendant was surprised that no inquiries were received regarding her grades."

"Normally, I would have stopped at that point," he added. "Instead of getting off a cold trail, I called the Post Office. I must remember that I owe them big time. They sent a clerk to their morgue, as they call it, and his search showed absolutely no change of address. I thanked them and was almost ready to cave in when I remembered one thing that I had overlooked. Our files only list births, deaths, and marriages. To go further I needed police help. I called a detective that I knew in school. I also owe *him* a big favor. He checked the missing person book and made a strange discovery. Are you ready for this information, Katie?"

"Hell yes! I'm hanging on the edge of my seat," she answered impatiently.

"According to police reports, two families, a total of seven people, landed on a small stretch of land near Fort Lauderdale. They arrived in a small sailboat, lunched for a short while and then sailed from the beach. A sudden storm with gale force winds blew up in the area. The stormy squall lasted for almost an hour and when it was over, according to the locals there, their boat was gone. They were never seen again and were listed as missing. My detective friend tells me they will be declared legally dead next summer. Is this an amazing story or what?"

She sat quietly for a few moments. Was it disappointment, or relief, that caused her shoulders to sag? This is not what she expected from this trip? Her hastily formed plan back in Socorro made no provision for this type of news. She had envisioned finding a live female of approximately her own age and well schooled. Was this to be a totally wasted trip?

He watched her face closely and saw her look of disappointment.

"Well! I guess I didn't do you any good," he said. "I'm sorry Katie, but your agent will have his proof of death when summer comes."

"No, you've done excellent work and I'm very pleased. Not many men would have continued to search through such a dead-end street. I'm somewhat dejected because my quest was wasted on deceased people. I had hoped to find them alive and see them inherit their birthright."

"You had me worried for a minute. I don't deserve all the praise though. The detective was the deciding factor. They do an awesome job down there. Look at this and see the detailed account of their findings. I noticed that the teener had a name similar to yours," he said as he passed the sheet to her.

To satisfy him, she took the document and began scanning it with an early lack of disinterest. Her expression changed rapidly and she began reading aloud from the page.

"In the matter of these individuals: Henry Ryan; husband and father; age forty three; white, male Caucasian; Leona Ryan; Wife and Mother; age forty-one; white, female Caucasian; Katherine Loraine Ryan; age fourteen; daughter and only child of Henry and Leona. It has been finally concluded that these three people and their companions, the four as named in the connected case below, on the twenty-ninth day of June and in the year of 2004, were swept out to sea. If there is no official report to the contrary after the legal time has elapsed, they will be considered to have perished."

She paused and with numbed fingers, put the sheet back on the table. Katherine Loraine Ryan, the sheet stated plainly. This put even more mystery into the possibilities picture.

If a ghost had suddenly taken a seat beside her, the shock could not have been greater. What was happening here?

Twinges of loneliness and feelings of depression instantly struck her when reading the names of Henry and Leona.

No such feelings were present in reading their names from the sheet that David had earlier provided.

The arrival of food halted any further talk and gave her a chance to recover her wits.

Marrioti's kitchen served excellent food and if you ate before you examined the bill, you were certain to enjoy it much more. With both of them being hungry, they ravaged the delicious food until it totally disappeared. Their bottle of wine was drained to the last drop and only then was she able to proceed with a plan.

Carefully she took the food dishes from the small table and placed them on the tray cart. Moving to the door, she rolled it outside to await the return of the waiter. As David sat by puzzled, still and quiet, she wiped the table down with a damp napkin.

With purse in hand, she turned toward the table where David watched expectantly. Out came her checkbook and pen. She began writing an amount on the check face. When finished, she handed the check to him and spoke.

"Please David, no arguments with me. Without your help, I would have gotten nowhere. I simply could not have done this alone. This check can only reflect a portion of my gratitude. I will be leaving tomorrow and I doubt that I will ever return. I want nothing said between us that might cause sadness. I detest saying good-bye. I've never found anything *good* about that word."

He took the check without even looking at it and his face reflected his despair.

"You're leaving and I can't say a darned thing," he muttered sadly. "I really think I deserved more than this."

She rose from the table with him and slowly walked him toward the door. Here, she placed her arm on his shoulder and kissed him firmly and squarely on the mouth.

"You deserve more that this too, but this is all you will ever get" she said softly.

After he left, she returned to the table and reread those frightening words from the missing person file. Was it possible that some fragment of psychic power caused her to use the name of Katie Ryan and moved her to come to Florida?

She wanted to acquire roots, making it easier to be employed. It would put an end to repeated lying. Instead, she was more involved in this deepening mystery. At the moment, she was unwilling to accept the possibility of being the Ryan girl that was about to be declared dead.

For several reasons, the puzzle pieces failed to fit. In the first place, Alexi had strongly hinted that she was from some other world and if that was a lie, where did that leave her.

Without a memory to work with, she had very few options. But for her to consider being *that* Katherine Ryan would be carrying coincidence to an incredible plateau.

If she adopted this scenario, she must contend with the mystery of her missing parents and their four friends.

If she *were* that person, they might possibly be alive and stranded in some far corner of the world?

Her thoughts raced wildly. "If I had memory of anything that existed beyond that Socorro boulder, I might be able to sort things out in my mind. But there's just nothing solid for me to grab onto."

I start getting a headache when something tries to surface. This state of not knowing the missing pieces of my life is driving me stark raving mad, but I'm unsure if I'll be able to connect the pieces."

With a throbbing headache ripping at her mind and a souring stomach that threatened to destroy her body, she began pacing like a caged animal. In total anger and frustration she questioned aloud.

"Is there no end to this madness? Have I done something in my past life to deserve punishment like this?"

Quickly she undressed for bed. She would sleep little this night, but she could try to rest. Hurling herself onto the bed, she glared with fury toward the ceiling.

Katie silently tried to make sense of things. Reviewing the last weeks of her existence, she recalled instances when her memory tried to come alive.

Each of the instances had to do with a particular sound, or the lack of friends and family. Love for others seemed so far away and unreachable. Yet, she felt certain that was one of the things that she needed most. Tonight, just the reading of the names of Henry and Leona Ryan tore at her heartstrings.

It was unfortunate that she was unwilling to be their child at this moment because it seemed that the hand of fate might already be dealt. Before sleep took her away, she spoke through wet tears.

"Oh Mom, I doubt if I could recognize you and still, I feel that I miss you very much. Will we ever meet again?"

By calling the Miami airport early, she managed to get reservations. Her next action was to call Sam and give him the flight data.

He reminded her twice that Steven would be waiting in case her plane was early.

After waiting several minutes for a cab, she finally got underway.

The ride was a quiet one, but she did not want conversation. At the airport, her luggage was quickly and efficiently handled, leaving her with nothing to do until departure. No overly friendly souls pestered her and she liked that too.

Before take-off, she discovered that the seats next to her were unoccupied and that pretty well made her day.

It should be a quiet and restful flight toward Albuquerque.

"You had a fast turnaround, Miss Ryan," Steven told her pleasantly on arrival. "I hope you had a good trip."

"It will be a little while before I know the answer to that one. I'm bringing as many problems back as I took there."

"My money is on you. Whatever it is, you'll work it out. I've seen a certain glint show up now and then in your eyes, like when you were trying to learn to drive. I've never known anyone with such a glint that's been a failure at anything."

A certain warm feeling came over her at that moment and hope sprang from her chest. This was part of what she had been missing, but for how long she could not know. Friendship and family love were things that she must have been a part of once. What else was missing that held the ability to hurt so damn bad?

For two weeks, she stayed away from everyone. Her days were mostly spent in hard physical exercise. Early morning and late afternoon jogging sessions became long endurance running efforts.

Her tightly wound body became as firm as a professional athlete. On one particular afternoon the route took her to the campus.

As she turned into the compound, Fred Wallace was moving in the same direction.

"Join me please, Miss Ryan. I'm tired of running alone."

Breathing easily, she allowed her pace to merge with his.

"I will if you promise to stop calling me, Miss. I'm Katie to my friends and you certainly fit that category."

"Then I'm Fred and I accept your friendship with the greatest of pleasure. Understanding people represents a vital portion of my business life. There is something very special about you, but I'm not nosy. I'll simply enjoy your friendship as long as I can. I have a feeling that your stay here will be much shorter than I would like it to be."

"I have no long range plans. I don't feel very good about my life, but I don't know how to improve it. At this moment, I feel that I'd be satisfied to be here the rest of my life. I have good friends who care about me. I have a nice house and I have money, but I'm very unproductive at present. I'm a fairly intelligent woman and I need to put that intelligence to work."

"I understand completely. Everyone needs a life and for some, that life needs to be fuller than others require. A beautiful young lady needs more than Socorro has to offer, that's for sure."

Later that night, Katie was roused from sleep by a constant beeping noise. The sound seemed to grind into her brain, forcing her to act quickly or lose her mind. Wide-awake now, she swung her legs over the side of the bed and reached for her purse. With a soft touch to the transmission unit, the irritating sound stopped and the deep voice of Alexi was heard.

"You have done well except for your impetuous trip to Florida. Will I be forced to give you a list of things that you must not do, as well as the list of things that must be done? In the future, you will not take independent actions. You will clear it with me before taking any action that varies from your scheduled activities. Is this point clearly understood?"

Katie considered her situation carefully. She wanted very much to blast out at this arrogant tyrant, but quickly relented for he held the key to this sorry puzzle. Unless she could personally solve this mystery, he was her only hope. She must remain a slave to his wishes until this riddle was solved.

"I understood what you said, but why is a simple little trip such a big deal to you."

"All you have to understand are the orders that you get. I will issue new orders now, and you will not question my motives again. There is a company in Albuquerque that seeks contracts with the Federal Government. The company name is Visions West and much of their work is in the confidential type security classification. The background checks for that classification should pose no problem for you and it is a good beginning for an employment history."

"Can't I keep my house and come back on weekends? I want to keep my friends."

"That is acceptable for the present, but I will not allow you to remain very long. Our long range plans might be compromised by absences from your new location."

"I'll get a motel room until I can find permanent housing," she told him eagerly. "I'll buy new outfits suitable for work. What type of work do you think I should apply for, Alexi?"

"You were trained as an executive secretary. I know nothing about the requirements of that position, but experts trained you. There is no doubt about your ability. You will excel and the market for your talents will be great. Express farewells to your friends and leave for your new assignment within two days."

The voice died and the low glow from the instrument went dark. She was vacillating between a high mood and a low one.

Leaving Socorro might not be too bad, since she could return on weekends. A new job might create new friends and interests that would overshadow Socorro's offerings.

Katie spent several minutes bringing Sam to date on her plans and he was trying to adjust.

"If you're sure this is what you want, then I'm happy for you. It won't be the same without you. We'll be looking forward to the weekends though."

From her coat pocket, she withdrew four necklaces that she had taken from her deposit box. He was then given further instructions.

"Sell these to Pepper, if he'll buy. Your percentage will be fifteen percent just as I told you. Don't give me any argument, they're mine and I can do with them as I please. I don't need to okay your deal with Pepper. If you turn the deal before I return, put it in the bank. I'm leaving for Albuquerque in just a few minutes."

She left him shaking his head in amazement and went to her car. For her, another adventure was about to unfold. The drive was pleasant and upon reaching Albuquerque, she parked in a space near a public phone.

Thumbing through a worn phone book, she found the name of the target company.

The Visions West Corporation was located in the triangle near the juncture of I-40 and I-25. It seemed logical to secure a room near that address and she found several motels available. Despite the absence of a credit card, she obtained a room by writing a check for a one-month stay. She found her room and then sat down at her phone table. After punching in the numbers, she waited patiently until Sam answered.

"I want you to know that I'm here. You might need my room and telephone number."

She was not through with doing phone work.

"Fred, I'm calling from Albuquerque," she said after punching up her second call. "I'm looking for a job and I need a favor."

"Ask away and I'll certainly try."

"Can you suggest a way for me to get a credit card here in Albuquerque? Strangers don't like to take checks and I don't like to carry much cash."

"You're one smart lady. I'll handle the card deal for you. My bank will issue a standard charge card, with a Twenty Five Thousand dollar limit and we'll put a hold on your account for that amount. I have an agreement with the Cattlemen's Bank. Go in and ask for Dave Potter, he'll take care of you."

"I'll do something nice for you someday," she said softly.

"You already have by giving me your friendship," he spoke gently.

CHAPTER THREE

The Visions West Corporation complex of twenty acres was purchased many months earlier while it was still affordable. The assembly and manufacturing buildings were set back deeper on the grounds. A large employee parking lot used up much of the middle property. Their attractive main office building stood guard at the front and immediately reflected the high-class taste possessed by the owner. That he was an ex-senator and doing business with the Pentagon meant he had waited out the necessary time in compliance with the laws. It also meant that the man was getting on in years.

Todd Whatley had a silver mane, was tanned and extremely glib. Rising higher above these things, he was known as an honest gentleman. During his long honorable period of service as a senator, he had almost perfected the art of conversation. If he had chosen to apply himself to any type of illegal activities, he might already own a big piece of the world. He was that good. This was one of the few days that the ball did not bounce Todd's way. It was in his small conference room that he received the shattering news from his long time secretary.

"Maggie, give me the doctor's prognosis in his exact words."

"He told me it was a treatable form of cancer, but it would consume considerable time. I wish I could give you more notice, Todd."

"I'm concerned about your welfare. I can get by with temps for a while. I refuse to let you quit. You've been with me so long, I think of you as family."

"I thank you for those thoughts. It's always nice to hear things like that when you reach my age. By the way, I checked with our employment pool and there is simply no one available. I know our clerk and filing personnel like the back of my hand. You don't want anyone from out there."

"All the Electronic plants have sucked up the real talent, but I'll manage just fine. I'm more concerned with your getting proper health care. Are you fully certain about your doctor's ability?"

"Doctor Woodward is a capable man. He is no stranger to the practice of treating cancer. Good-bye, Todd, I'll stay in touch," she said.

The two weeks that followed seemed like a nightmare to Todd. In every direction he tried to lead his temps, they failed consistently.

Help was on the way, but he could not know that. Katie was at that moment nearing the office building.

The receptionist looked toward the half open door as Katie entered.

"May I help you, Miss?"

"I'm sure you'll be able to help," answered Katie. "I want to apply for employment."

"I can give you an app form and I'll take it to the interviewer when you're finished."

It was a standard form and simple to complete. In a matter of minutes, she returned it to the receptionist. The woman took the form, turned it face down, and then spoke.

"It may be a while. We are really busy today."

In seconds she was back at her desk and answering the phones.

Todd was elbow deep in mail when his phone rang. Pushing the mail stack away from the noisy instrument, he lifted the handset.

"Todd Whatley here, what can I do for you?"

"This is Paul from Industrial relations. I have an applicant waiting that I can't figure. Some answers are vague and some are shockingly impertinent. Still, I have never read an app that so quickly grabbed my attention. Want me to give her the old bum's rush treatment?"

"No, Paul, but I thank you for bringing this to my notice. I really need a change of pace. Bring her app to me and I'll take a look at it."

Todd studied the form, wondering why any adult intent on finding work would submit such answers. It could be a hoax, it could be just an attempt to get in the door, or it could be that this woman was very good and resented the filling out of such a standard form.

Without interviewing her, he would never know. Since he had lived this long with a deeply rooted sense of curiosity, he buzzed the receptionist.

"Please escort Miss Ryan to my office and hold my calls while I'm interviewing her."

"Yes sir, right away," she said quickly.

When Katie entered Todd's office, he came to his feet swiftly. Nothing in her application gave clues to her impressive beauty.

"Please have a seat, Miss Ryan," he said cautiously. "My name is Todd Whatley. Might I have some coffee or tea brought in for you?"

"Thank you for offering, but I don't want to take up too much of your time. I can tell by the way the receptionist acted that you are an important and busy man. I can't imagine why you would choose to interview me, instead of having it done."

"Come now, Miss Ryan," he said. "You can't fill out an application form in such a manner and expect normal treatment? Just re-think the answer that you gave an important question that reflects one's typing ability. The question how many words per minute can you type, brought an answer of, 'whatever the required number.' Please explain that answer, Miss Ryan."

"I *am* an expert typist, but not a braggart. If I told you how many words per minute I can type, that might seem to be bragging. I am expert as a receptionist, file clerk, stock girl and script girl. I have had training for a position as an executive secretary. Are there other questions on my application that bother you?"

"If I *had* other doubts, I'd be afraid to raise them. I'm still trying to digest your explanation for that first question. Seriously though, I notice that you show a lack of normal education on the form. Is there a reason for your leaving high school and being taught by private tutors?"

"That is a fair question and deserves an answer. After a terrible family separation, I went to live with my aunt. She traveled extensively throughout the world, but she never neglected my education. If necessary, I could probably track those tutors down and get certificates. I may still have some of their addresses."

"I see no reason for that, Miss Ryan. I've simply had my fill of temps as secretaries. You could be as good as you say. I seldom make risky moves, but I'll make one now. If you report to work tomorrow morning at nine, we will give it a try. If you need employment as badly as I need an executive secretary, we may be able to co-exist."

"Mr. Whatley, I'll do my best to prove that you made a wise decision."

When she left, Todd buzzed Paul and told him to prepare a new file.

"How good is she, sir," he asked in a surprised filled voice. "I didn't even get to see her. Helen told me that she was a tall and very pretty woman."

"Helen is more efficient at judging beauty, than acting as a receptionist. Miss Ryan is the most attractive lady I have seen in years, but that had nothing to do with my hiring her. A few weeks trial will determine whether Miss Ryan has the ability to function sufficiently as my secretary."

Katie dug into her new job with determined vigor by taking product lists and descriptions to her motel to study. She learned that Visions West not only made electronic equipment for aircraft and ships, but for space vehicles as well.

Most Vision West products were accessible to her, but some were classed as top secret and only the name, along with the product number was shown.

Still, in only a short time, she became familiar with most of the Vision West products. Products with the highest security classification were first handled by the senator and had the top secret portions blacked out for Katie's viewing.

Alexi had not overstated her training. The duties that she performed for the senator went so smoothly that he seemed in awe of her. She not only carried out his assignments, she anticipated many duties and had them available before he requested them.

In a few days, she began to accompany him on trips and sit in on his important conferences. After Katie's first month on the job, he realized what a huge find she was and offered her a raise in pay. Though very pleased by this turn of events, she refused his generous offer.

"I am still a temporary employee and will be for sixty more days. I refuse to break the company rules. You can have the best of my ability for as long as I'm a temp and it won't cost you a dime more. I have not spread my resumes throughout Albuquerque. No one will hire me away from here until I'm ready to go," she said with a smile.

"You're not the first dedicated employee that my company has hired, but you may prove to be the most resourceful and talented one that we've ever had," he said grudgingly.

Later that day as she was stepping out of the shower stall, she heard the menacing signal from her purse.

Though she was not expecting a communication from him so soon, Katie reacted obediently. Quickly, she draped the towel around her shoulders and reached for the noisy contraption.

"I have an assignment for you," Alexi said. "You are to attend the first of several yearly events. Make a note of this address and be there promptly at eight, tomorrow night. Someone will introduce you to the proper people. It is known as a charity benefit and you are expected to donate money toward what they term a worthy cause. An invitation is unneeded for these events," he advised her.

“Three of your first four introductions are of value to us,” he added. “Be especially interested in those three. Give them reason to want to see you again. I expect you to develop friendships with these people. You do not need to know more than I have told you.”

He severed contact from the device and the sudden continuing silence nearly devoured her. With a slight trembling of her body frame, she finished drying off and stepped into a comfortable pair of slacks. As she dressed, questions began filling her mind. How was Alexi able to keep track of her? He had known of her trip to Miami, but how did he? He seemed to know that she had nothing planned for tomorrow night, but how could he? Was someone watching her movements? He admitted that he had other people in his employ. If he was so certain that she would meet the proper three people, an inside person had to be at this charity affair.

She was dressed to fit the occasion when she arrived at the benefit. As she stepped through the doorway, several eyes turned toward her in open admiration.

A long sign-in desk was strategically placed inside the entrance to the large room and manned by three people. Guests were unable to avoid registering and most of them were making their donations at that time.

She failed to bring the purse with Alexi’s device. A smaller clutch bag was her choice and from this bag she removed a previously prepared check.

Having duly registered and her donation delivered into their hands, she joined a small throng at the refreshment bar. Arriving five minutes early was not a coincidence; she wanted time to look at the guests before her first contact.

With an uncola in hand, she did a slow turn around the room. After a few shrewd looks at members of the gathering, she decided that one of two men was the most likely contact. Though both men cast looks of interest and appreciation, they stayed in place.

A slim graceful woman soon appeared. Katie eyed the female carefully as she stopped by her side. Her large expensive earrings cast spangles of light that reflected from the overhead incandescent fixtures.

“Hello there,” she said gaily. “I was told to take you in hand and introduce you to some people, but I can’t do that until you introduce yourself. I am Teresa Sandusky and you have the looks of an interesting person. I always love to meet people who interest me.”

"I'm Katie Ryan, but you're wrong. There's nothing very interesting about me."

"The people at the desk think you are and said you were entitled to some VIP treatment. I intend to see that you get it."

She linked an arm inside that of Katie and led her toward the two men that Katie noticed earlier. Teresa began talking in low confidential tones.

"These men are important people, Miss Ryan. They have a little power in the political arena. Try to avoid angering either of them. It would not be beneficial to your career."

The men were still engaged in conversation as Teresa drew her into their midst. Their talk quickly stopped as both men looked with interest at Katie.

"Hello Teresa, it looks like we have a new lady in town," one man remarked.

"Yes, we do. Katie Ryan, I want you to meet Bradford Whatley and to the right of Brad, I am just as equally pleased to present James Simpson."

"Still covering your bases, right Teresa? I am very pleased to meet you, Miss Ryan. I want my bid in to have the first dance."

"It is a real joy to meet a new and lovely lady," James said boldly. "I have many questions to ask, but they can wait until you've danced with Brad. I'll try to atone for his lack of ability on the dance floor."

Teresa moved along with Katie toward another group, but they were interrupted by a man with an irritated look on his face.

"Teresa, you must stop monopolizing every new guest at these affairs," he said curtly. "You've never been named as our official greeter. I could have made this lady acquainted with the proper people. I don't know you, Miss Ryan, but I do know your name. I am Sergai Valenkov."

Taking her hand to his lips, he gave it a caress and then dawdled with the holding of it.

Irritated by his boldness, she withdrew her hand with firm strength. Lacking a warning from Teresa, she was unsure how to treat this overbearing man. She decided Teresa was afraid of the swarthy fellow.

"Mr. Valenkov, how do you fit into the charity game?"

"I believe it is the duty of everyone to support charity. Unfortunately, we can't all give as much as you have. Perhaps our funds are not as plentiful as yours, nor as easily obtainable."

"Are you insinuating that you know my financial situation? That's hard to believe. I've never seen you before and I doubt if I'll see you again."

"You are wrong on both charges. I made no hint toward your sources, but you will see me again if you circulate in our society. I'll see you around soon, my dear."

Upon delivering this small speech, he departed and left a void of silence until Teresa broke it by speaking cautiously.

"I'm sorry about this, Katie. I had no way to warn you. He owns a rather evil reputation, but he dabbles in so many events that it's hard to avoid him."

"Don't worry about it, Teresa. I've never experienced an argument with a man of his type, but I am confident that I can deal with him."

Their talk was ended by the arrival of another man that appeared to be in his fifties. His style commanded attention.

"You must be new here. I'm Robert Hartley. I'd like to meet you."

"I'm Katie Ryan and I'm sure it will be to *my* advantage to make your acquaintance."

They exchanged light handshakes and looked each over while he waited to allow her the next move.

"What line of business are you in, Mr. Hartley?"

"Heck! Just call me Bob," he said easily. "I have a corporation here in town that keeps me busy, but I have a plant on the desert. What keeps your wheels of life turning pretty lady?"

"I'm a secretary, Bob."

"No! You're joking. Secretaries are *taken* to charity events when they're as lovely as you. They don't go unescorted and donate their hard earned money."

She answered with some annoyance.

"Bob, this one does. I'm a good secretary, but not just for the money. I do it to keep the wheels of life turning as you so aptly put it."

"I didn't mean to upset you. I beg your pardon for my blunder. You *must* be an exceptional secretary. If you ever need a change of scenery, look me up. I'll find a place for you or create one."

He placed a business card in her hand and without further words, went in another direction. She placed his business card in her clutch bag.

"This is turning into a busy evening for you. I'll be back later. I have to go freshen my drink and say hello to a man that likes me."

Teresa smiled as she left in the direction of the bar.

Katie expected to meet four people, with only three being of interest to Alexi. Having met five, his contact was still unknown. Bradford and James did not fit the supposed role of an Alexi disciple.

Sergai seemed much too offensive to be a yes man. There was only Robert Hartley left, unless one considered Teresa to be a candidate. Since she so resembled a butterfly flitting from one blossom to the next, Katie was doubtful that she was Alexi's contact.

Hartley was unlikely to be owned by anyone. Unless she was wide of the mark, he was not the one. She was very eager to stem the constant flow of mysteries and puzzles that always lacked sufficient clues to solve.

Little by little, her tolerance level was being fractured and would soon spill over her mental dam. It would help if she could solve one of the many things that persisted in troubling her.

Her uncola having lost its fizz, she angled toward the bar. The barman quickly moved toward her, took her glass and replaced it with a fresh one. Raising the new drink to her lips, she accidentally made eye contact with the man on her right. She could have turned away, but her interest stirred.

He was somehow different from every other man in the room. His skin color was darker than average, but not from the sun. He was not swarthy in appearance, as was Valenkov, but still dark enough to set him apart from the norm. In some strange way, she sensed having met him at an earlier time. The face of the man was certainly unfamiliar.

Her curiosity was aroused and on the chance that she might recognize his voice, she decided to talk with him.

"I'm Katie Ryan," she said while boldly offering her hand. "This is my first charity affair and I'm trying to meet a few people."

He showed irritation at her interruption of his drink. Briefly, a small scowl flashed across his face before recovering. Ignoring her outstretched hand, he gave a surprise response.

"I am Amahd Rashooti," he said. "I am surprised that you present yourself to me with so many available men in attendance."

Annoyed by his unfriendly attitude, she decided to give him a parting shot. With glass in hand, she faced him in her full height.

"If you're not one of the available, Mr. Rashooti, I'll blot your name out of my little black book," she told him coldly and turned away.

She moved to the room center with no further concern about him.

Her attention was swiftly taken by warm-up sounds from the small orchestra.

In moments, Bradford was at her side for the promised first dance. She had to admit that he was an exceptionally handsome man. Getting him interested should not be too difficult.

Would he be a talkative partner or the strong silent type? This was part of the excitement that came from meeting new people. She looked forward to discovering his personality.

Uncertain if he was one of the three that she was meant to enchant, Katie intended to concentrate on Bradford and James. Pretending to have interest in Sergai and Hartley would take a considerable amount of acting on her part.

In the beginning of their dance, Bradford was quiet. She pushed small talk until his mood lightened. With the music continuing, his wit peaked and he had her laughing like a schoolgirl.

"You're a lot of fun. I'd like very much to see you again. There are places I could take you where the food is out of this world and the music is heavenly."

"That could be arranged, Bradford," she said in pleased tones. "I'm not in the phone book, but I can give you my number."

The music died away and James appeared from nowhere.

With the beginning of a new tune, she saw that he had not overstated his ability as a dancer. He had her floating across the floor like a leaf on the wind. In trying to impress her with his ballroom ability, he only murmured small talk. After nearly half of the number was gone, he realized his mistake and began to quiz her.

"I've been enjoying your company so much, I haven't found out anything about you. Do you have a career, or are you in some type of business. I'm certain that you're not on the old nine to five grind."

She answered with a laugh

"Then you are certainly wrong, James. I'm a secretary and my hours are almost as you described them."

"That's incredible! Not that there's anything wrong with being a secretary, but you seem so in charge. I'd have guessed you to be CEO of some corporation at the very least."

"I've disappointed several people tonight. I believe everyone expects too much of me. Let's talk about you for a little while. What do you do to keep the wolf from the door?"

"Well, mining was my first interest and I found a bit of success in that field, but other things have come along to turn my direction. I've been able to parlay my mining knowledge into a new venture that looks promising. It hasn't paid off yet, but it's coming along."

She spoke eagerly, "This sounds very interesting. I'd like to hear more about your venture."

"I'm not free to give details about the project."

As he said this, his attitude quickly changed. Noticing the difference in his facial expression she laughed easily.

"Oh God, I hope it isn't a military secret. I *am* the Mata Hari of the future you know."

"I apologize, Miss Ryan. I'm getting off on the wrong foot with you. I'd like to see you socially and get our friendship going in the right direction."

"You're an interesting man and a very good dancer, James. I'll give you my phone number and we'll see what develops."

No way would she seek out Sergai unless Alexi clarified the plan a little more. In making sure that she dodged him, she ran smack into Bob Hartley.

"Won't you please dance with me, Miss Ryan?"

She spoke pleasantly, "Thank you for asking, Mr. Hartley."

As they turned about the floor to a slow oldie, she questioned him in a delicate manner.

"If I decided to work for you, would I have to move to the desert?"

"Heck no, Miss Ryan. If you're needed there, I'll have you flown down in the chopper."

"I'll keep your offer in mind, but things are going real well at Visions West."

"So, you're working for the Senator. I see why you aren't job shopping. If he values someone's work, he won't allow them to leave."

She spoke with some heat evident in her voice.

"That's rubbish, Bob. He employs me, but I'm not owned by him. If I want to leave and find other work, his money will never hold me."

"It is said that he makes offers to people that they can hardly refuse. The Senator has powerful friends, but he also has some formidable enemies. I've never been on the outs with him, but he's taken some contracts that I thought were locked up. Hell, little lady! I don't want to talk about him. I want to talk about you."

With the number's end, she fled to find another uncola and skillfully dodged everyone but Bradford.

"Miss Ryan, I can't let you get away again. I was unable to find you after we left the dance floor. You're just too much in demand to suit me. I need to get you away from all this competition."

"You're just saying that to be kind," she said with a smile. "I'm sure you can handle a lot of competition and do it with style. Are you a native of Albuquerque?"

"Yes, I was born here and got my early schooling here. We had several years away though while my father was serving as a Senator in Washington DC."

Unable to control her surprise, she tried to mask the quick look she had thrown his way. She spoke quickly to him.

"I should have made the connection when we were introduced."

"I should have found you before tonight. You're an interesting person. I'd like to know more about you, but the evening is slipping away."

"Yes it is, and tomorrow is another work day. I must leave right away, or I might get fired tomorrow."

Without giving him a chance for more talk, she turned and left the building. As the valet was bringing her car around, she saw Bradford watching from the entrance.

The next morning, Whatley delivered various pieces of mail to Katie's desk with a dark scowl on his face. Having helped him over hurdles before with fresh ideas, she just might give him a new slant on this odd situation.

"Katie, I can use an idea toward solving a problem. A competitor is getting to be a pain in the butt. Normally, I wouldn't see this as a challenge, but I think he's found an inside man in the government contracts section."

"Bring me up to date, Senator. How could an inside man give your competition an edge?"

"In as few words as possible, I'll explain one way an edge is obtained. Every contract that goes to public bid is first analyzed for specification content by an engineering section. The estimating section then establishes a reasonable budget price and money is appropriated for the proposed contract. Are you with me, so far?"

"I see the framework and purpose. Please continue, Senator."

"With the initial procedures complete and budget established, blueprints and specifications are printed for public bidding. It looks like an even playing field for all contractors at this point. However, an engineer could purposely leave a gray area in the plans or specs. Careful reading by the contractor engineers might pick up the gray areas, but that does not severely alter the playing field."

He waited for only a moment. "If my competitors knew the government's estimated value of the contract and submitted a bid based on that value, this would alter the playing field. If he won the bid, he could cash in on the gray area through the change order system."

"What a neat little arrangement," Katie admitted. "If an insider gave this contractor the budgeted figure, he could trim his bid to accommodate the feds estimated cost. The government would then be in a hostage-like situation once they became contractually bound."

"Exactly what the contractor wanted when he submitted his bid. Now you must understand that I'm unable to prove these allegations, but Hartley Industries won the last sizable bid. They also left a pile of money on the table in relation to the other contractor bids."

"Is this company owned by Bob Hartley?"

Todd looked at her with suspicion. "Yes, how do you know of him?"

"I met him at a charity function. He offered me a job, but I told him I was quite satisfied here at Visions West."

"Sounds like an interesting meeting. Did he make you a terrific offer?"

"No, he didn't mention money at all. He hinted that you try to own your key employees. I told him I refuse to be owned by anyone and if I chose to, I would walk away from Visions West."

"I don't want to see that happen," he said with color rising to his face. "I have little doubt that you are among the finest executive secretaries in the west. Margaret may never return to a full time job and you are even more qualified. It is imperative that I have *you,* in this position. I'll try to do whatever it takes to keep you here."

"To better understand you, let's clarify a point here. Is Bob's awareness of a government estimate worse than using past Washington influence to gain a foothold in the system?"

"Hell yes! Any edge that I may have held from time to time came from a favor for a favor. Though unethical, it is still legal. Hartley, though, may be part of a conspiracy scheme that intends to defraud the federal government."

"Thank you for the explanation. I'll try to see it in the same light that you describe. I'm certain that I'll see him again. It will be interesting to bait him a bit and see what I can learn."

"I don't own you, but I still prefer that you don't see him. He may be highly egotistical, but he's a wise old fox. If he can use you to any advantage, he'll jump at the chance. Better let well enough alone, Katie."

Though only a few weeks had passed, Katie's mail brought an invitation to another charity affair. Alexi did not order her to attend, but she decided to make an appearance.

After entering and signing in, Teresa took her in hand. This woman was a bubbler of conversation and never seemed to tire.

At the bar, she asked for a Vodka Collins and Katie swiftly ordered for her usual uncola.

Noticing Amahd at the bar's end, she quizzed Teresa about the man.

"What's with this Amahd Rashooti guy? He is the strangest fellow I've ever seen."

"I've tried a few times, but he's a cold fish. James told me that he's an art dealer and collector. He buys from the art colony in Taos and exports back to the Middle East. A friend of James says that the man also has Washington connections."

Teresa darted off to see someone and Katie was left to manage on her own.

She carefully looked the room over, hoping to see Bradford or James and found neither. Robert Hartley could not be seen, but Sergai was present and circulating.

She exercised great caution in avoiding his path and decided to call it a night. Without someone decent to talk with, the entire evening would be a pooper.

On a partially clear, but breezy Saturday morning, she drove down the interstate toward Socorro in a happy mood. The powerful car was barely laboring, but still doing the speed limit with ease.

Twenty miles away from Albuquerque she saw a dark cloud line nearing the interstate. Unless it veered from its present course, the main body of the squall would cross her route in only a matter of minutes.

The storm system was less than two miles in length, but it was a mean and menacing foe. She decided be to let it pass ahead of her and angled her car to the road shoulder to wait it out. Though fully insured against storms, she opted to be safe rather than sorry.

Relaxing at the wheel, though attentive to the approaching storm, her eyes strayed to the rear view mirror. Another vehicle apparently opted for the same idea and parked about seventy yards behind her.

Other cars bravely passed on by and were challenging the storm. In a few minutes, the entire squall line had passed on across the sage cluttered wasteland.

She powered the window down to smell the freshened air and breathed deeply. The wind and light rain had totally purged the air. She sat quietly for a moment, carefully checked the road behind and then entered the interstate slow lane. The parked car behind her was still there as she accelerated her speed.

Entering the area where the storm crossed the road, she saw a small car on the shoulder.

A man was alongside the vehicle and examining it. Because it was such a remote area, she hated to see anyone stranded with car trouble and pulled in behind him to see if she could help.

He came toward her car, with a look of distress on his face. She lowered the window to talk.

"I can send a tow truck if your car won't run."

"It sure won't run," he said dryly. "I guess I need a ride to Socorro. The car is only a rental. I'll call the agency from there and let them worry about it."

"Is Socorro your destination, or just a place to use the phone?"

"I have a cell phone, but I'm going to the College to do research. The library will be open today. I must have the information for Monday's work conference."

She mulled the situation for a few seconds.

"Get your things from the car and I'll take you to Socorro."

He smiled his thanks and rushed to his vehicle.

On returning with his articles, she saw a small piece of luggage and a briefcase. She also saw that he had an athletic type body and extremely good looks, but no wedding band. Everything about him seemed to appeal to her taste toward romantic possibilities. The fact that she had no memory failed to cloud the issue.

"I sure appreciate your kind offer. I didn't hold much hope of getting a ride. You can't trust people these days and I sure didn't expect a ride from a lady. You probably wouldn't have stopped, if you hadn't been traveling with that other vehicle," he spoke with certainty.

"I'm not traveling with anyone. I'm traveling alone, but I can take care of myself."

"My mistake, I saw the car pull over at almost the same time you did and I drew my conclusion from that move."

She checked the rear view mirror and saw the same vehicle that was behind her before the storm hit. This was not a coincidence. For some mysterious reason this car was following her.

"Must have been a coincidence," she said softly.

She continued to watch from the rear view mirror as she drove.

"My name is Katie Ryan. Why don't you introduce yourself?"

He answered with a nice smile. "Besides being a very lucky fellow, my name is Justin Wade. I might have spent most of the weekend back there and it could have cost me my job."

"I know you're an engineer and you're going to a mining school to do research work. Still, several types of engineers are involved with mining."

"I work with alloys. Many things come from the earth in one form, but they're often converted into hundreds of other forms. The entire world is focusing on metals and minerals."

"You are so correct, I see this trend every day," she replied. "I work for a concern called Visions West."

"I suppose that makes us friendly rivals, Katie. I started working for the Hartley Corporation two years ago."

"It *is* a small world. I met your boss a few days ago. He was kind enough to make an offer of employment."

"Are you considering taking him up on that offer? The company pays exceptionally well; at least that's my opinion."

"I haven't decided one way or the other."

Entering Socorro, she slowed for the restricted speed limit and checked the rear view mirror. The tailing car was not in sight. With a sigh of relief, she pulled in at the motel where she had previously stayed. Justin might need a room for the weekend.

"Have you made reservations anywhere, Justin?"

"No, I've never been here before and I wanted to see what I was getting before I took it."

"I've stayed here," she said "It's a quality place and you'll like it."

"You've been extremely nice. I'd repay you, but I can't offer you anything that you don't already have more of than me. Your car would cost most of my yearly salary and if my boss offered you a job, you must be pretty well up the totem pole in the business world. I *can* thank you sincerely and wish the best for you in the future," he said.

"Well there *is* one thing you could do for me," she said. "I could pick you up about eight and take you to dinner. I hate to eat alone."

He gave her an incredulous look and answered.

"I'll be here, if you're serious."

Later she entered Dugan's Digging's and Sam beamed his best smile.

"It's always a good day when you visit us, Katie. How's your new job going? Are they treating you right, or must I come up there and straighten them out?"

"The job is going well, but I don't know how long I'll be able to return for the weekends. My boss is demanding about work."

"Aw, you'll manage. You're a real smart lady. Whatever it takes, you'll work it out before you get to feeling trapped."

Later in the evening she drove to the motel for Justin. Sliding into her automobile upholstery, he eyed her with appreciation.

"Where are you taking us for dinner, Miss Ryan?"

"Nowhere, if you keep calling me Miss," she said. "I like to be called Katie by my friends."

"Katie is it too late to tell you that you look very pretty tonight?"

"It's never too late to hear kind words. I'm taking you to a fabulous place. The food is usually marvelous, but you might get killed if you don't compliment the chef" she said dryly.

He fell silent for a few moments as she motored through the residential area. Puzzled, he watched her pull into a private driveway.

"This is awfully small to be a Bed and Breakfast place," he said. "Do they serve dinners at a B and B place?"

"Hey! We can check it out," she said quietly.

Pulling her keys from her purse, she opened the front door and only then did he understand that she was teasing. She showed him through the place by leading him past her kitchen that had filled with enticing aromas. Not only was she the most beautiful woman he'd ever met, she apparently was an excellent cook as well.

Once finished with dinner and into the wine, she led the conversation to her chosen direction. He looked closely at her, as she began to speak

"You're my first guest since I rented this place. I'm usually up in Albuquerque. I only come down here for the weekend."

"It's a nice little place. I think putting some distance between you and your job is a very smart move," he said.

"I'm not really satisfied with my job at Visions West. I probably should have contacted Hartley to see if he was serious about the job offer."

"I hope you do work for Hartley. I might see more of you then."

"He gave me his business card, but I don't want to contact him through his office. I don't want it on record that I've ever been in contact with him. The senator is a very thorough man and is quite likely to have spies everywhere."

"Hartley has a fax at his home. That would leave no record to take back to Whatley. Hartley would probably kill me though if he learned I had given the number to an outsider."

"Then don't tell him. If he quizzes me about it, I'll tell him that it's on file at Visions West. Justin, you're a refreshing change from the people I deal with on a daily basis. I'd like you to have my phone number. If you're in Albuquerque with free time, maybe we could get together."

Despite using Justin for selfish purposes, she enjoyed their time spent together. The rental agency had delivered another car to him and he would soon leave for the Hartley desert location.

She learned that this site was a super secure testing facility. If she read the light in his eyes correctly, they were testing for something very important. She felt sure that in a short time she'd learn much more about this facility.

Sam's shop was closed Sunday and he likely needed a day of rest. She need not visit him before returning to Albuquerque. The necklaces had sold well and if the buying frenzy continued, she would soon be a wealthy woman.

Sam saw his bank account bulging. He could hardly believe his good fortune. There were many items still to be sold, but she had not told him about those. She intended to feed them to him in small lots and bank the money for future needs.

It was expensive to maintain stylish clothing and keep appointments with her beauty salon. She moved from the small motel to an upscale condo. The monthly payments were easy enough to handle.

In keeping with the times, she purchased the finest personal computer that was available. Most of the top software programs and applications were now in her computer cabinet.

Thanks to a salesman with romantic hopes, she was able to escape with some of the latest and most elaborate software search programs.

It came as no surprise to find that she was a computer expert. She wondered with dry humor if there was anything of importance in which she lacked training.

Katie decided the fastest way to dig into the Hartley organization was by the computer route. If she could break into their system, she might learn all that she wanted to know. By using the fax number that Justin supplied, she tested several combinations of numbers.

Getting nowhere, she decided to go with her intuition. Hartley was a busy man and surely must work with many numbers every day. He would need combinations of numbers that could be retained by memory and to make it even easier to recall, they should be consistent in their numerical form.

Ready for a full-fledged hacking attempt, she punched up a number that resembled his home fax number. After three rings, a voice came on the line.

"This is Mr. Hartley's residence. May I take a message?"

"Yes! I need to talk to Bob about a confidential matter. Would you please tell him that Katie Ryan is on the line?"

"I would if he were here. He is out for the evening though and is not expected back until around midnight. You might try calling again tomorrow."

She thanked the woman for her trouble and hung up the phone. Now, she had Hartley's home number and the pattern was holding. With the third try, she was into his computer phone line.

"Now for the acid test," she thought silently.

By using her training and best intelligence, she broke into his system. In browsing through the Hartley Corporation projects, she was amazed by the magnitude of their product diversity. Their product tree ran through five full screens of scrolling. Their desert testing facility drew immediate attention because of her chummy conversation with Justin.

It was their alloy section that she targeted and soon drew first blood under the astrophysics heading.

Hartley's group had developed a strong, yet lightweight material that was highly heat resistant. That was important sure, but it paled in value when coupled with its radar-deflecting capability. She dallied here for awhile before moving on to Hartley's file of contacts. In that file, she struck pure gold.

Listed were names and numbers along with job titles. She wanted to browse them for follow-up information, but she could return later. She exported a copy of the document and did a printout of the screen of names and phone numbers before shutting down her system.

The Senator would love to have this information, but she was not ready to offer it to him. Something told her that Alexi might not want this given away to anyone. Things might be simpler if he told her what he wanted and from whom.

She had been followed on that stormy road to Socorro. Alexi's accomplice may have tailed her. If there was a different player, he should be made aware of it. She decided to reveal her suspicion in the next conversation with him.

At this moment inside Fred's bank, a serious conversation was underway between Wallace and Dugan.

"Sam, I called you here to talk about Katie. Have you made inquiries from your buyer about her collection?"

"I know nothing about her personal life. I like her very much and I trust her. I didn't check on her collection, but Pepper did. He laid out a lot of money and made sure the goods were legal. Why is this suddenly becoming a worry to you?"

"My worry is for her best interests. I have to keep records and with her account ballooning, we need to protect her. I won't proceed without your blessing, since you're her partner. Your records also need to be updated. I can set it up in a way that won't get either of you eaten alive."

"Well, you're our man. Do whatever you have to do and charge us accordingly. With her in the big city we sure can't ask for her opinion. From my heart, I believe she's worth some extra trouble. I don't think we should tell her though until everything is in place."

CHAPTER FOUR

Bradford Whatley ate his lunch from a fast food sack and watched the squirrel activity at a small local park. Despite the restful setting, the actions of the creatures began causing him some discomfort. They were having a problem similar to the one that he might soon be facing. The bushy tailed rodents pulled pine nuts off the tree and threw them on the ground for later stashing. Their action indicated a bit of intelligence, but was short on common sense. Rival squirrels made off with some of the harvest before the pickers could race down the tree to protect their goods.

Now, comparatively speaking, Visions West was Bradford's tree. At least it would be his when his father retired or passed away. He wanted no interference with his family tree or its products. He was getting a little suspicious of Katie. She had known who he was, but failed to mention her position as the top secretary of his father. He could have forgiven that omission, except for his father's ceaseless admiration of her. He was vocal about her excellent ability.

Though his father was past middle age, his eyes still seemed to stray toward a lady of beauty and intelligence. Katie Ryan could definitely become a major threat to his future and fortune. At the charity thing, he'd been impressed with Katie. He meant to pursue a relationship, but that changed as his father began singing her praises. Though not presently involved in the daily operations of Visions West, he had learned the operation during their start-up days and then drifted into other types of business.

By this stage of his life, he had ably proved that important attributes aren't necessarily passed along through the family genes. He gained fast experience in these new business ventures, but real wisdom came slowly. Bradford sometimes had regrets for leaving to work elsewhere, but his pride kept him away. With sudden inspiration, he reached for his car phone and punched up the number of James Simpson.

"Jim this is Bradford. I want to discuss our common girl friend, Katie Ryan."

"You're using a very loose term of description. I've discovered there is nothing common about Miss Ryan."

"What the hell do you mean? If you've dated her already, then you're much faster on your feet than I've been led to believe."

"No! You're wrong as usual. I haven't *dated* her, but I was ordered to check her out thoroughly and I've drawn a blank. This woman must have something to hide."

"You used the wrong people. My people are pros. I may decide to run her through them."

"Hell, Bradford. The senator would have checked Ryan out thoroughly before hiring her. I'd give a bundle to learn if he hit a dead end too. "

"You keep losing me with your loose word expressions. Please explain the words blank and dead end."

"I'll make it simple for you to understand. She was born in Fort Lauderdale, attended school there and then dropped off the face of the earth until this year. My source told me that she first came to the surface in Socorro. She has a partnership deal with a man in Socorro and he's so clean that he squeaks when he walks. Her banker thinks she walks on water. He refused to give my guy any information except that she had an account there."

"Yes, she probably has something to hide. So, all you really have is that she came from Socorro. I'll send a man to Florida that can get the job done. The family might be in a witness protection setup, but my guy can dig it out. He still has ties to the FBI and claims that he has several favors due for hazardous duty."

"Spend your daddy's money if you wish. You'll end up with the same poop. Remember we answer to the same man and he hates weak information."

"You don't need to remind me of our common bond. My involvement with him has become one of the most stupid things that I've ever done."

"At least he jerked your butt away from threat of jail. An embarrassment like that would have killed your daddy. We may not like each other much, but circumstances keep us tied together."

* * *

Across town inside Visions West, Katie moved restlessly to the opposite side of Todd's desk.

"Senator, I have information that you might like to hear. Please don't ask how I got it. With your lily white reputation, you don't want to know.

You mentioned insiders within the system sometime ago and I've tracked down something of value. I've written two names and phone numbers on this sheet. They work in the contracts system. You can handle this anyway you wish."

"As grateful as I am for your efforts, I won't accept this information if you've broken any law to get it. If you're ridiculing me for being lily white, I guess you have a right. I've spent most of my life in public service and I'm proud to challenge anyone to find legal fault with my service."

"I intended no ridicule," she said hurriedly. "It was only a small test and you passed with high marks. I'm still getting to know you. I found it hard to believe all the good things that I've heard. At least, some of them are true. No, I broke no laws to get this information. My ethics may be questionable, but the people involved in this conspiracy will never make their complaints public."

"You passed a little test yourself. As much as I like you and need you, I *will* fire you for any illegal act that you carry out. Now my dear, give me a few minutes alone and I'll try to call up a favor or two. If you sat in on these conversations, you might think *I* was bragging."

She did not see the senator again that day. He was often tied up in phone talk and she did not interrupt him. Instead, she left the office a few minutes early and went home. She was tired and needed a break.

Following a hot and refreshing bath, Katie relaxed by the television set. She caught the news and weather before punching the off button. A certain problem was puzzling her and the noise of the television ruined her concentration. In the quiet that followed, she resumed her thoughts.

With the amount of interest that James and Bradford had initially shown toward her, why had they not pursued their interest? Why had their feelings cooled toward her?

Even Hartley, the old warrior, was not shaking her tree. It seemed unusual that neither of the three would make a move. She was sure of her desirability factor. Alexi had instructed her to make these men interested and she had certainly tried. Something had gone wrong with the plan. *Darn! If I didn't have all these mysteries, I'd have no life at all.*

The signal from the phone brought her off the couch and she picked it up reluctantly.

"Katie I'm sorry to bother you at this hour. Am I interrupting anything?"

"I'm not involved with anything, Fred. What's wrong down there? You wouldn't be calling at night if it wasn't important," she said cautiously.

"Something *is* going on. I don't know why, but I've had several inquiries about you. Most of the queries have come in just the last few days. They claim to be checking you out for possible employment, but I know you're not leaving the senator. Two of these callers claimed they represent the Federal Government. One man even came to the bank and talked with me. He showed me an outdated badge and ID. I told him to come back when he had upgraded his ID and he left in a huff. Can you explain any of this?"

"No, I can't. I haven't applied for another job. My resume is still unused and will be for quite a while. I'm beginning to like the senator."

"You should. He's the only important political man in this state that can honestly wear a white hat. I wanted you to know that I made moves toward legalizing your income. I have papers for you to sign on your next trip down here. It's important that we don't get out of step with the tax people."

"I thank you so much for seeing to my interests, Fred. You're just like family to me and you should know that by now. I *will* call you when I get back down there."

"Just be very careful up there. Something big must be going on. If you feel uncomfortable, call the senator. He'll know the right steps to take to get these people off your back."

The next day Todd did his homework on the people whose names she furnished.

Knowing that these men had ties to Hartley, Todd's contacts finally found a holding company with checks deposited to the accounts of the two men. Todd punched several numbers into the phone. Now it was time to see if something could be done inside the government system.

"Mr. Speaker, we may not see eye to eye on many things and I'm not in a power position to ask favors, but I will. I'm certain that you would never sanction an outright conspiracy to defraud the government. Now having said that, let me give you names, dates and cases where this act has come to pass," the senator said grimly.

"Wait just a minute, Todd. As Speaker of the House, I can act on this if I choose. But why are you calling me? Your power base was in the

Senate. Why aren't you dealing with your senator from New Mexico? I don't want to step on his toes."

"I'm borrowing an old phrase, but I believe he's a little too close to the forest to see the trees. You won't be doing any favors for me, or yourself, if you make him aware of this conversation."

"I hope you're wrong, but I'll play this out just like you've dealt it. If you'll bring me up to date, I promise to begin taking action right away."

In a later conversation with Katie, he recounted his call to the House Speaker. Though Todd was promised nothing, he held high hopes and commented in a wry manner.

"I put the ball in their court. They can clean up their system now if they have the desire. Thank you again for finding those names. One day, I should ask you how you managed it."

"One of these days, I'll tell you. You've made working for Visions West much easier than it might have been and I appreciate it. This is a top of the line company. I'm surprised that Bradford isn't involved with you. You never mention him; am I getting too personal here?"

"You're my personal secretary and it's normal to wonder about the lack of father and son association in a plant of this size. It's big enough for both of us, but not until he makes some major adjustments. I'm not proud of my son these days, but he was trained in an ethical and moral background. He left the company and went out to conquer the world his way. Most of his present friends should be in the pen. If he's not awfully careful, he may eventually wind up in jail."

"I'm sorry to hear that. I was impressed with him at the charity affair."

"I know of his charming manners," Todd replied. "In several instances though, people have complained about being used by him. I hope he will mature enough to see the error of his ways."

"He has a friend that I met on the same night, James Simpson. Do you know him, Senator?"

"Unfortunately, yes. My son has been a different person ever since he came to know this man. Brad invited him to a little outing that I threw and that's how I met him. I advised Brad to avoid the man and he came unwound. It has been a downhill slide ever since that night."

The next day was another long and tiresome one for Katie.

It began with an early charter flight to Phoenix along with a middle of the morning conference downtown. Following that, they held a late luncheon meeting with a valued customer and an afternoon conference with a software coalition.

On the plane ride home, the senator was kind enough to be quiet and let her nap.

From that short rest break, she looked eagerly forward to a good night's sleep.

Alexi's noisy communication signal from her purse deferred her intended plans. His voice was cold and stern.

"Why have you not carried out my orders? These men should be fighting for your attention. I wanted important pieces to fall into place because of your intimacy with them. You seem intent on being a disappointment to me."

"I'm doing well considering that both my hands are tied. I might handle your tasks if you weren't so mysterious. It might help if you'd give me a full briefing instead of these piecemeal handouts."

"Certain circumstances prevent me from telling you more than the minimum required. My best explanation is that the less you know, the less danger you present to us. These people with whom we are dealing are not naive. They have ways of making you tell everything you know. Time is slowly slipping away from us and your contributions are falling far short of target. I expected much more from you."

"As a test, give me a specific person's name that you wish me to connect with and one particular item of information that you want to draw from him," she suggested.

"I must admit that your request makes considerable sense."

After a short pause to reflect, he spoke again.

"I shall give you one chance to work on your terms. If you are successful, we might try the same tactic with another individual. Robert Hartley has some insiders in the federal buildings. It would be most helpful to learn their identity."

"I can handle that with ease," she said quickly. "You'll have that information very soon. Meanwhile, I need more level talk with you. In more than one instance now, someone has followed me. If they are your people, it's an unnecessary burden for you. I know nothing of my past and I have no memory before arriving in the Socorro area. If I'm to learn anything to enhance my memory, it must come through you. Willing or not, I'm on your team until this quest is complete and I learn my true identity."

"Perhaps this compromise will be good for both of us. I am surprised to learn that you have been under surveillance. It is not of my doing. This news forces me to act quickly to protect our backside. I will have my associate look into this disturbing new angle. It is almost impossible to function properly if someone is on your trail. Your promise to have the Hartley information; was that offer made in total honesty?"

"Yes Alexi, I'll have names and numbers ready and waiting for your call."

The following evening, almost ready to retire for the night, she got another delay. The telephone was signaling for attention.

"I apologize for calling at this hour and at your residence, but you left a message for me. I'm pleased that you called. I was told it might be important," Hartley said.

"I'm not in the book, Bob. How did you get my number?"

"I may have obtained it in the same way that you got mine. I'm not in the book either, but you came up with my number."

"Your number is on file in the senator's office. What's your story?"

"There's no use in being rich and influential, if you can't pull a few strings. I'm waiting for you to explain why you called. Have you reconsidered my job offer?"

"I did consider it momentarily. However, the senator is thinking seriously about opening an office in the nation's capital and I find that a thrilling prospect. Who knows what exciting new frontiers that move might open for me? I could possibly meet a young and powerful senator, or congressman. I think I'll stay with Todd Whatley a little while longer."

Hartley laughed heartily, "You're turning into a first class little gold digger. I like you more all the time. You know, it's sort of like ranching and cows. Other pastures may certainly look greener, but when winter comes and the grass is gone, the man with the grain elevators will always be the biggest winner."

"I had nothing important to discuss," she said with a laugh. "I wanted to mention the possible Washington move. I thought it might interest you."

"It's a very interesting idea and I do appreciate your call."

With a polite farewell, she closed the conversation.

Unexpectedly, the device inside her purse gave a signal and she punched it on. The voice of Alexi came forth swiftly.

"I am ready to take notes on your findings," he said. "Please do not disappoint me."

After delivering the information, she decided to question him about a future point.

"How long do you expect me to work for the senator? I've had other employment offers, but I turned them down."

"You have done well with the senator. Continue to work for him and gain his confidence. If we need favors from him, you must be in a position to request them. The next time we talk, I may give you another name and challenge."

On the weekend in Socorro, the hot Saturday morning sun soaked Katie's body with warmth as she marched to the bank.

The tax papers that Fred prepared must be signed today. She was expected and greeted at his desk.

"Hello again, it's good to see you. We miss you terribly. You don't visit often enough."

"You're telling me. I'd be living here and loving it, if I didn't have such need for a purpose in life."

She signed the papers, noting that Sam had co-signed in every proper spot. There were several different items and it obviously had taken Fred a considerable amount of time to prepare them. Because of his generous time and pleasant companionship, she felt an overwhelming obligation to reward him.

"I need to get into my safety deposit box. I'll continue our visit when I return."

Katie opened the cloth bag of valuables and sorted through them. She had no idea what she would choose, but one flat oblong piece had a profile and crown that drew her full attention. Removing it from the sack, she closed her deposit drawer. This piece looked adequate for the occasion. Back at his desk again, she faced the banker with a prepared speech.

"Fred, simple words fail to describe my appreciation for all the things you've done. I'd like you to have this object as a token of my feelings. The crown that you see on this piece indicates that the man is a Prince. I will always consider that you and Sam are my Princes and sent to me in a time of need. There will always be room in my heart for thoughts of you."

Fred was overwhelmed with emotion and struggled for words as she hurriedly fled the bank. She also was overfilled with tender feelings. Again she approached the mental brink and failed to remember the love and tenderness of her past. It was there, but she could not reach out and grab it.

Back in her Albuquerque condo, the musical tones from her door were unexpected.

The hour was not late, but she was ready to retire for the night. Glaring in frustration, she went to check out the uninvited caller.

Teresa was at the door clad in light brown slacks and a creamy toned blouse.

Obviously, she was cold from the night air and from being without a coat.

"I'm sure you have a reason for being at my door in a half dressed condition. Can I get you something hot to drink?"

Teresa answered in low tones.

"I could certainly use a cup of coffee if it's not too much trouble."

In the kitchen preparing coffee, Katie racked her brain to guess the reason for this woman's presence.

Two meetings between the pair did not lay enough foundation for paying a social visit.

Teresa watched her go about her chores and waited for the proper moment to make a full explanation. It was plain to see that Katie was irritated by her visit. It would take a thorough piece of explaining to satisfy this lady.

"We don't know each other well enough to be visiting buddies, but I had to come for your safety, but we're both in danger unless we're careful. I'm so scared that I'm talking in circles. Let me start at the beginning. I dined alone at the Fat Calf restaurant earlier tonight. I was almost done with my meal when a waiter seated three men in a booth behind me. Once they began talking, I recognized the voices of two of them. It was Bradford Whatley and James Simpson. You met them at the charity thing."

"I remember them, Teresa

"As they talked, their conversation turned ugly. After the charity thing, I grew curious about you. It seemed strange that a woman with your looks and money, would be unescorted at a high-class affair. After checking around, I learned you were working for the senator. They talked about a woman that was becoming a problem. When I heard Bradford say that he wanted you eliminated because you were making a play for his father, I nearly choked on my wine. James said you'd been checked out three times by different people. He said all they could learn was that you came from Socorro. Mr. Unknown said he was waiting for a personal report and unless it firmly established your identity, you'd have to be erased. I've been on the fringes of bad people and I've seen some bad things. Men that have important names and yet do evil things make me cringe."

Katie was silent for a moment. Though her heart was thumping at a faster rate, her brain remained surprisingly cool. Teresa's news was shocking, but incomplete in detail and only added to her stack of mysteries.

"Why are you so frightened by this? If they were talking about me, that doesn't make you a target."

"I'm sure they recognized me. I paid my check and could have left safely at that moment, but I'd left my jacket on the booth seat. It's an expensive article and I went after it, but James turned as if to look for the waiter. I'm almost sure he saw me. I left the place and drove here as fast as I could. I'd never be able to live with myself, if I didn't warn you. If they think I overheard them, they'll eliminate me too."

In looking at the tear-stained face of Teresa, she knew truth lay in her words.

Could Bradford be so mixed up as to believe she was interested in his father? Why was she now a target of Mr. Unknown and his two henchmen?

She made a fast decision. Alexi could be of no help to her in this mess. She couldn't ask the senator to go against his son either and yet, she desperately needed help. She had no evidence to give the police. Without proof, they would never take action. If trouble came, she would have to handle it alone. Tomorrow, she would either buy a gun or apply for one.

"If you wish, you can spend the night here," she said to the woman.

"I'd like that very much. James knows where I live. He even has a key," she added in a low voice.

In their conversation before bedtime, she learned Teresa's address and phone number.

The day dawned with a strong yellow glow. The night had passed swiftly and Teresa was still asleep. Katie drew the drape and turned to the coffee pot. Waiting for the coffee to brew, she took time to consider her position and how it was affecting her. She was not frightened about being a target.

Could this lack of fear stem from a phase of her earlier training? Would she have the ability to shoot straight, or would she need practice at a gun range to acquire marksmanship?

Teresa had dressed and as she neared the kitchen table, Katie poured coffee for her. Dark circles were diminishing the beauty of her lovely eyes.

Her worries were becoming quite evident.

"I hope you rested well. You were tense last night and I never thanked you for warning me. I don't have many friends, Teresa. I hope you'll become one of them. If I can help in any way, please give me a call."

Teresa's shrugged and spoke again.

"That reminds me of something James said about you. In his view, you were a loner. He said other than the people at Socorro and Whatley, no one would know if you were eliminated."

* * *

Katie marched up to Todd's desk in a hesitant manner.

"Senator, may I discuss something with you without going into all of the little knotty details? I know you aren't the type of man to take half a drink, but please cut me a little slack."

"I'll give you all the rope as you want. If something is bothering you, spit it out."

"How well did you check me out after you hired me?"

"A noted investigative group looked into your background. It's not my choice to have our employees investigated. A federal requirement requires all new hires to be thoroughly checked out if they work within security areas."

"Senator could you be a little more specific regarding the findings of their report?"

"They found practically nothing. Oh sure, they furnished the normal date of birth, birth site, and parentage. The schooling record stopped upon completion of your sophomore year. You disappeared from all public record. The report simply indicated that other than the early years in Florida you came from Socorro. Of course, as you and I discussed in our pre-employment talk, that background void was caused by the travels with your aunt. You've created a tremendous amount of curiosity in my old brain, young lady," he said cautiously. "Does this have anything to do with the Hartley information that you gave me some time ago?"

"I'm unsure of anything. Someone is doing background checks on me. I know I've been followed more than once. I received a reliable tip that some of Bradford's friends are involved. I'd be better prepared by knowing his friends."

"Having been in public office, many people want political favors and try to reach me through him. My son is an example of what can happen when you live in a goldfish bowl. Brad has few real friends, but his acquaintances are many. I believe it's time for me to ask how you got the Hartley information."

"Fair enough, Senator. I have some ability with a computer and I put it to use. Bob Hartley seems to be a vain and egotistical type of person. Recognizing these weaknesses, I was able to break his codes."

"I wish now that I hadn't asked you about it. If I was put under oath and asked for my source, I'd have to betray you. I will never lie to a legal investigative committee."

"We must prevent that coming to pass," she said quickly. "There is a slim possibility that Bradford may be involved in this action. Even an indirect involvement would hurt your reputation."

"I can't think of this in selfish terms. My days in the goldfish bowl are over."

"Consider the plight of hundreds of people that work for you. If scandal hits the Whatley name don't you realize the damage that would do to Visions West?"

"Hell Yes! We'd lose our government contracts and the opportunity to bid for others."

"Your employees are loyal. You're a man that rewards loyalty. You can't do it by waiting until trouble strikes first. I'd like to make a suggestion for your consideration."

"Please do so. We're speaking in hypothetical terms anyway. If you have a suggestion, put it on the table."

"Brad thinks I'm romantically involved with you. He sees the evil stepmother inheriting things that should be his alone. He must learn that you *aren't* interested in me that way. It's critical that you not divulge that I'm aware of his feelings. To put Brad on the right track, you could call him for a talk. I don't like sounding so all knowing, because I'm not the answer lady. My suggestion is to express disappointment and warn him that you may change your will. If you threaten to leave everything to charity, he might open up about me. This might give you a chance to clarify our relationship. If I'm stepping over the line as an employee, I'll back off."

"You've shown me a way to reach Brad, but this hardly relieves our situation with a federal investigative body? I'm worried because if charges are pressed against the two employees, their attorney has a right to know how the evidence was obtained."

"I'm hoping that reaching accord with Brad will cause him to leak the names of his important friends. He may never purposely reveal them, but you might learn through an accidental dropping of names. Whoever this person is, he's big and he stays in the background."

"Give me a few days and I may think of someone big enough to qualify. Less than twenty people come to my mind that could possibly fit into this category."

After leaving the office, she went to a nearby gun shop. When the lone salesman came to the counter, he eyeballed her with interest.

"Something for you today, Miss?"

"Yes, I want to buy a hand gun. What is your policy on gun purchases?"

"There have been many changes and the policy may change again tomorrow. At the moment, the rules say you apply, you wait ten days and if your record is clean, you can buy. Do you want a copy of the document to fill out and apply?"

Watching her attractive face closely, he saw the instant flash of major disappointment.

"How about buying a target pistol, Lady? I can sell you one of those if you have a driver's license. It's usually referred to as a twenty two, but it will kill most anything at close range."

Leaving the shop with the pistol and two boxes of cartridges, she felt much more secure. She wouldn't go hunting for trouble, but she'd be better prepared if it came looking for her.

Katie drove directly to Teresa's place and found her in a tangled situation. She watched as a very frustrated Teresa packed a small bag of personal clothing and other items. The place looked like it had suffered an explosion from within. It was a mess from wall to wall with drawers dumped in the middle of the floor. Closet articles were tossed onto the carpet and even the bathroom was trashed.

Whether the damage was done by a frantic search for something or as an act of spite, the only wise thing left to do was to vacate this place in quick fashion.

Katie thought things out swiftly and as it was evident that Teresa needed help, began making suggestions.

"You should be safe at my place in Socorro. I'll give you a map and a spare key. The area people are not prone to be nosy, so run like hell if anyone asks questions. The banker will be your best source of help. Tell Fred that you're a friend of mine. I have provisions in the pantry, but a small market is less than a block away. I'll be there Friday afternoon."

"I have money, Katie. Don't worry about me, I'll play things very cool and wait for your next visit. Make sure nothing happens to you before Friday."

As a precaution, she trailed Teresa's car to the city limits. At this point, they exited the interstate and parked side by side in the lot of a supermarket. After talking through the car windows for several minutes they felt safe enough to go by separate routes to their destinations.

At home, Katie felt that her personal load had just about reached the maximum that she could handle. A relaxing hot shower could not hurt a thing. With a sigh of relief, she stepped from the stall and toweled her body dry. If some easy chair time with soft music in the background could be had, it would be a soothing relief to a trying day. It appeared that her wishes were coming to pass, until the phone blared sharply. Irritated, she spoke sharply into the instrument.

"You'd better not be selling anything. I've had a bad day and I don't want it to get worse."

"I'm sorry, Katie. I'm in town on business and you said I might give you a call. If I've caught you at a bad time, I'll go away quietly."

"Justin! No, No, don't go away. I think it would be good medicine for me, if we got together. Where are you? I'll come and meet you."

"I'm at a coffee shop near my motel. I'll give you directions and it's just off the interstate."

She pulled on a dark pair of slacks, a plain white blouse and a soft green sweater. Her interest had peaked and her disposition mellowed into a smiling face. She began looking forward to the meeting with unusual excitement. She parked in a space and entered the eatery with a smile.

Justin stood and greeted her warmly.

"It is so good to see you. I've thought about you often since being rescued near Socorro."

She gave him a gentle cheek kiss and squeezed him lightly.

"I certainly haven't forgotten you either. You made a very good impression on me, Justin."

"Have you had dinner? I'd love to share a nice meal and conversation with you tonight."

"I was just out of my shower when you called. I needed to relax and get my head together, but I don't want to talk about that right now. I want to enjoy my time with you. I love to eat and this place is known for its fine food."

"I waited before ordering drinks. How do you feel about margaritas?"

"I'm not sure. I don't recall ever trying one. What is it like?"

"Trust me! You'll like it, but we only need one. They have a strong kick and unless you drink them slowly, you can get a headache. They're very cold and filled with finely ground ice. The rim of the glass is sometimes brushed with salt."

The waitress brought menus and Katie chose the steak dinner. Justin echoed her selection and ordered margaritas. Minutes passed as they sipped their drinks and talked. It was easy to relax and enjoy his company.

During the Socorro meeting, he seemed in awe of her and seemed shy. She was drawn to him at that time and now the feeling persisted. He grew quiet for a moment and searched her face with a serious, yet steady gaze.

"You're a very beautiful lady. I'm sure you've heard that a lot, but not from me. I feel a bit overpowered in being with you."

"Please don't feel that way. I'm trying to be friendly without scaring you away. I was very impressed with you at Socorro and I've not lost the feeling."

Katie must lead this relationship in the proper direction. Without his apprehension, Justin might prove to be quite a man. He was very attractive and a cool companion. Her interest stirred in a strange way that she could not fathom. She wanted to know him in a personal way, but that could be difficult if he thought her lifestyle was above his.

They ate silently with each of them knowing they were on a special threshold. He cast several curious glances toward her. She expected him to voice his thoughts first, but he didn't.

"Let's live recklessly, Justin. I want another of these margaritas. How do you feel about another drink?"

"I need another drink. I may never see you again. I want to stretch this time with you and I'm searching for enough nerve to ask you to my motel room. I know it sounds fishy, but I swear my intentions are honorable."

"I sincerely *doubt* that your intentions are ever questionable. I'm getting to be a fair judge of character and I intend to consider you as a very nice guy unless you prove me wrong."

Justin paid the check and they strolled across the parking area to his motel. She walked in silence, but deep in thought. She wanted to explore intimate moments with him. She wanted to feel his arms circling her in a strong caress. These thoughts were overpowering her usual caution against romantic involvement.

Why am I feeling so emotional about this meeting with Justin? Am I suddenly developing a hunger for someone's love and attention, or is it a natural reaction to an attractive member of the opposite sex? My whole life is turning into a complete mystery.

He held the door open for her.

"As you can see, it's only a simple room. I doubt if the company would go for a suite. I'm only here for two days and one of them is nearly gone. Would you like some soothing background music on the cable channel?"

She nodded and rethought the situation as he searched. As she sat back in a seat, a surge of feeling swept over her. A memory rush tried to break through her mental fabric, but it only brought more anguish. If he could be enticed to show romantic attention, the memories might emerge.

"I'm sorry that I have no ballroom to offer you, Katie. Do you think we can dance on the carpet?"

"I'd love to try. I don't dance often, but I want to dance with you."

Without shoes, they moved to the music. The big surprise was their feeling of familiarity and the ease they found in togetherness.

She felt a tingling sensation that surprised her and saw his look change from meek to persuasive. He clearly had romantic feelings above and beyond her wildest expectations. When the music paused, he pulled her tightly to him in a possessive way. She allowed him to gently lift her chin to better reach her lips and then the kiss started tenderly, but progressed into a powerful search. She felt an exhilaration that was completely unfamiliar to her.

His hands moved to explore parts of her body and this sent even more tingles racing through her nerve network. She underwent feelings of a kind that she never dreamed or expected to experience.

This was the promise of future love fulfillment, but it was based on a relationship of extremely short duration. She returned his kiss with equal fire and passion, but the moment was soon gone.

"Justin I can't do this to you. You would be so easy to love and if I knew you better, it would only increase my feelings. In a few minutes, I'm leaving this room and I'll take along a most tender memory of the man that I want to learn to love. It's a selfish request, but I'd like you to wait for me. I have things in my life that must be corrected before I pledge myself to a relationship. I deeply believe in honest love and that's impossible until I straighten out my life. Things are messed up for me right now and I don't have answers, so please don't ask difficult questions."

His face was suddenly twisted and his eyes held a stricken look, but she moved close to him again.

With hot lips, she met his until he gave a quiver and then she broke from their embrace to hear him speak.

"I have few skills in the ways of love, but our case must rank as world class. I felt beneath your level in society's eyes and I was extremely pleased that you accepted me as an equal. I'm willing to wait, but it won't be easy. When you find answers, please call and give me an update."

The moment was difficult for her. More than anything in the world, she wanted to make love to this man with all her heart and soul, but it could not be. At some later time, she would return to him. When that day came, she would make absolutely certain that his wait had been worthwhile and his patience fully rewarded.

* * *

Before noon, at his Visions West desk, the senator took a phone call.

"Thank you for calling, Mr. Speaker," Todd said respectfully. "What can I do for you today?"

"For openers, you can tell me how you came by this information that you gave me."

The senator responded by asking an important key question.

"This sounds suspiciously like a show and tell game. Are you getting ready for an indictment? Do you anticipate a legal demand for source exposure?"

The Speaker answered carefully.

"The answer is no to both of your questions. We are not going with an investigation at this time."

"Then I see no reason for exposing my source. I've given you something, but I've got nothing from you. I don't understand where you're coming from, Mr. Speaker."

"Senator, you've turned over a real can of garbage. You've seen stonewalling at a high pitch, but this is something else. I may be Speaker of the House, but my hands are tied. I'm calling because I was told to stop digging. Since you're the one who initiated this probe, I must tell you to shut down all ongoing action in this matter."

"I'm no longer an active member of a governmental body. You can't throw orders at me. You'll need to give me something substantial, if I honor your request to back-off," Todd said.

The Speaker almost screamed at Todd. "In the interest of National Security, back off? Will that buy satisfaction from you?"

"Mr. Speaker, that plum's been rolled across the senate floor so many times that I'm hardened. Give me a specific and sound reason that I can swallow and swear me to secrecy. I'm unconditionally loyal to America. I'd never do anything to hurt this country. You're asking me to forget that someone is allowing graft and corruption. I feel I deserve better than what you're offering."

"I'm truly sorry, but I vowed to disclose no more than I already have. You certainly do deserve more than I can deliver and at some later time, I'll bust my butt to make amends. For now, I've done my job and you have a direct order to cease and desist. Good day to you, sir," he said tersely."

SHE CAME FROM SOCORRO

CHAPTER FIVE

At Katie's condo, Alexi's communicating device signaled for attention and she responded in rapid fashion. Each session with this mysterious man, gave her a little more hope that substantial answers might be forthcoming.

"I am pleased with your last piece of work. If you can do as well on this next assignment, I must find some way to reward you," he said gruffly. "You met James Simpson at the charity party, but you failed to build a relationship with him. We need to know many things from him. Simpson has connections with some powerful people. I wish to learn more about his connections. You must use extreme caution with him though, for he has neither morals nor ethics. Have you anything of value to report?"

"Whether I have anything to report, might depend on how you expect me to pry this information from Simpson. I'm experiencing some difficulty that you might need to hear about, but I'm uncertain if you care that much about my problems," she said.

"You simple minded wench," he screamed. "You could never fathom the amount of time and money that has been poured into your training and tutoring. A vast fortune in money and hoarded treasures was poured into this effort. We are on the threshold of success, but your stupid actions may keep the door locked. Listen closely! I can only care about your problems in the way that they affect the team. If you wreck the team, our quest is doomed."

Equally angry, she replied heatedly.

"Listen to this. I can do damn little for you if I'm dead. A friend overheard talk between Simpson, the Senator's son and an unknown man. They discussed my elimination and my friend is now in hiding."

"I sent her to my place in Socorro," Katie added. You mentioned a team, but the team seems to consist of you and me. Since I never hear from you except out of my purse, I believe that makes *me* the team."

The silence was nearly unbearable. Had she gone too far with sarcasm?

If she had a life and memory, had she just destroyed all hopes for the recovery of those precious items?

"What you have just told me may force me to alter the plan. Why would these men plan your death? What else have you done? Whatley is a weakling, but he is not a killer. You could not have offended Simpson, since you failed to socialize with him outside of the charity instance."

"I followed your instructions. You told me to stir their interest and I gave it a good try. They never responded in the way that you hoped. My friends in Socorro told me several inquiries have been made about my background. The unknown man with Simpson and Bradford said he was waiting on a report that concerned me. He made the statement to the others that if this report didn't identify me, I was to be immediately eliminated."

"There is something that you are not telling me. In this entire country, profit and revenge are the regular reasons for committing murder. Though sometimes there *is* a third. I need to meditate on this for a moment to find an answer. If one is seen as a threat to the life or security of another person, it might create an incentive for murder."

A momentary pause in his communication followed before his voice was heard again.

"Since there would be no profit from your death and the revenge factor is non-existent, we must examine this threat theory. In what way have you become a threat to Simpson? You don't even know this third man, but you must have become a threat to him. How about young Whatley? What does he have against you?"

"Well, he thinks that I'm after his father and the Whatley fortune. In his eyes, I may have become a threat. But you don't consider him to be a killer and I agree."

"Being incapable of killing does not prevent him from arranging the act," he said. "However, I have strong doubts that the other two would help him in this instance. It appears such a personal issue that I am sure they would refuse to get involved."

"Unless you have other plans for me, I'll be down at Socorro through the weekend and maybe I can get some clear thinking done about this."

"Your search for the connections of Simpson can begin after the weekend. Remember now, his important contacts have priority over his private business. Dig into his research operations once you have gathered the names. The next time we talk, I may have something for you that could be beneficial to your safety."

Long after Alexi had de-energized the communication device, she carefully considered their conversation. He failed to make any suggestions toward infiltrating the defenses of Simpson. Apparently, he considered her fully capable of making such decisions alone.

On Friday afternoon, she left work early. Several things were needed for her stay in Socorro. Hurriedly, she packed and stowed the luggage in the car trunk. Some daylight would remain when she reached her destination and she preferred it that way. She did not intend to be stranded on the road during darkness. Flat tires sometimes appear at the most unmerciful times. A few blocks from her condo, she decided that a sport car was tailing her. To reinforce her belief, she made three route changes.

The tailing car stayed with her. Familiar with the area, she turned onto a street with four paved lanes and traffic lights. Timing her speed to one of the lights, she quickly pulled over to the curb. The tailing car was forced to go past her and toward the signal light. The quick glimpse of the driver was not enough for recognition, so she pulled into the lane to his left.

Accelerating to the speed limit, she pulled alongside the car at the next signal light.

Sergai was behind the wheel and wore an angry face. With the green light, she moved away from his vehicle and he made no attempt to follow.

When Katie arrived in Socorro, Teresa gave a report on the events of the week.

She appeared very relieved to see her new friend.

"It's been a real scary week. For two days, a dark blue van was parked on the street. I watched closely, but never saw anyone coming or going from the thing."

"It was probably a surveillance rig."

Katie said this without thinking and then asked curiously.

"Now why did I say that? I don't know about such things."

"I've read and heard about them. They're equipped with snooping devices that can eavesdrop on conversations, even if you're on the telephone. I didn't make any calls and since I had no one here to talk with, I guess they just gave up," Teresa said.

"We must stay alert. If they show up again, I'll call the police and tell them someone is stalking me. You may be surprised to hear that Sergai was tailing me, as I left my condo. I faked him out and pulled alongside his car, but he wouldn't even look my way. This is a strange bag of goodies that we have here, Teresa. We're in need of help, but I have no one available. The most unfortunate thing is our inability to explain the reason for this mess. Without a believable reason, it's useless to seek help."

The doorbell announced a visitor and Katie peered through the peephole.

"Come in, Rosalie. It has been quite a while since we visited."

Rosalie spoke with a pleasant smile. "I saw your car here and wanted to say hello."

While introducing Teresa to the Indian woman, Katie remembered something Rosalie had said many weeks ago. This might be a good time to learn if she was as psychic as she appeared. When a conversational lull appeared, Katie opened with a question.

"You told me that you would be here for me if I needed to talk. Your offer was very much appreciated. If you're still willing to help, let's try it. I may not want to open the door to all topics, but let's take a shot at it.

"I'll try to help in any way I can. What you've done for Sam and me is very important to our future. I hope I can repay that kindness."

"I don't have any answers, so bear with me. Three men want us dead, but we don't know the reason. One of the men mistakenly thinks I'm after his father's money and wants me eliminated, but I can think of no sane reason why the other two want us dead."

Katie sighed and continued. "They're all in this mystery together. Teresa overheard their plans and now they're after her."

"Are you a believer in hypnotism?"

Katie answered with complete sincerity.

"I have absolutely no idea. If you believe in it, give it a try. If I don't respond properly, you can just cancel the trial."

Rosalie looked at Teresa questioningly. The dark eyes of the Indian woman gave all the order that was needed.

"I'll run up to the store for a few things. It may take about twenty minutes." Teresa said.

After the slim woman had gone, Katie readied a question for Rosalie.

"Why did you send her away? She's as involved in this as I am."

"Maybe she is and maybe she is more involved than you think. Trust no one else until we get a fix on your problem. There's no danger in a hypnotic spell if the hypnotist is qualified. I began early in life after finding I was different from most people. I consider myself ably qualified. You must cooperate fully for this spell to be successful. You must relax and listen carefully to my instructions. If you'll let my voice enter your mind and thoughts, the spell will be unbroken."

"Whenever you're ready to begin will be fine with me."

"Take my ring and look closely at it. Hold it up toward the light. See how it flashes and sparkles? It has special powers because it was made by an ancient medicine man of our tribe. He made great magic with this ring. We'll try to make some magic with it today."

As the full attention of Katie was drawn to the ring, the voice of Rosalie continued in a repetitive tone.

"Please give me your name, young lady."

"My name is Katie Ryan."

"Would you tell me your place of birth?"

"I was born in Fort Lauderdale, Florida."

"How long have you been in Socorro?"

"Several weeks, but I don't know exactly how long."

"Why have you come to Socorro?"

"I'm not sure," she replied after a pause. "I don't seem to have a reason."

"I see," Rosalie said quietly. "You've made several friends here in Socorro. Do you have sincere feelings for these new friends?"

"Oh yes! I have much love and affection for my friends in Socorro."

"Have you discovered any friends in Albuquerque?"

"I really admire Senator Whatley."

"I didn't ask if you admired anyone there, Katie. I want to know if you have friends in that city. Do you know the difference between friendship and admiration?"

"I don't believe I could be friends with someone that I didn't admire."

"We'll go on to something else. Listen carefully to my voice. Where had you been before Socorro? What town were you coming from?"

A long silence prevailed. Katie showed worry lines across her face as she struggled with this query from Rosalie. It was becoming obvious that she could not furnish the desired answer.

"I'm trying, but I'm not doing any good. I remember being outside Socorro, but I don't know how I got there. I'm mixed up now and it's getting worse. I can't even remember the face of the man who stole my purse."

Immediately, Rosalie clapped her hands sharply and spoke softly.

"I'm going to call you back now. We've done enough for one day. When you hear the next sound, you will return to me and we'll continue our visit."

She clapped her hands again and the eyes of Katie opened wider.

"You're back," the Indian woman said. "Are you feeling all right?"

"I feel just fine. Was the session worthwhile? Did you learn anything of value to help me with my past?"

"I wanted a lot more than I got. It will take more thought and planning than I hoped. You don't have much memory, do you?"

"Please be specific. I'm really tired of not knowing things. Do you think you can help me?"

"I'm not sure I can, Katie. I'm almost positive that you've been brainwashed, but you could be suffering from a fall or head injury. The after effects are somewhat similar."

"Did I say something to convince you that I've been brainwashed? That thought scares me more than ever."

"In a way, your story gave me all the clues we need to consider brainwashing. There's a snarl in your memory if you know that your purse was stolen, but can't remember the face of the one that stole it. If we could even dig up one absolute fact from your past, we could begin to build on that fact."

"You knew there was a problem when you met me and hinted as much. How could you tell, Rosalie?"

"Our eye contact gave up the secret. Our eyes tell much about our mental make-up. At times, your eyes reflected a little fear and at other times they showed much confidence, but no happiness at all. I saw no sparkle from your eyes. I may have oversimplified the answer to your question, but this ability has been handed down through my family for years and for me it is very simple. Sam told me that you rejected a man with romantic urges. Because you rejected him, he made you walk. This male throwback also stole your purse. Most any woman would remember that face for a lifetime."

"To be totally honest, I heard myself telling that story to Sam and until then, I didn't even know it had happened. I've lost track of the difference between real and imaginary images. I wouldn't know my parents on sight. I don't even know if I *have* parents."

"It's too bad that your Aunt Clarita is dead. Do you suppose her other relatives could give some information that might shed a little light on your past?"

Getting into the fabricated Aunt Clarita bit was a little too much, since that was nothing but a story.

She had been told earlier by Rosalie that it is nearly impossible to lie while hypnotized. Now, she was puzzled in recalling her purse theft. She was almost certain this story had also been fabricated. It appeared certain now that she must dismiss the relatives of her aunt as neither knowing nor caring about her welfare.

"They were so far away and cold toward our family, they would never be of help to me. I think I can work this out before long. I have moments when memories try to flood into my mind, but I can't pull them on out."

After a moment she spoke again.

"When I see loving, caring people and when others are exceptionally nice to me, I get these flashbacks. All that we have talked about though has done nothing to ease my mind about these men that want to harm me. I was hoping to find relief from that worry."

"From what you tell me, your present memory has been excellent since your arrival in Socorro. If that's true, you should remember if you made an enemy. It may be that in working with the senator, you've seen or done something that they see as a threat. I could never pull that information from your mind. I do have a little ESP ability, but not enough to handle that load. I still say beware of Teresa. She might seem to be a friend now, but she might also become a threat."

Back at her office desk the next day, Katie used free moments to consider her options. With Teresa deciding to remain in Socorro for some time, her only concern now was for herself.

She intended to take precautions to prevent an ambush or sudden attack. The preventive actions she had already taken were only a start.

Few preparations could be made to pluck secrets from Simpson without knowing more about him. Perhaps the senator could give her some leads. Rising from her chair, she quickly headed for Todd's office.

In response to her light tap at the open door, he spoke thoughtfully.

"Come on in. I have been sitting and dreaming for the last half hour. I am such a fool to have spent all those years in the Senate and neglect my family. When Brad really needed a father, I was trying to pump bills through committee. When Mildred needed the comforting presence of her husband, I was locked up in chairing another committee that could not come to agreement. Shortly before she died, she asked me to take a week off and go fishing with my son. I simply could not fit it into my schedule. Now, if it isn't too late, I have another chance to get better acquainted with Brad."

"Senator, that's wonderful. Please tell me more."

"I phoned and asked him to visit me for the week-end. He was not enthused about my offer, but he agreed and we began the visit with an argument about his friends. I was extremely stern with him and stated if his friends were so important, charity could probably find a better use for my estate. I was not making a baseless threat and he knew it."

Todd paused for a moment and smiled weakly. "We were then able to find common ground for conversation. He told me about his suspicions of you and I set him straight on that score. Through our talk, I learned that he has strong feelings about the years when I was too busy to be a father. I promised to atone for the failure in some manner. I told him things were happening that threatened to bring down some important people. Unless he wanted to risk his future, he simply had to clean his house. We finished the week-end with one of the most enjoyable times I can recall."

"How did he accept your advice? Was he argumentative and angry or had he mellowed out enough to listen?"

"He listened well enough to ask me for a week to close out his ongoing deals and then he wants to return to Visions West. You helped make this possible and I'll be eternally grateful."

"I did nothing that you wouldn't have done soon. Did he mention anyone or speak of anything that might help us in identifying Mr. Big?"

"No, he did not and I was hesitant to push my luck. I had already gotten more from his visit than I expected."

"Well, I'm back to the drawing board with my problems. Hartley called to ask if I had reconsidered his job offer. I'm afraid I lied to him. I told him that you were considering an office in Washington and the idea intrigued me. I mentioned all the important young lawmakers that such a move might allow me to meet. That turned him on and he asked to see me socially. Am I boring you with this talk, Senator?"

"Hell No! I'm getting a bang out of it. In fact, I'm tempted to do the very thing that you lied about. Brad could run the plant here and you and

I could try to improve our company relations with the federal government. Also, such a move would get you away from whoever has been trailing you."

When her workday was over and she reached her condo door, close attention was paid to the tiny particle of paper wedged in the crevice between door and jamb. Since the small sentinel was still there, she knew it would be safe to unlock and enter. This type of safeguard was necessary if she wanted to live and complete her mission.

Her answering machine had just one simple message.

"The truck with the big ears is back. I wish they would go away."

Nothing else was on the tape. It was Teresa's way of telling her to stay alert. These agents should know that she was here in Albuquerque working for the senator. Could they somehow know that Teresa was staying at her Socorro place?

For lack of anything more productive to do, she went to her computer. If Hartley was not using his system, she might browse for a while. After inserting his password, she waited patiently for his company logo to appear.

Instead, the screen came alive with words. It took her a moment to understand that Hartley had used the machine as a word processor. She could not see the beginning of the message and the recipient was unknown, but the importance of the message was never in doubt as she read the words.

"I did not choose to be in this position. I was placed into this spot like a piece on a game board. I realize that you may not have suggested the action, but I know you have the power to make my troubles disappear. I don't make threats, but I do take active steps to protect myself. Some steps have been taken and others will soon follow. If you want my advice, I'll tell you to take some bidders out of the game. I am one of the few bidders with America's best interests at heart. Your influence is felt in America and much of the world. I leave you with this question. What have you done for our country lately?"

Katie read these words in complete admiration. She had not imagined Hartley as having this amount of guts and grit. Knowing that he might go to print or review his message at any moment, she decided to exit.

When she shut her machine down, her mind clouded with doubts. What had she bumped into now? Snarls of mysterious activity seemed to wait for her at every turn. She earlier believed Hartley to be a top gun and crooked as anyone. It was a surprise to learn *he* was also being used. He made a strong statement to someone holding a tremendous amount of power.

If she knew the identity of this individual, she might begin unraveling this mess. Going back into his computer would accomplish nothing. He would never leave the complete message on his machine for an extended time.

Alexi could not help her with this riddle. He still expected her to extract information from Simpson.

The senator's standing was different because he could probably name the man that Hartley was challenging. When the situation called for knowing present power, or power of the past, Todd knew most of the seats of clout. She decided to seek his advice. His problems with Hartley had not lowered his integrity and for that, he was entitled to more information.

The next day, she marched resolutely into his office and spoke boldly.

"It seems if I come in here, I want something. Today, I'm hoping that you can help identify another Mr. Big. Are you interested?"

"I'm extremely interested. Give me what you've got and we'll go to work on it."

"I'll set the stage by describing Hartley products that are being tested and evaluated. Then we can open a complete sheet of Hartley contacts and phone numbers. I'll end with a partial message that Hartley intends to send to a person of great importance. If you view these bits of information as a trespass into the privacy of Hartley and prefer to be unaware of them, I'll stop now."

"I have reasons to risk this invasion of privacy and we'll discuss those reasons later, but please proceed with your disclosures."

Katie was either gifted or trained in the art of memory retention. Having this ability, she was able to repeat each item of value.

When she repeated the intercepted message that Hartley was composing, Todd was stunned.

"I am certainly glad that you're working for me, instead of against me," he said. "This is valuable information. It fits in nicely with the brick wall I met in trying to blow the whistle on the contracts department. Even the esteemed Speaker of the House, couldn't push an investigation. He called back and told me to cease and desist. He said that I was to do no more prying into the General Procurement Administration."

"Is that not considerably odd?" she queried. "You would expect them to appreciate early information that might prevent a later red face."

"Only the highest level cabinet people would be able to swing this weight. The face of this unknown man seems to be taking on the appearance of our Secretary of Defense. I'd wager my life that he can't be bought. Why he's interfering in the private business sector and allowing illegal activities is more of a mystery than I can swallow. I'm going home early. Why don't you do the same? The world may have a cleaner look tomorrow."

Across town, phone lines were busy. "What do you mean, Whatley? Do you think this is a simple little game that you can play until you tire of it? I'd bet you've given no thought to the serious consequences of walking away. Are you getting scared now that the pressure is building?"

"No, it isn't fear that makes me walk. I suddenly realized that everything I ever wanted is just a heartbeat away. If I don't break my ties and return to Visions West, the Senator intends to change his will and leave everything to charity. When I walk away from you and the man, my lips are sealed. I'll never reveal anything that could bring damage to this corporation, or to its people. It will become a closed chapter of my life. I hope everyone can understand why I must do this thing."

"I understand. Still, the best bet to save your butt is to hope the man understands. He may insist that you have your tongue cut out as an insurance policy. You haven't the guts to squeal. You'd regret seeing the last year of your life exposed in the media."

"Stop it, James. None of us have clean hands. If the big man was exposed, our government might become worse than the stink on a four-letter word. You have an independently thriving and stand-alone business. Why do you persist in this association with undesirable people?"

"Who makes the call on what is undesirable? Very few people in our government are more respected and important than the man. Life must be exciting, even risky, if it's worth living. Go on back to your drab father and his humdrum plant and live your drab life. If you ever get another urge to live a little, give me a call. I may not let you back in, but it will furnish me with a laugh."

Later in the same day, from her desk, Katie made a personal phone call.

"You may not remember me, but we met several weeks ago at a charity affair. This is Katie Ryan and since we are in a year of the sexual revolution, I have an option. This option says that if an interesting man fails to call me, as he hinted that he would, then I have the right to pursue for the reason."

There was a few seconds of silence before the sound of muffled laughter.

"Please excuse me, Katie. I shouldn't laugh, but that is so funny and unreal that I can't seem to help myself. I can't believe a beautiful lady would pursue anybody for any reason. Maybe you should slow down and let them catch up."

"I'm nearly twenty two years old, funny boy. If I wait until some shy fellow gets enough nerve to come knocking, I might find myself on Social Security and still unconnected."

"Maybe I should do something about that before you give up," he said. "I have a dinner appointment tonight, but I'm free tomorrow night. Would you be interested in dinner, around eight?"

"Certainly, that was my reason for this call. It was so gallant of you to ask," she said.

"Before your claws get too sharp, you should give me your address."

Later, she walked to the bathroom and splashed cold water on her face. It had taken much nerve to make that call. To go through with this date would be even more of an ordeal. Well aware of the risks, she knew this was a dangerous game. Still, she knew of no other way to learn the things that Alexi wanted. It was foolhardy as walking into the web of a giant poisonous spider.

James was a conspiring member of a group that wanted her dead. She did not know their reason and it would take considerable luck to avoid learning too late. Once out of her condo and away from the senator, the danger intensified.

The following day was mostly uneventful and as it drew to a close, she spoke to Todd on the intercom system.

"Senator, I'm leaving a little early and I want to tell you something before I leave. It's important that you know where I am tonight. Everything may go well, but I'm going out to dinner with James Simpson. Even though my source says he is conspiring to kill me, I pressed him for the dinner date. I've reached the point where I must know with whom I'm dealing. I can't let Mr. Big remain unknown much longer. I might dig enough information from James to fill in some blanks."

"I don't approve of this move, Katie. Why haven't you told me that your life was threatened? I can't help much at this late date, but I'll make some calls. Associating with the likes of Simpson can be harmful to you socially and physically. Find an excuse to call me just before dinner is served. I want to know exactly where you're dining and if the date extends into dancing. I'm looking for the proper time to begin worrying. I can't possibly sleep until I know you're safe at home."

Later in the evening, James escorted her into the posh and exclusive country club dining area.

It had been a quiet ride from her place. He complimented her on her looks and dress, but other talk was at a minimum.

The waiter held her chair and Simpson declined when the man asked if he wanted a wine list.

"I'll have my regular, Albert. The lady may make her own choice."

"I'll go along with your selection, James. I can try it and see if it works."

"It's a rare combination of grapes and bottled by a small winery in Mission San Jose. They're growing slowly, but they're destined to become a tremendously successful operation."

"Sounds to me like you may have some seed money tied up in this company."

He laughed wickedly as he remarked with a knowing wink.

"You *are* a smart girl. Schools must be much better in Florida. You seem so knowledgeable and in control. I'd wager that at seventeen you led the boys a merry chase."

"What a lucky guess you've made. Of all the possible states, you picked the winner. Are you a mind reader, sir? Must I keep my mind free of all personal thoughts to hold them safe from you?"

"We can dispense with the games. When someone stirs my interest, I check him or her out. I freely admit that I was attracted to you at first sight."

"Why did you not pursue this attraction? Why did you wait for me to make the first move? Did you find something negative that made you reluctant to call? A girl has a right to know."

"You lead a strange life. I hear your family got involved with the federal government while you were in high school. You were put in the Witness Protection system and your parents are still involved. Somehow, you've gotten released. I'll expect you to bring me up to date on the details."

She took a moment to stare at him, seeing him for the first time in the dangerous light that he projected.

As an adversary, he might possibly be the meanest one that she would ever face. All of her wits might need to come to the forefront on this night.

"Have you ever seriously considered writing a novel? You have the most imaginative mind that I've ever seen. Don't give me that old negative headshake. You certainly didn't pay private detectives for the worthless drivel that you've just described."

"Because of your interest, I have a right to know your background?"

"My past life is personal until I decide to reveal it. I might add that if you choose to socialize with me, what you see is what you get."

The wine was deliciously zesty, just tangy enough to be exciting and she got into it quickly, trying to quell her rising temper.

He had color rising to his cheekbones and seemed to welcome her sudden quietness. The appearance of the waiter, seeking to take their dinner order, was a blessing.

They danced with little conversation, until time for their food and then returned to their table. Unless she could melt some of the ice that formed so quickly, this night would be a waste.

"A few days ago, I talked with Hartley. He offered me a job and I'm considering it. What do you think of him? Would he make a decent Boss?"

"Why work for that old goat? If you're unhappy with the senator, you can work anywhere. Word has spread of your ability, thanks to that old fool. You'd be trading one has-been for another in my opinion. The senator has had his day and Hartley is headed for a downward spiral."

"Well! Excuse me! How can a girl get ahead if her only contacts are losers? The senator is considering opening an office in Washington. I took that as a sign that things were looking up. That's the main thing holding me at Visions West. If Hartley is going downhill, I may have to leave town."

"If I get to know you better, I could probably do you some good. I have friends that make opportunities happen. It would not be wise to introduce you though until I can vouch for you. They are important people and they are very security conscious," he bragged.

She excused herself and headed for the powder room to call Todd.

"I'm here, Senator. I haven't learned anything yet, but I'm still safe. We won't be going out to dance. We're at the *Desert Winds* country club and it has a dance floor."

"I know of it. Will you be there very long?"

"I'll try to get away early. I'm sure I can think of something."

Back at their table, the conversation dwindled toward comparing the entrees to those of other eateries. She pushed her plate back and he refilled her wine glass.

"You caused me to re-think my future, James. I'd be stupid to sit in the senator's office until the roof caves in. I need to find deeper pockets and opportunity. Can you really open doors for me? I've been told to beware of men that promise candy to young girls."

"In these days, a good business manager would tell you to get the candy first. I can't open doors for you until I know more about you."

"What can I tell that you don't already know? Your detective must have a tie-in with the FBI. They swore that no one would learn our identity. We lived a quiet life for several years, but I got tired of the surveillance. I sneaked off one night and put many miles between my parents and me. I'll go back and find them some day. We were being protected from an old man and when he dies, the threat will disappear. I can't reveal more for it might cause harm to my parents. If I sound bitter at times, I wish you'd try to understand. This has been six tough years that I'll never forget."

James stared for several seconds. It was just a wild stab and it looked like an error when she covered up so beautifully. This made things different. He'd dig into her past now and find something to hold over her head. Knowing she was in the Witness Program would let his detectives do their work. Using the threat of exposing her parents, he could totally dominate her.

"I feel very sorry for you. I know it must have been rough, but better days are coming."

"I can't help being excited. When can I see these people?"

"I can't reveal their identity until I get everything set up. I can give you a hint of one man's importance. A senator from this state comes running when he calls and he calls often."

"I'm impressed and I would like to know more, but I'll trust you to do the right thing."

On delivering Katie to her condo, he expected to be invited inside. He looked dismayed, when she only kissed him lightly on the cheek and closed her door. In seconds, she was on the phone to the senator.

"I'm home, sir. I've got something, but it can wait until I see you."

The next morning as Katie entered her office, Todd was waiting. Coffee was brewing and he wore a frown and rumpled clothing. She had never seen him in such a state.

"Senator, please get your robe on and let me run an iron over those clothes. You have an appointment in thirty minutes."

He answered in terse tones.

"I will if you'll promise to talk while you iron."

She smiled patiently at him. "Done deal, I can iron and talk."

"You've become very important to me," he told her earnestly. "I value you not only as an important aide, but as an individual. You have the most magnetic and powerful personality of any woman I've ever met. Your aura manages quietly and quickly to infiltrate the minds of others. I care for you very much and I couldn't have worried about you more if you were my daughter. I hope you won't take any more risks with your personal safety."

When he returned to her office, he wore a robe and a better expression.

"I'm sorry to see you so uptight, Todd. I don't want to cause you more worry than you already have."

He looked at her strangely and then grinned across his weathered face.

"This is the first time you've called me by my name. We may be beginning to like each other. Well, spit it out, what did you learn from Simpson?"

"He said his agents checked me out. Their report said my parents and I were involved in a witness program. I let him think this was true. He said if he got to know me better, doors could be opened for me. He knows someone big and powerful who supposedly owns one of our senators from New Mexico."

"What were his exact words regarding the senator?"

She repeated that part of the conversation, word for word.

"I'm almost positive that Senator Hildon is the man Simpson was referring to. I'll certainly make some calls and try to verify this information. You've made a very important discovery, Katie. Please don't do it again though, I'm uncertain if my old heart can stand the strain. You have no need to place yourself in further danger."

* * *

In Washington, eight men gathered around a large expensive conference table. Most were from the Contracts and Procurements section, but the House Speaker was also there. The most notable of the group was the Secretary of Defense, and he opened the meeting.

"Gentlemen, I have a problem that must be fixed. All of you except the Speaker are involved to some extent. An outsider brought him into this situation. We're involved in a program to develop a new weapon. Our original approach has turned complicated. Ordinarily, this program would be completed in a legal, ethical, and moral manner, but we had to make some adjustments. I'm not usually involved in the daily operation of this system, but I was asked to get involved due to complications."

He rested his voice momentarily. "One of our important vendors notified us of an impending bankruptcy. Without funding for extended development or an immediate contract they would belly up. I tried the proper channels, but they wouldn't budge. Since time and the vendor's products were of such priority, I took the suggestion of an aide and made sure that this vendor won a contract. Somehow, other vendors learned of our compromise and it suddenly became a problem."

Wiping his brow of moisture from the humidity, he then continued.

"I accept responsibility for my adjustments. I made the decision because our country needs this system. Such heavy competition can breed graft, corruption, and a tremendous amount of greed. The worse case scenario has happened, Gentlemen. Now, it's time for our House Speaker to share the infamous spotlight."

"I'm not sure if I should thank you, Mr. Secretary," he said carefully. "I'll do what I can to put my spin on this sorry state of affairs. A few weeks ago, I was asked to investigate a charge of conspiracy to defraud the government. The details involved a private contractor and two members of our contracts division. The contractor was given a rigged contract over several other bidders for product development. His product was no better than an equal and deserved no edge in the bidding war. My source gave me names and dates of the inside men, along with the check numbers from their payoff. A very thorough job, huh? I began to hunt for an investigating committee and our esteemed Secretary stopped me in my tracks. I'm waiting for an explanation, but we'll likely get one today."

"These people from contracts have actually done nothing wrong," the Secretary explained. "Their payoff money was returned to the general fund. They were merely following our orders. I pressured the Chief of Contracts into this situation, so I can't allow him to take any heat either."

He waited a few moments and surveyed those about him. When it was apparent that no one was leaving, he prepared to speak.

"Three companies are developing engines more powerful than any we have, but they are surprisingly quieter. Listening devices cannot detect their noise outside a ten-mile area. Each of the contractors' engines has similarities that could be the result of engineering leaks. Three of these contractors show possibilities of marketing the most durable, lightweight metal in existence."

He paused and drank water from a glass provided by an aide before returning to his subject.

"As if this product wasn't important enough in that light alone, its radar deflecting ability puts the stealth bomber to shame. Again, no qualities exist to give either company an edge. Five companies are engaged in a race for the most sophisticated guidance delivery system that has ever been developed. Again, our engineers tell us that neither of these companies have a product that is greatly superior to the other. Though multiple sources for a vital product looked like a blessing, this thing has turned into a disaster."

He used another pause to gaze at the faces before him. "I received word from reliable sources within these companies, that threats are in the air to peddle their wares on the open market. If they can't get additional funding to develop their products and/or favorable contracts to manufacture diversified products, they want to take their show on the road. We know it was a mistake to pacify the first disgruntled company. We caved in the first time and the domino effect followed. We're almost held hostage and I simply don't know what to do about it. When the

Speaker began to unwind my detestable ball of yarn, I had to stop him and try to regroup."

He took another short breath and continued.

"I have another thing of importance, before I yield to questions from the floor. I received a very surprising communication from an instrumental contractor in the State of New Mexico. In his letter, he advised me to take some of these other bidders out of the game. I'll say that even as we speak, records are being turned to see who can be eliminated from this bidding program."

A flurry of hand rising broke out as the Secretary finished and he acknowledged them one by one. To each questioner, he was polite and patient.

After questioners had been pacified and a few had taken leave, the House Speaker looked hard at the Secretary before asking a question.

"Are you at liberty to disclose the name of the contractor from New Mexico? It seems we've been keeping secrets from each other long enough."

"It was Hartley and you are entirely correct. We need to have more meetings of the minds and try to avoid these disgraceful incidents. Was it Hartley that turned the conspiracy news to you?"

"No sir! Todd Whatley put me on the trail. We've done a terrible injustice to that old patriot. As an honest citizen and former trusted senator, he was appalled by this conspiracy."

"Rightfully so and I applaud him. He's one of the few that failed to join the scam. We'll have to find a way to make amends to him and soon."

CHAPTER SIX

Back at his hotel, a very powerful man received another phone call.

"Sir, I've kept watch on the Sandusky broad for two weeks and learned nothing. She knows I'm here and she's staying cool. Do you want me to continue the surveillance?"

"She's another Simpson mistake, Quince. It's time to erase this mistake, but don't do it in Socorro. Take her away and make it seem a road accident. Your next job will be to cover Simpson's activities in a covert manner. I have a call on my other line."

The man punched the phone button and then raked his fingers through his thinning thatch of hair. A man of little patience, he spoke tersely.

"Yes, I'm here. What can I do for you?"

"I'm sorry for disturbing you, but Hildon is missing. We've been unable to find him."

"What do you mean, missing? I want a full update immediately."

"He's not been on the senate floor for two days. I got no answer at his apartment, so I broke in. He either packed and left, or was taken away."

"His absence will cause an inquiry by the FBI. Stay still for a few days. "

Things seemed different now. The wheels of his once powerful machine were falling off. Years of seeding the proper pockets had brought him to the present stage of his success. Only a few people knew the power that he held.

To unravel his business interests would challenge the finest of investigators. In forming his group, he carefully chose aides considered worthy of trust and he believed his selections were wise. He endured enormous expense in attempting to sail a firm course. It was now becoming apparent that someone was rocking his boat.

* * *

At lunch, Katie punched in the number of her Socorro home phone. She tried again later, but got no answer and was puzzled. Teresa may have grown enough courage to return to Albuquerque. At home later, she checked her messages and found nothing from Teresa. After a shower and snack, she called Socorro again without success.

A movie, edited for television, kept her occupied until almost bedtime. She decided to have a bite of fruit and went to the kitchen. Removing the peel from an orange, she heard a news bulletin and eased toward the TV set. She was unprepared for the following news item.

State Police today discovered the partially burned body of a local woman. The body was found off the Interstate near Socorro. The woman's car may have blown a tire and careened into the deep, dry wash where she was found. The car was partly consumed by the fire, but the license tag was legible. Through the tag and other articles, they identified the woman as Teresa Sandusky. Always one to volunteer for civic and charitable affairs, Ms. Sandusky will be missed by all who knew her.

There was more, but she had heard enough. This news cast a cold and bitter feeling like an enormous damp shawl on a winter day.

Teresa had not lost control of her car. Somehow, they had gotten to her and committed an act of murder. Unless she felt safe, Teresa would never have left Katie's home.

With anger burning from her insides, she dressed for a trip to Socorro. As she drove, her mind spun like a finely tuned machine. Things sometimes fall into place as a natural course. At other times, you have to kick-start things if you want forward movement. It wasn't just forward movement she was looking for now, she wanted revenge.

At the same time, she was taking out some of the frustration she had accumulated since she first came to Socorro. She sought retaliation for loss of memory and for the many mysteries that had been dumped on her. By the time she reached Socorro, she was in a killing mood.

Outside her door, the porch light broke the darkness and shadows. The night was quiet and nothing seemed amiss. Carefully, she took the gun from her purse and gripped it firmly. It felt good and it felt comfortably normal.

A feeling of calmness settled about her and she turned the key in the lock. Once inside, she flipped a switch and the entry was lit with a warm, safe yellow glow.

Stepping carefully across the carpet, she reached the phone desk. If Teresa had left any type of message, it would probably be here. Staring at a note pad that lay near the phone, she tried to recapture the last moments that Teresa had spent here. If the situation was reversed and she was leaving, what would she do? *I'd leave some kind of message*. But if someone took Teresa away, there might not have been time for a message.

She picked the notepad off the desk and looked closely. Nothing was written on the top page or on any pages. To sort the possible actions of Teresa, she began doodling with the lead pencil and then stopped. With the pencil held in a slanted position, she shadowed the top page with a coating of lead and saw numbers appear like magic.

Teresa may not have tried to leave a message, but she did. Unless Katie's best guess was off-base, the top page now contained the license tag numbers from the blue van that had long worried Teresa. Because the page was missing, someone had taken Teresa *and* the written note.

* * *

The man of power sat in a rented hotel suite awaiting a phone call and scowling impatiently. This was like the hated earlier days when he waited for things to happen because he lacked the power to speed things along. Now, with even more power than he ever dreamed possible, he was completely stalled. Years had been spent to create a splendid offense. Could a weak defense bring him down at this late stage of the game?

He knew Hildon lacked the guts to run away on his own. Someone must have taken him out of the game. Who would have enough gall to snatch a United States Senator? What could anyone hope to gain by holding or killing this lawmaker? It had been five days now and no word of Hildon had surfaced. He would never stay off the senate floor this long unless he had a severe problem.

The senator was one of the hearts that pumped vital information into this man's network of industries. A foreign bank account had been established and the solon was paid lavishly for his efforts. The man had no regrets for paying such an excessive amount to Hildon and he would be nearly impossible to replace.

A burst of intuition suddenly struck the man full in the face. Someone had learned of his ties with the senator. Only three men knew of this connection to Hildon and one of those was above suspicion. Either Simpson or young Whatley must have sold him out. What could either of them hope to gain by betraying him? The phone signal jarred his stream of thought.

"Yes, this is me," he said tersely.

"This is James, sir. Has Whatley mentioned that he wants out of our organization?"

The man carefully controlled his voice.

"No! He has not said a word."

"His daddy threatened to cut him off without a dime unless he breaks his ties and returns to the Senator's company."

"Thank you, I'll take it from here. I have to go now, I'm getting another call."

He waited a few more seconds before punching the phone button.

"I congratulate you on the handling of your last chore, but put a temporary hold on the Simpson deal. I've got another important chore for you. Young Whatley wants out of the company. He has already spilled to someone about our organization. He must be taken out before he can cause more damage."

"I understand, sir. Consider it done. Do you want a report, or would you rather read about it in the newspaper?"

"The media should tell me everything I need to know."

The man needed the comfort of his place above Albuquerque. He would not go there again though, until some of this mess was resolved. Why was his contact in Washington not calling? It seemed that competent help could no longer be found.

This scenario seemed like a return to the old days. Many restless minutes passed before the phone signaled.

"Yes!" he spoke gruffly into the transmitter.

"I know who I'm speaking to, but it's not necessary that you know me. The important thing is the message that I'm to deliver. We've taken your eyes and your ears from you. What happens next is strictly up to you. You chose to make this game rough instead of competitive. Now, we'll find out if you're up to the rough game. You know we have him, how else would we know how to reach you? How much more can we learn from your stooge?"

The man sat in total surprise and looked at the phone for several minutes after the caller's disconnect. The other games that he had played and won had not been like this one. Suddenly, the man's phone again signaled for attention. He reached for the instrument with hands that were trembling. The situation was becoming a severe test of his courage.

This time he spoke in a flat tone.

"Yes! I'm waiting for your message."

"I have nothing to report on Hildon, sir. I have other news that might be a tie-in though. I got an excited call from the engineer, Weede. He says our two men from contracts section are no longer there and no one seems to know where they went. What shall I do next, sir?"

"You have their home addresses. Check there and see what you can learn, but do it undercover. Use the surveillance truck and make certain that you're not spotted," the man instructed carefully.

His confidence was being severely tested now. He sensed that an unknown enemy was attacking him on all sides. Without answers that seemed beyond his power to obtain, he could no longer chart his course. Although he detested the thought of what he must do, no choice remained. The boss must be consulted and it would seem like an admission of failure. For years he had led this operation alone and received high praise for his efforts. He, along with Simpson and young Whatley, had traveled to exotic places during the times of success to celebrate. Now, he might learn how the boss would treat his people in times of failure. He punched in the feared numbers and waited patiently for the security precautions to begin. He knew all the steps, though he had only used the number on rare occasions.

First, Caller ID checked the calling number. Next the caller's line was switched to the desk of his boss, where the caller's ID was shown on his personal monitor. At this point, the big man made the decision to use the regular line or a secure channel.

The deep voice came promptly. "Go ahead Sergai. The scrambler is on."

"Sir, things are happening that may require your attention. I would not bother you if I had a decent option."

"Explain why you can't handle this problem in your usual capable way. I rely on your fine ability to keep me out of the daily routine of our operation."

"I'm not admitting failure on this end, sir. I begin to worry though, when my contacts are suddenly unable to find Senator Hildon. We also discovered that two men from contracts have similarly disappeared. Due to the magnitude of these circumstances, I felt you should be notified."

"You are quite correct, Sergai. I'll begin a quiet little probe into this matter and I'll get back to you as soon as possible."

* * *

In Albuquerque, the Hartley receptionist eyed Katie carefully as she approached the desk.

"May I help you, Miss?"

"Yes. Would you please tell Bob that Katie Ryan is here? I have no appointment, but he might find an open spot for me."

"I'll try, Miss Ryan, but he is very busy today."

She punched some buttons and after delivering the message, rolled her eyes in surprise.

"He says you should come right in. Take the door to your right."

Smiling sweetly at the astonished woman, Katie went quickly to the door where she tapped gently.

Hartley opened the door and motioned her inside.

"I'm surprised, but happy to see you. What's on your mind? Can I put you to work today?"

"Bob, I'm not sure that I can work for anyone. There's a lot of turmoil in my life now. I can't go much longer without answers, so I came to you."

"I'm not solving many of my own problems, but I'll try to help with yours. If you'll lay one on me, I'll see what I can do."

"Without naming a particular reason, let me say that my opinion of you has changed. Several days ago, I couldn't have brought problems to you. I don't know why, but someone wants me dead. This is not a case of paranoia. Teresa and I were both marked for elimination and now she's gone."

"Teresa died in a car crash. How could you possibly connect her death with murder? Give me something solid if you want my help."

"Solid? I'll give you solid. Listen! She came to me in the middle of the night. She was scared silly and wanted to hide out from James Simpson. She overhead a conversation about eliminating me and they recognized her. Someone sacked her place looking for something and I sent her to my house in Socorro. She would not leave my place without a note or a call. A blue surveillance van was parked on the street and she was terribly scared of it."

"Are you positive Simpson is involved? I can't see him as a major player in any kind of game. I consider him a fringe man trying to take advantage of the research and development of everyone else. Have you taken your theory to the senator?"

"I don't know enough about Simpson to take to anyone, but he spoke of developing an exciting new product. Since his evolving was in mining, I thought your paths might have crossed. You're still into mining and I hoped that you could give me some leads. I never learned the name of his company or what they produce," she said softly.

"I'm not a gullible man. As much as I admire you, it would be impossible for you to sweet talk information from me. I *do* consider myself an excellent judge of character and I'd wager my company that you're not here on the senator's behalf. I'm in deep competition with the senator, but I believe he's a square man. I'll tell you what little I know about Simpson."

Simpson's only company, according to Hartley, was named Phantum Enterprises and it began as a mining operation. There was a big demand for several types of ore, native to the area. As Phantum grew and prospered, it added a plant in Albuquerque and began to develop various products to manufacture.

They never expanded enough to seriously compete with Hartley in the mining operation, but their new line of products was getting a piece of the market.

"When he began competing for government contracts, things began going to hell," Hartley said thoughtfully. "When he opened his plant, I lost two extremely capable engineers to him. Without examining their fabrication area, there's no way I can prove they took my technology to him. If allowed to snoop around a bit, I might recognize a lot of their procedures."

"You should have a face-to-face with the senator. He's a real decent man and would be an honorable competitor. If the two of you talked and compared notes, you might learn more about your competitors," she said gently.

"You could be right. The way things are in business these days it couldn't hurt a bit. I just can't figure the feds position in this thing. They've waffled, meddled, and finally managed to screw up the whole process. I'd take early retirement tomorrow if I didn't have so much time and money tied up in the Hartley Company."

"Bob, I have to go right away. The senator will get alarmed if I don't call or show my face. I walked away from my desk and didn't leave a note. Now that you've given me a starting point with Simpson, I can begin to track down some of this mystery. I thank you for the help and I hope to see you later."

As she walked to her car, she considered her position.

Todd would have given her the name of Simpson's company, but Hartley had given her more. His remark concerning the entrance of Phantum into fields other than mining, gave her a burning desire to learn more details of that bold move. If the fortunes of Hartley Corporation began to slide at that time, did Visions West also begin to take some losses?

With her car in view, she began counting the safety precautions that she had taken.

The auto's security system was the latest and greatest. Her new cell phone also gave her a sense of security.

With each passing day, she found ways to increase her defenses. Punching the phone buttons, she readied herself to receive a scolding from the doting ex-senator.

She was very appreciative of his affection and she would be gentle.

"Senator, I just wanted to check in and ask for the remainder of the day off. Don't try to con me now, I know your schedule."

"I can work through the day without you, but please stay in contact. I can't do much for you when I don't know where you are."

The Florida search for records was good experience for what she intended to do.

Phantum had to be a registered corporation or it wouldn't be doing business with the federal government. Her objective was to learn how Phantum came into existence. It might also be valuable to learn the identity of the officers of the corporation. After spending hours of searching through several buildings and reams of records, she was exhausted and only partially successful.

Todd would not be happy to learn what she had discovered. Tomorrow, she would confide more in the senator and hope for new revelations.

When Katie arrived home, she did not immediately enter the condo. The fragment of paper was gone from the door crack. Someone had entered her living space and the unknowns began to sour her stomach. It was decision making time.

If the intruder had gone away, had he set a trap for her? What was waiting on the other side of that door? If he was still inside, could she get through the door without alerting him? These questions were flying at her mind like angry hornets. She'd never learn the answers to these questions while standing outside the door.

In examining the lock area she saw no visible damage and determined that the intruder had either picked the lock or obtained a key. Unless he had relocked the door, entering would be easy. With the gun in her right hand, she eased the other hand onto the doorknob and gently twisted. It clicked quietly and was now ready to open, but was she ready?

Steeling herself with some effort, she quickly pushed the door open and with gun upraised, stepped inside. Seeing no one as yet, she moved carefully into the kitchen. The intruder was not there either. Cat-like, she moved through the hall toward her main bedroom.

The unmistakable sound of a drawer closing alerted her to the intruder's presence. Grimly, she stepped through the open doorway and pointed the pistol at the back of the prowler.

"I believe you've found a hell of a lot more than you were looking for," she said to the startled intruder.

He whirled and stared at her for a moment. He could see that the gun was of small caliber and it appeared as though he was contemplating his odds.

"Try it, tough guy," she said. "It might keep me from answering a lot of questions from the cops. The first shot will enter near your eye. I don't know where it will exit. Want to guess along with me?"

He read the coolness of this tall woman. She was not putting on a brave front just for show. She was deadly serious and she would be a dangerous foe. His only choice was in living or dying and he must make that choice quickly.

"We all do what we have to do, lady. Some of us get caught, others don't. Since I'm caught, the next move is yours to make."

"You can empty your weapons and wallet out of your pockets. That'll do for openers, tough guy. I want to learn everything about you. Believe me, you'll tell me anything that I want to know. We'll get real chummy if you hope to be walking during the next few months. When we get to the real knotty questions, you may have to decide if you ever want to be a family man. This small caliber gun, if used in the right place, can relieve you of those fatherly responsibilities."

He was pale when she finished with her threats.

Removing a snub-nosed police special handgun, a small sized switchblade and his wallet; he carefully tossed them on her bed. He'd known cruel men, but she might surpass all of them. If he complied with her demands, would she still turn him over to the cops?

"Is this between you and me, lady? Do you really want the cops to get involved? Are you ready for the questions and hassles?"

She kept one eye on the prowler, while she went through his wallet. Pulling his driver's license up to the light, she read it carefully.

"Well, Gene Evans, I may not need the cops. If we get real friendly and discuss why you're here and who sent you, I won't need police help. I'm tired of these rough games. Someone is trying to get a history on me. When they kill my friends, I want it ended in a hurry. I intend to track down every single player that had a part in Teresa's death and I'm beginning with you."

"I had nothing to do with her death. I knew her only because she dated the man that I work for. As far as I know, she died in a car wreck."

"Teresa often dated James Simpson. Are you admitting that you work for him? Why did he send you to my place?"

"He told me to go through your personal things to learn more about your background. I was ready to give up when you walked in on me. I'm a good agent, but somebody lied to me. I called your workplace and they said you were working late with the senator."

"I'm really sorry about that," she said sarcastically. "I don't know why people want to lie to each other. It gets real tacky sometimes. Well! It looks like we're about through here. I don't believe you can be of any further help to me at all. You haven't been much help to our friend Simpson either. You really should look for another job. The next time I see James, we'll discuss this whole matter. I doubt if he'll have any further need of your services."

"No! You won't need those items any longer, Gene," she added as he moved toward his weapons and wallet. "Find some line of work that won't require weapons."

Throwing a dark look in her direction, he moved through the hall and scurried out the front door. She had damaged this man more than legal punishment could have. She went through his wallet with extreme care. In addition to an abundance of cash, she found a Phantum business card with a phone number penciled on the backside. Her curiosity intensified.

Lifting her cell phone, she punched the numbers and waited.

"Yes, go ahead," ordered a stern voice.

She had heard this voice, but could not remember when or where.

Now, she was thoroughly confused.

Carefully, she pressed the off button and dropped her phone back in her purse. Since Gene worked for Simpson, whose stern voice answered this number? Again, each new mystery seemed to stack on top of her other puzzles.

With the intruder gone, she felt her stomach growl from hunger and moved to the kitchen.

Soon she had a sandwich and drink ready at her table. Finishing the last few bites of the BLT, she grabbed the signaling house phone. She wasn't expecting calls and this could be from anyone.

"I'm relieved to find you at home. Brad is in a trauma unit at Hilltop General and I desperately need you to cover for me tomorrow morning. I intend to stay with him until his condition stabilizes. I wanted to prepare you ahead of time," Todd said in a strained voice.

"I'm terribly sorry to hear this news. What happened to Brad?"

"He's suffered a bad car accident. He's in a coma and it doesn't look very good at the moment."

"I'll take care of things at the office and I can use the cell phone if I need to consult with you. My wishes and prayers are with you, Todd," she said softly.

She paced an oblong trail in the carpet and stewed with frustration. With everything dropping on her head at one time, it was next to impossible to think with a clear mind.

Her showdown with Simpson must wait now until the Whatley crisis was resolved.

The purse device began to signal and she swore softly. Was there no end to this madness?

"Do you have anything to report on Simpson?"

Alexi's voice lacked the normal demanding harshness. He sounded considerably more humble than she had ever heard.

"Not at this time. I know he's involved with the Phantum Company, but I've really gotten no place. So many things are happening at the same time, it's difficult to do a decent job on anything."

"This *is* a difficult time. I lost my other associate a few days ago. She will be hard to replace. It may take a week to bring in a new agent."

Katie asked a key question and waited patiently for his reply, but she sensed his forthcoming answer.

"How did you lose her, Alexi?"

"A stupid automobile accident took her life. She was a sufficient agent. I know of only one mistake that she made on this assignment."

"Teresa did not die in a car wreck. As sure as stars shine at night, she was murdered."

"What makes you say that? How did you know that I was speaking of Teresa? Did she tell you that she was my agent?"

"No, but she was the one that warned me about Simpson. She's the one that I sent to Socorro to hide from him. If you had told me that she was on our team, we might have prevented her death," she told him angrily.

"What has been done becomes history. We must learn from our mistakes and press onward. I ask again, why do you think she was murdered?"

"She would never leave my house unless certain that she was safe. She knew a truck was watching the house and she wrote down the tag number. Do you think she would walk into their hands while they were on my block?"

"She was too good to make an error of that magnitude. Her only mistake was falling into the web of Simpson. What are you doing about the license tag number?"

"I've got that on hold. I wanted a face-to-face with Simpson, but that's on hold as well. Brad Whatley was involved in a car wreck today. I must run the senator's ship until Brad's condition stabilizes," she said.

"Is it possible that young Whatley's wreck was not accidental?"

"I had not thought of that possibility. I assumed that he was somehow involved in this messy puzzle. If they did try to eliminate him, it puts a new slant on things. I'm not prepared to go off in another direction."

"Unless we learn why these men want you dead, we must stop our operation until I have my new agent on the scene. You must cater to every whim of the senator. We may need him before our plans are complete."

The ex-senator's knowledge of the situation was limited. Having learned of the conspiracy, he attempted to put an end to it and had been rebuked. It seemed such a huge snarl that even the former senator was incapable of untangling it.

* * *

The FBI director, the Defense Secretary, the House Speaker, and the Chairman of the Senate Appropriations Committee attended a special meeting. The four men were there to share information and learn from each other. The Director stood in silence, before speaking.

"Since everyone is present, let's get this thing rolling. I'm with you today because of a serious problem. I'm sure you know we have a missing senator. Because he had appointments scheduled, something serious has likely happened. I have people working on this and we want it kept quiet. You're in this meeting because my sources say you have a crisis in your own ranks. I'll share what I can with you and you're expected to share with me. The senator's life may be on the line. I want to know about your crisis, Mr. Secretary. I'm told that you called that meeting; would you like the floor."

"Hell! I'll gladly take the floor. If we can put light on the senator's disappearance, you can count on us. Our meeting had nothing to do with the senator. We were dealing with a contracts and procurement problem at our meeting. The name of Senator Hildon was never raised."

"You have a talent for laying ten pounds of talk on the listener's scales when he gets only about twenty cents worth of substance. I want to know *all* about that meeting. I'll determine if it's pertinent to the problem of today."

"I don't wish to antagonize you, but I outrank you in this matter. My meeting had no connection with Senator Hildon."

"You've just made a big mistake. We should be on the same team and trying to solve a serious problem. Instead, I see you condoning a cover-up."

He made no further remarks and quickly left the room. When the door had fully closed, the Senate Leader rose unsteadily to his feet.

"The Director is as steamed as I've ever seen him and I've known him for twenty years. I hope you know what you're doing. I have a question for you and if it's out of line, feel free to decline. You came to me some time ago and asked for an emergency appropriation. Are your problems related to my refusal? Had I granted your request, would today's meeting have been necessary?"

The Secretary smiled tolerantly. "That's two questions, Senator. I cannot state with certainty that things would have worked out had you given me those funds. Although, with the requested funding in hand I could have bought time to make course corrections. Given that small window of opportunity, I would not be in the sorry position that I'm in today."

"Tremendous pressure was being exerted to justify each disbursement. The financial heat was nearly unbearable. You know how penny-pinching things can get when there is no threat of war. Everyone believes defense spending is wasted when peace is staring into your face. Well, I can only say that I'm sorry if I put you in a bind. I know you're working with hot items or you'd not challenge our esteemed Director."

He left and only the Speaker and the Secretary remained in the room.

"Mr. Secretary, I should tell you what Todd Whatley said in regards to Senator Hildon. You can take it anyway you want, but Todd still has some of his connections. I asked why he came to me, instead of Hildon and his exact words were, 'he's too close to the forest to see the trees'. I immediately took that to mean that he suspected collusion between Hildon and the Contractors. The FBI Director could be right on target and Hildon may be missing because of his involvement with some of the vendors."

"I still did not do the Bureau Director wrong," the Secretary argued. "He was pushing and out of bounds. If he could have made a connection, I would have caved in. He must go through channels just like I do."

CHAPTER SEVEN

In Washington Senator Hildon was neither bound nor gagged, but that's all the freedom he could claim. He was unsure who masterminded his abduction, but he knew these two men lacked the brainpower and motive.

His temper flared and receded, like waves breaking on the seashore. This treatment was so new to the pompous senator that he found it difficult to adjust. No one catered to his whims now. No one came and cowered when he barked. It had become a terrible experience for the corrupt lawmaker.

He was a captive and these men were treating him with total disrespect. One of the men spoke insolently while he waved a white page of paper.

"You could make it easier on yourself by answering these questions."

"Yeah, we're getting tired of you stinking up the place. It sure smells like a rat in this room. I'd like to turn you loose and be rid of you."

Hildon told the men quietly.

"I don't have any idea how much you're being paid for this, but I'll top it. I can fix things in such a way that you won't ever have to work again."

"Well, that makes things come nearly full circle. We can fix things so that you'll never get a *chance* to work again."

The senator turned eyes that were filled with hate toward the speaker before quickly averting his gaze.

He had no stomach for this and they were well aware of it. He'd read the questions on that sheet, but his mind was still in turmoil. If he answered the questions and signed his name, his political life was dead. At some point in the future, he could be assassinated as revenge for his act. If he refused to cave in and sign the sheet, what might happen to him?

Without knowing who backed this kidnap action, he could not possibly guess about his fate. All he could do was delay. The authorities were probably already looking for him.

At the same moment in New Mexico, Hartley's phone signaled for attention and he glanced quickly at his watch. It was time for a report. The men who worked for him were very efficient.

"This is Hartley."

"Sir, nothing has changed except the subject is edgier. He's to the point of making personal offers above whatever compensation we've been promised. You can draw your own conclusions about his state of mind from that bribe attempt."

"Keep offering the paper to him for signing and see that he has anything that he wants to eat or drink. Hang in there and remember that I take full responsibility for this action."

* * *

Sergai answered the gentle rap at the door and found food service waiting. They delivered his breakfast and a newspaper. After a great gulp of coffee, he placed the newspaper on a table and looked at the front page.

Former Senator's son lies in coma as a result of car wreck. This headline was blazed across the page. Mouthing a vile oath, he reached for the phone.

"Quince, I just read the headlines and it failed to tell me what I wanted to hear. Having never let me down before, you may have a good reason. I'll withhold judgment until I listen to your story."

"I'm sorry, but it was out of my control. I ran him off the road and was ready to go down in the ditch and finish the job, but a helicopter showed up."

"A helicopter, you say? Why the hell was a chopper on the scene?"

"It was that commute reporting chopper from the TV station. If you'd read all the paper, you'd know that it was coming back from a police action on the interstate. If they hadn't come along when they did, the medics say he would have died at the scene. He's in a coma and may die anyway."

"If he lives, will he be able to recognize you? Think carefully now," Sergai said.

"Well, he doesn't know who I am. When I forced him over the side his last look was directly at my face. He might be able to find my picture, I do have a record. You knew that when you hired me."

"Take it easy, Quince. I'm an understanding man. To prove it, I have another job for you."

"Thank you sir, I'll handle this one without a hitch."

"I surely hope you do, Quince. This one is a good looking broad, but she is tougher than I first believed. She got the best of one of my men just a few days ago. I had to send him to our Phoenix site. I'll give you the details and you can handle her departure in any manner that fits the occasion."

* * *

Bob Hartley's phone rang relentlessly until he reached it.

"Report time again, sir. The subject is still mad and uncooperative."

"Then keep the heat on him. I've got a few questions and a suggestion to make."

The man answered in a calm tone. "Go ahead, sir. We know it's your ballgame and your rules."

"How are you giving the subject proper exercise and how are you managing room service with the subject in tow?"

"We planned for a long stay and took two suites. They're two floors apart, but we take the subject between floors by the stair route. We keep the door locked until the room is cleaned."

"You're doing a fine job and my next suggestion might prevent another problem. I don't know his medical history, but we must keep him healthy. If it takes severe arm twisting, find out if he is on any type of medication. Tell him he may be there for several more weeks," Hartley said with a laugh.

At Visions West, Katie's day passed surprisingly well and she detoured toward Hilltop General Hospital to touch base with the senator.

He was glad to see her and his eyes clearly displayed that fact. She was greatly alarmed by the senator's general appearance. He was much thinner, hollow eyed and his color was extremely poor.

He was in desperate need of good food, exercise, and sunshine. It was a waste of time to browbeat him about his health though for he was totally focused towards staying in sight of Brad.

"I talk to him much of the time," he told her. "We can't know if he hears, but it would be terrible if some part of his mind was working and no one was here for him."

"I won't argue with that logic, Senator. We all do what we have to do."

She finished her visit and continued on home. It was very difficult to dislodge the Whatley crisis from her mind and she entered her condo in a blue mood.

A hot shower helped some. A speedily prepared frozen dinner gave her an even better perspective. She selected an unread book and cranked the chair into a reclining position. If she could get involved in a book, it might help keep her mind free from these nagging problems. After two hours of reading, she closed the book and went to the lavvy.

Her eyes were tired from the day's busy schedule and the reading activity. The cold water relaxed her stress.

After donning pajamas, she crawled under the sheet and felt that nothing could keep her from getting a good nights rest. She fell asleep listening to the rising wind as it hammered a bough against her wall. In the early hours of the morning she awoke with a tremendous shiver. Suddenly she felt cold and needed a blanket.

In moving her hand toward the bed lamp, she touched her purse. Hastily, she drew the handbag to her pillow and reached toward the switch, but swiftly stopped her movement.

Strangely, she no longer felt cold. From a corner of her suddenly alert mind, intuition provided the fearful answer. She had felt the cold air because her door had been opened, but now it was closed.

She eased the gun from her purse. With extreme stealth, she moved to the other side of the bed. Bending low to the carpet brought her below the bed line. Instants later, a beam from a flashlight struck the spot where she had been laying. In a split second, a slug tore into the area of her bed.

Seconds later, the beam came on with another short burst and two more slugs struck the bed. The lack of sound indicated that someone was using a silencer.

When the light switch clicked and the overhead fixture blasted the room with light, she was much better prepared than the intruder. She knew exactly where he was, but he expected to find her in a crumpled heap inside the bedding.

When she rose from behind the bed with the gun in her hand, he gasped in surprise and lifted his weapon.

He was too late, as her bullet caught him full in the face and he was dead when he hit the floor.

The blast from her small gun filled the room with sound and a small wisp of smoke hovered for a moment over the bed before dispersing to the ceiling.

She stood for a moment in total surprise at her accuracy. It must have taken a ton of training to attain such an extreme degree of marksmanship.

In the ensuing quiet, with ears still ringing from the blast, she hoped none of her neighbors heard her shot. She turned all attention toward the body.

Why had he shot into an empty bed? He used a light, though sparingly, on the very spot where she had been sleeping. She moved to the nightstand to turn the bed light off. Next, she went to the wall switch and turned off the overhead light. Now, she moved to the spot where he had been when he first fired his shots. Staring at the bed, she saw how the gunman was fooled. A human head appeared to be at rest on her pillow. The purse that she placed beside her pillow was as dark as her hair. In fleeing to the far side of the bed, static electricity from her pajamas must have left the sheet in a heap and that result evidently fooled the uneasy gunman.

She knelt beside the still form and felt for a pulse. There was none and now she had a huge problem. Should she call the police and be involved in a situation that she couldn't explain?

She considered the situation for several minutes before angrily punching up Simpson's home number. When an obviously sleepy voice came on the line, it came on angry.

"This better be good," he said with heat.

"This *is* good," she replied equally angry.

"Katie, is this you? I'm sorry for yelling. Is something wrong?"

"You know full well that something is wrong. I was mad as hell when you sent Gene over here, but I'm livid about this last creep that you sent. He put several bullet holes in the place where I usually lay my head. I considered coming to your place, kicking down your door and blowing you away, but I backed off. I wouldn't know what to do with two bodies on the same night."

"Listen to me, Katie," he said hastily. "I sent Gene to prowl your place because I wanted to know more about you, but not to harm you. I didn't send anyone else. I have absolutely no idea who you may have over there. That's the God's truth, Katie."

"Do you have any suggestions? The cops won't believe that I don't know who wants me dead. They'd probably lock me up on suspicion. You know I can't stand a deep investigation."

Seeing a big edge, he snickered wickedly. "If I help with this, you're going to owe me big time."

"The hell with you, Simpson," she said with deep anger and punched the off button.

There was not much night left to work with, but she would do what must be done. Pulling denims and a western shirt over her body parts, she dressed for the occasion. Dragging the body of the gunman to her door, she peered out into the early morning. No one was stirring and the street was empty of vehicles.

She stepped directly to the trunk of her car and raised the lid before returning to her door.

Katie was well aware that her strength was greater than most men. Now, she used that strength to gather the dead man over her shoulder like a sack of potatoes and carry him to the car. With grim determination, she deposited him in her trunk and quietly closed the lid before driving away.

Finding Simpson's place was easy enough. After checking the place out, she placed the man on a grassy spot near a ground floor apartment. Her task finished, she returned to her condo and built a pot of coffee. While it was brewing, she put her clothes in the washer and by using a shampoo, removed the bloodstains from her carpet. It had been a short night and if the beginning of this morning was any indication, it promised to be an extremely long and tiring day.

Only an hour later, the area around Simpson's apartment complex became a hive of activity.

Police units were parked at the curb and unmarked cars were double parked beside the Medical Examiner vehicle. Members of the police investigation team, looking for clues, were stalking the entire area. The tenants that were up and about were being held in the entry lobby area. Though it was still early, a newsboy had discovered the body and reported the sighting to the police. The routine action of the cops now involved the taking of names and statements. The kid gave his statement and left to finish his route.

Simpson was not an early riser and the call from Katie had caused him to sleep even later. He lay listening to the commotion from outside, wondering if it would ever subside. After several minutes, he gave up all hope for sleep and decided to get an early start at Phantum. As he put the finishing touches to his dressing chores, a gentle rap was applied to his door.

"Good morning sir," a calm and friendly voice said. "I'm Captain Victor Lopez, of the local Homicide Division. I need a few minutes of your time. I'd like to ask you a few questions."

"I'm James Simpson and I'm CEO of Phantum Enterprises. My time is your time, Captain. I must be at a conference at ten. That's my earliest commitment of the day."

"I won't take up much of your time, Mr. Simpson. Did you hear any unusual noises during the night?"

"I heard nothing, but then I'm a sound sleeper. If Homicide is here, it means there is a body present. Have you identified the body, Captain?"

"No sir, that's the main reason for these questions. It would be a lot easier to move the investigation forward if we had a make on the body."

"I'm sorry I can't be of more help, but I have nothing to report," Simpson said carefully.

"You were my last hope, Mr. Simpson," the detective said sadly. "All eight occupants of this complex deny hearing anything or having company during the night," he said slowly. "It sure beats me how a man could walk up beside your unit and die without anybody hearing anything. Even a small caliber gun sounds loud, when it's fired next to your house. Well, I'll take your phone number and if anything turns up to put a name on this guy, I may be talking to you again."

Once he got downtown and inside his office, Victor Lopez kicked his chair away from the desk and placed his heels atop its grainy, worn surface. Something reeked to the sky about this murder case. It simply didn't happen in the way it was painted. There was only one bullet wound in the victim, but the shooter could have missed with other shots.

Still, no spent slugs had been recovered though an exhaustive search was made of the entire area.

The lack of empty cartridge cases was another clear sign that the murder had occurred elsewhere. Now that part was okay. He didn't give a damn that it happened somewhere else, but he was highly irked that the victim had been delivered to this complex. The victim was carrying a weapon that had been recently fired. A silencer was still attached to the gun. The main question appeared to be the reason why the guy was hauled to this particular spot? There were dozens of safer places to dump a body than this living area.

Lopez had reached his present position by not being satisfied with easy answers. He didn't run for a deodorizer can every time an odor arose. The Lopez way of curing an unpleasant smell was to remove the body of the odor. As sure as his ancestors were Spanish landowners and cattlemen, someone at the apartment complex knew why that body was in the yard.

He would run the name of every tenant through the grinder until something clicked. He reached for his desk phone and punched in a number from his notepad.

"This is Lopez from Albuquerque Homicide. Please connect me with Inspector Beam."

He waited patiently for the transfer, knowing that the FBI man was on another line. It was a reach, but they might track the dead man's gun.

"Good to hear your voice again. It's been a long time since our last case. I'll get right to it, Frank. It looks like I may have a mob tie-in. There's a body here with pockets emptied and no ID. He has a silencer and an automatic pistol. I'll fax you his prints and the gun will be expressed. If this is mob related, I'll hold everything until you arrive and I know you'll come."

* * *

Sergai Valenkov paced the hotel room floor. No word had come from Quince and the paper failed to mention the Ryan woman. The news was normally printed around midnight though, and it could have happened in the early hours of the morning. Quince had been very effective except for young Whatley.

The phone signal broke his thought stream. The voice from the receiver sounded strained.

"This is James, sir. I have a strange report for you and you're not going to like it."

"Feed it to me, Simpson. Lately, I'm finding much that I don't like about our present situation."

"Last night, the Ryan woman called to jump me for sending someone to her place. She was mad as hell. She had a body there and wanted my help to get rid of it. It may not be connected, but the cops found a body outside my place. If she brought it here, she's stronger than I thought."

"If she's killed Quince, she's a bigger *threat* than I thought. He was a pro and he came to me with the highest credentials. I told you that she was a federal plant. A normal citizen couldn't have taken Quince out. Are the cops on it? I saw nothing in the papers and seldom watch the box."

"They questioned the tenants and came up with blank, according to the top cop on the scene. I cannot believe she's a plant, sir. If that were true, she'd never ask me to help with the body."

"Simpson, so much is happening lately that I'm unsure about several things. I thought Whatley squealed and I asked Quince to silence him. The pup is in a coma. If Quince is dead, there's no more threat to us from Whatley."

"Is there any word on Hildon? Do you know who snatched him?"

"Have you nothing but questions? I'd like you to make more contributions to the organization. I could have any fool fronting Phantum Enterprises," Sergai said.

He replaced the phone unit on the charging stand and stared thoughtfully toward the hotel window. Having taken several setbacks now, it was time for the ball to bounce his way. The phone's sudden signal drove him to the instrument in haste.

"I am here. Go ahead with your message," he said tightly.

"I'm sorry to be so late in reporting," the voice said. "We've been working on the Hildon thing nonstop and we just now got something worthwhile. Boss, we've got him pinned down to one of two suites in the same hotel. We're setting up listening devices in the stairwells now, so we should pretty soon know which suite they're using to hold him."

"You've done fine work, Ollie," Sergai told him in incredulous tones. "If you get a positive fix on the senator, eliminate him immediately. He is of no further use to us. Each added hour that he lives, increases the threat that he poses to our safety."

It was later in the evening in New Mexico when Katie's communicator signaled for attention. The bullets fired in its direction had not damaged it. She pressed the buttons and heard a concerned voice.

"Have you learned anything from Simpson?"

"He's associated with Senator Hildon and Sergai Valenkov seems to revolve in everything associated with Simpson. I checked the corporate records of several companies that are in competition and found a smelly, orbiting circle of officers. I may get more information later."

"Under the circumstances, you have done well. I will have another agent on the scene today and things should begin to improve for us. You will meet this man and work closely with him. Your cover story will be that he is an old school mate and you accidentally met at the Mall. He has no memory and it must be that way to protect all of us. There is no need for you to make prying attempts at his memory, for it is safely locked away from the reach of anyone."

"How will I know him? Are we to be like ships that pass in the night? Will we have to collide to know each other?"

"He will be at your place soon. I expect you to share your wealth. I also expect you to share your Condo. It will make a far more believable cover."

"The hell with you," she retorted angrily. "I'll decide who shares my Condo. I'll share my funds without a fight, but the man that lives under my roof will be chosen by me."

"You will make an exception here if you have hopes of returning to your original life," he said with anger. "You are not in a position to make rules or set conditions. You will do as I say or you both will suffer the consequences."

The device went blank without further sound. She was boiling mad, but helpless to escape his orders. If she rebelled, she might find herself stranded in this world of no memory.

The new man would be here soon according to him. Soon, could mean minutes, hours, or days. These words belonged to Alexi and he often used words in strange ways.

Angry at this new situation and frustrated by other problems, she needed something to perk her up. Hot tea might repair some of her depression.

While the water heated, she mulled the possibilities that could arise from having a live-in companion. If he kept everything on a strictly business level, things might be bearable. Even if things did work out, it held no advantage for her. Since she had accumulated several friends, it would not be good for him to answer her phone if they called. She must set hard and fast rules for him to follow, lest there be an ugly altercation.

As simultaneous signals called for her attention, she decided to get the door first; the kettle could wait.

He looked nothing like an agent under the porch light. His blond hair was barbered short; his pale blue eyes looked worried and unsure. He was dressed in jeans that seemed molded to his athletic body; Alexi's new man had arrived.

She questioned him in a strong voice.

"Why do you press my doorbell at this time of night? City ordinance allows no soliciting after eight in the evening."

"I was sent here and told you would expect me. I think we work for the same people."

"Do you have a name? I may judge a man by the name that he carries."

"Will we stand on the porch all night, Katie? I can answer questions from inside the house."

In surprise, she stepped back from the doorway.

He entered with only a small carrying bag in his hand. He would need many personal things if he expected to stay under her roof.

Despite her initial anger at having this agent thrust upon her and the reluctance that dwelt in her mind about sharing the condo, she softened considerably. He was neither obnoxious in looks or voice and in spite of her stiffness during the first moments of their meeting, he remained pleasant.

"My name is Don Brim," he said softly. "It is a name given to me by Alexi and that's all the background I have. I awoke outside of Socorro and he gave me a few instructions through this transmission device. He gave me your name and address and I caught a ride to Albuquerque."

After he spoke, he pointed to his traveling bag and she nodded.

"Yes, I have one also. He told me our cover would be that we were schoolmates. Where did you go to school?"

"Fort Lauderdale high school, but don't ask for the names of our classmates. I have none to give you."

"It does not matter, as I have no names either. We're only pawns in his game whatever it may be. What were your orders?"

"I was given no orders, other than to come here and join you. He said I would be assigned tasks when the need arose."

"I was about to have some hot tea. Would you prefer some coffee instead?"

"No! I love hot tea," he said with a nice smile. "I'm also quite hungry. Is food a possibility at this late hour?"

"I'll show you where I keep the sandwich stuff," she said quickly. "It's never too late for a good sandwich."

They talked at length about Alexi and about themselves, but they found little comfort in their common situation. It was horribly obvious that for them to return to their own world, Alexi's quest had to be resolved. Another thing that seemed certain was that if Don had no inkling where he came from, he sure couldn't enlighten Katie about her roots. She showed him the guest bedroom, the linen closet, and the towel storage area. She apologized for having just one bathroom and he simply shrugged indifferently.

"Until I get a job, it doesn't matter. If mornings suit you better for showers, they're yours. I can use it after you go to work. Other than for baths, I spend very little time in the bathroom."

She retired with problems laying heavy on her mind. He'd have to learn to drive and he'd need his own car. If he didn't know the bus system, he'd be lost trying to find his way around town. She'd have to take him to the mall tomorrow, so he could buy clothing and other personal things. He didn't even have a toothbrush. He might never be worth all the trouble he'd likely cause.

Across town, Bob Hartley's phone signaled again and he grabbed it eagerly.

"It's report time, sir. Our man has no medication needs, but he's eating like a hungry old wolf. He's unhappy with the situation, but he won't spill his guts. I don't think we'll get anything soon."

"I can last longer than he can. You may have to change your attitude toward him. Try acting like you're getting cabin fever. Tell him of the trouble that he's causing. Within hearing range, tell your partner that you'd be rid of a big headache if you dumped the old man off somewhere."

"That's a smart idea. I can't wait to try it. I want to see that smug look gone from his face."

* * *

At Hilltop General Hospital, Todd sat by the bed of the young man and patiently held his hand. Brad's breathing pattern was of the same boring rhythm and Todd grew increasingly sleepier with the passage of time. In moments, his hand grew still and the older man was sound asleep.

He was becoming physically weaker due to his insistence on maintaining his bedside watch. For many minutes, he slept with his head buried in his chest. When roused from his sleep, it was not done by the nursing staff.

Bradford was gently shaking the senator's shoulder.

"Dad, what are we doing here? What am I doing here? What has happened to me?"

Most of Whatley's cuts and abrasions were healed by this time and he felt weak from inaction, but he saw no bandages. He looked with alarm at the breathing machine that he'd torn off and the needle that had been feeding him. For the first time, he realized that he was in an intensive care unit. Then his memory began flooding back and Todd saw fear strike his son's face.

"It's okay, son," he said quickly. "You've been gone a while, but you're back now and I think everything's going to be just fine."

The senator tugged the nurse's call cord. In seconds, a nurse was at the bedside. Without a word, she began taking vital signs and then punched in several numbers.

"We need you in room two-four-three at your earliest convenience, Doctor," she said in calm tones. "Well now, Bradford, you've taken your own sweet time about returning to us. I trust you'll be with us for a while now?"

* * *

Katie pushed back in her office chair and leaned hard against the cushion. The senator's ship was sailing along smoothly, but she needed a break. Todd's office seemed to have a full work calendar every day. She innocently thought silently, *Just give me ten minutes of rest and I'll be okay.* It was not meant to be though for the phone signaled its impatience.

Hartley was on and laughed boyishly before commenting.

"I made it through your armed guards. It's just the beginning. I'll wear down your resistance and one day you'll be my executive secretary."

"Now that you've had your laugh, you'll want to tell me why you called. I needed a break though and you've given me that," she said.

"I want you to meet me somewhere for dinner tonight. I'd be happy to pick you up, but that would look like a date and I'm too old to be dating you. I'd really like some serious talk."

"I'd love that, Bob. I'll be at the Fat Calf restaurant at eight. Does that sound workable?"

"Expect me to be waiting."

When the day was over, she practically flew home.

There was promise of a hot shower, a refreshing drink and a few moments of relaxation before going to meet Hartley. What did this strange man really want? Before the shower was through draining, she heard the phone.

She spoke softly into the transmitter.

"This is Katie."

"I glad I caught you at home. I wonder if I might come over for a little while and set up a meeting. I have someone that wants to meet you?"

"That is impossible tonight, James. I have a dinner date scheduled. Perhaps we can make it another time," she suggested.

"That's too bad," he said dryly. "I don't know how long the man will be in town. I'll try to get back to you later with something."

Choosing an outfit to wear was not a problem. She had a very blue evening thing that would cause all eyes to focus in whatever direction she decided to take the dress. Tonight, she wanted to look lovely for Hartley. Since she intended to unload on him, it was the very least she could do.

Hartley was waiting and his eyes showed just how successful her choice of dress had been.

He seated her slowly and carefully with tremendous pride. All the men in the vicinity of the table struggled with the puzzle of how the old bull had won the right to feed this vision of loveliness.

Hartley spoke no words for a few moments; as he was much too busy admiring her. He had always known that she was beautiful, but tonight she was something very special.

"You're well dressed tonight and you look pleased as a peacock," she said. "Is there something in the air that you want to share?"

"I'm pleased that you've made yourself extremely beautiful. I'm a cagey old bird. You've set this up to give my ego a huge boost and I appreciate it. You don't give a hoot about my money and you can get top dollar from any executive in the country. For some reason you've decided to honor me by making jealous idiots out of every man in the house. I ought to have a medal engraved for you. You seem to have everything else."

"I have great hopes of meeting a young man someday who has the courage and fire that you possess. I want to have children and I want them to have an active father until after they pass their teens. None of us have a long term lease on life. You may outlive my dreams and me, but I want to be as honest with my future husband and children, as I'm being with you. If you were twenty years younger, you're the one that I'd set my mind on."

"Your words hit me hard. No one wants to be reminded of his or her fragile hold on life, but you manage to do it with less pain than most. I love honesty more than my history might suggest and you've shown a great deal of it. Why don't we turn in our orders and get down to business?"

The food was ordered and wine poured before their talk turned toward business.

"I know the senator may not be one of my supporters, but I don't think of myself as a bad egg. Sure, I've done some unethical things and so has most everyone else that struggles with a business. Todd finagled some deals and I won't knock him for doing it. I just wish he would cut me the same slack."

"He's had reason to wonder about many things. He's lost out in the bidding wars to other vendors when they left much money on the table. He knows there's something kinky when that happens. He refuses to deal in anything that might be illegal. He even refused to accept information that I wanted to give him, until I swore that I didn't do anything legally wrong to obtain it."

"Can you give me more detail on that? We're being honest here, remember?"

"I certainly will. I learned the names of two men in the Federal Contracts section who were selling out to a vendor."

"How did he treat this information that you gave him?"

"He called someone at the Capitol and requested an investigation. He told me that he had given them a chance to clean up their act."

Hartley let out a low whistle of breath. He didn't expect show and tell to be like this, but he might as well learn as much as possible.

"I won't be tacky and ask how you learned this information, but I would like to know if you got more detail than you told the senator."

"No, I leveled with him and I'm leveling with you. I found most of your products, your R and D programs and your testing capabilities," she said.

"Oh, don't worry," she added. "None of this will ever be used against you, not in any way. I told you that I greatly admire your courage and determination."

"I am totally surprised. I believe everything that you've said, but a terrible error must be corrected. You believe that I corrupted these contracts men and you are wrong, wrong, wrong. Just like the senator, I lost a bid that I should have won. I cut my profit margin to the bone to get that thing. When I saw the bid results and noted that Simpson's company had won with a stupid low bid, I knew there was a fox in the henhouse.

I placed a call to the resident Engineer and demanded an investigation. He promised to take action and I backed off."

He paused a moment before continuing.

"A few days later, I got a call from a man who identified himself as a contracts technician. He said that if I was having difficulty, he and his partner could help. He told me there were ways to improve my chances of winning a contract and for a fee; they would help me to get the next one. You know I'm not a gullible man, but I fell for this ploy. I didn't dream they would be conspiring within their own section. When I got the bid package and saw their materials, I almost balked. My only excuse is that if I didn't get that contract, I'd have been forced to lay people off. I absolutely detest telling people they're being terminated due to the lack of work."

Katie raised her hands in almost helpless anger.

"Todd knows that things are going downhill, but he isn't sure of the reason. My question to you may be vital to both of you. Think carefully before you answer. Have you taken notice of other contractors that have won such cheap bids?"

Hartley quickly replied. "Sure, I went over some of them last week after I got fed up with the system. A local company, Blue Horizon, got two. Desert Enterprises from Phoenix got one. Lower Sierra and Associates, from Bakersfield got one. Two companies from the east coast scored low in the bidding and I don't recall their names, but they aren't as competitive as the west coast bunch."

"Bob please excuse me for being deliberately inquisitive, but it's a very important question. You mentioned that you got fed up with the system. Do you mind telling me what steps you took, if any, to induce them to modify their system?"

"I don't mind telling you of my first step. Since most of these contracts are let by the Department of Defense, I sent a message to the Secretary of Defense. I made the message interesting enough that he would begin an investigation. I haven't heard anything and I doubt if I will. For your own safety, I can't talk about the other action that I've taken. I'll say that I came onto some highly sensitive information that involves conspiracy. If my plan works out, the bidding process will get much better in the future."

"And if it doesn't work out, what could happen to you? Do you have a back-up plan as a safety net or might you find yourself in legal jeopardy? I don't want to see anything happen to you."

"I should ask you the same question. You think Simpson wants you dead and you believe Teresa was murdered. Are your goals and intentions worth becoming a target for Simpson?"

It was almost time for their food to appear. She stood and walked around the table to Hartley's chair. Leaning down to his height, she gave him a lingering kiss.

"You're becoming a very dear friend. I want you to be more careful from now on."

She followed the sign to the ladies room and along the way, considered her present situation.

She had come a long, long, way since her arrival at Socorro. She had accumulated precious friends, many puzzles, and yet the threat of death lurked close at hand.

Once again, an emotional encounter with Hartley was raising her memories close to the surface. She fought the blue feeling that came with not knowing her past.

One day soon, things might begin to look better. Carefully, she dabbed at her face and returned toward her table.

Partially screened by a room divider, she got a view of three men dining at a nearby table. Simpson was one and Valenkov was another, but she failed to recognize the other man. Without turning in their direction, she moved on to her table. Her arrival harmonized with the coming of the food. As she ate, she kept stealing glances toward the table of Simpson.

Hartley picked up on this and gently chastised her.

"Please don't be looking at some young buck while you're on my time, Katie. You'll have lots of chances when I'm not with you."

"Shame on you, that's a jealous side you're showing and it's totally unnecessary. I couldn't pull such a silly stunt. I have too much respect for you. I saw someone at another table and my curiosity is aroused. Sergai and James are dining with a man that I've never seen."

"I know him. He's CEO of the Blue Horizon Company, Arnold Montgomery."

"I spent some time digging through the records office. There are some interesting things to be seen there and especially with corporate officers."

A look of alarm struck the face of Hartley at hearing this news.

"Oh no, Honey! How much digging did you do? If you've found what I discovered, your life *is* in danger. I must make a confession. I hate to admit it, but I spied on you. I was suspicious from the beginning and tried to figure the role you were playing. I had an agent working for weeks to dig into your past, but you have no past. He took my pay and gave me nothing of substance. You were born in Florida and disappeared. You came here from Socorro. Honey, that's the reason they want you dead. Without federal help, it's almost impossible to cover up a past. To them, you're a Fed trying to infiltrate their scam. I believed the same thing until you opened up to me."

"Don't apologize for checking me out. I don't blame you at all, but satisfy my curiosity and tell me why there's more danger in my checking of records than you?"

"I've got an ace up my sleeve and that's all I'll say."

"I don't like hearing that kind of talk."

Depressing thoughts weighed on her mind at home. Although she reached a new plateau of sorts with Hartley, she uncovered more problems.

* * *

Back at the Fat Calf, the three men were into the wine and the waiter was clearing their table.

When he finished and departed, their talk resumed.

"I paid the records clerk a chunk to report inquiries for that concern our interests," said Sergai. "I told him we expect a take-over attempt and need time to prepare. He bought the story and this is his second report. Now, two people are interested in our corporate structure. His description fits that of Katie Ryan. We can't silence Hartley at this particular time. He has dirty linen of his own, but we must do something about this detestable woman. I say she's a federal plant and digging for an indictment"

"I don't agree," James said. "You're the boss. I'm not crossing your insight, but I don't see her that way. She told me that she hopes to meet someone to boost her importance in the world of business."

Sergai spoke sarcastically. "Just like the Sandusky woman I suppose. We turned Teresa's apartment without finding anything, but that didn't make her any less of a federal spy."

James colored deeply and remained silent. Montgomery listened to the hostile flow of words between the two and saw the possibility of moving upward in rank.

"I agree with you, Sir. If she's a snooper, we should take her out of the game."

"I'll get it rolling tomorrow," Sergai said tersely.

Later at Simpson's apartment, he paced the length of his kitchen floor and returned to the phone. Stress was building inside his body because of the unknown possibilities.

If he were dragged into this murder investigation, his problems would surely multiply. If Quince could be linked to Sergai and his own connection established with Valenkov, he could be in big trouble.

Once into these links, the cops would trace every tie that existed among these companies. If they bothered to check with the feds, they might find out a great deal more. The Ryan woman, if she was federally connected, may have given damaging reports to her supervisor.

Quince's report stated that Teresa had been tailed to the Ryan woman's condo. It was time to learn whether Katie was a plant, or just a mysterious woman with a past to hide. He punched in her numbers.

"This is Katie Ryan," the phone voice said clearly.

"This is James. I need an answer from you. As long as it's an honest answer, I don't care if it is negative or affirmative. Are you a federal agent?"

"That's an easy question, Simpson. I can honestly say that I'm not an agent for the feds."

"I accept that as a fact. Now, I'll do you a favor. You're way out of your league here. You simply got lucky with your last visitor. The next man they send will be forewarned and ready."

"You are admitting that you know who's trying to kill me. Do me a simple favor, James. Just who *is* the guilty party behind the crap that's been going on lately? I intend to find out anyway and when I do, the feds won't be your biggest threat. You haven't fooled me an ounce. You're puzzled by my ability to fight off two supposedly tough men and ticked off that I dumped a body on your doorstep. How is the police investigation going? Have they started digging into your affairs? Can your sordid connections stand the light of day?"

There was a lengthy delay before he answered.

"I really wish it hadn't been like this, Katie. I could have helped you get a good start in the world of business."

He replaced the handset, while worry lines played across his face. She was certainly not with the feds, but that didn't decrease the danger factor that she presented.

She was hot on the trail of something and that something might bring his prosperous lifestyle to an end.

CHAPTER EIGHT

In the Washington Arms hotel room, Senator Hildon made a decision and faced his captors.

"It's quite clear to me that the two of you are not qualified to make a field decision," Hildon said firmly. "I think the time has come for me to meet with your employer. By now, you should know that I'll make no statements to you."

"I think you've taken advantage of our good treatment," one of the men said heatedly. "I think we should have slapped you around. It's not too late yet. I'll pass your suggestion on to my boss, though. It's up to him to decide your fate."

The man sped to the other suite to use his cell phone and left Hildon to the care of his partner. With eager fingers, he punched in the numbers.

"I think he's ready to spill his guts, but he wants to talk with you," he told Hartley.

"I'll be there on the next available flight. Don't give him the silent treatment. Keep him off balance until I get there."

After a plane change and a lengthy flight, Hartley landed at Dulles airport and flagged a cab.

While riding toward the hotel, his mind spun with possibilities. How much light would this corrupt lawmaker shed on the shady dealings that had taken place?

He arrived at the hotel much quicker than expected because the traffic was exceptionally thin. Having been told the room number where Hildon was held; he took the elevator to the proper floor. The senator would swiftly recognize Hartley, but that was of no consequence.

Bob had no fear of the results. Enough evidence was present against the crooked senator to keep him forever silenced. The only problem was in knowing the proper person to whom this evidence should be presented. On walking through the hotel room doorway, the face of Hilton took on a dark red glow. His anger and frustration seemed near the explosion point.

"I half suspected you were behind this scheme, Hartley," he said heatedly. "Why the hell couldn't you have been satisfied with your windfall and stayed neutral? If you felt you weren't getting a fair share you should have told our men. They could have set up something bigger for you. Taking me away from the Senate action will energize an investigation that may bring us all down. I suppose it's too late to fix this terrible situation. If you turn me loose today though, I'll do my best to offset the damage that you've done."

"Good try, Senator, but it's impossible for me to turn you loose until I have more details. We've put most of this thing together, but your version of the facts is very important. With what I already know about you, I could turn you loose right now and you couldn't do a damn thing."

Hartley waited a few seconds to observe the pale face of Hildon.

"You're already finished as a senator and if you want to stay out of the pen, you'll cooperate willingly. The Secretary of Defense knows where I stand. I may get slapped on the wrist, but you're in deep trouble. There may be a legal way out for you, but your career is over. If you sign this paper and name the other members of the conspiracy, we'll say you helped break a gang that was sacking the government purse."

Again Hartley grew quiet as the senator still seemed confident. He gave the corrupt politician several moments to reconsider his abominable position. It finally dawned on Hartley what Hildon's hang-up was about.

"You might be able to quietly retire without public disgust. But if you're thinking I'll be facing a kidnapping charge, let me correct you. We took you for your own protection. There's been at least one murder committed since this conspiracy began to break apart. The son of Senator Whatley is in a serious coma and may die. I doubt that his wreck was an accident. What do you think they would do to you if they suspect you've squealed?"

The face of Hildon went white with fear. He had little doubt of his fate, if Sergai could get to him.

If anything was salvaged from this situation, it would be with Hartley and it must be soon.

"Give me the paper. I've read it a hundred times already. I'll sign it and take a chance that you'll do the right thing."

"You're being extremely smart now. I'm certain that you'll never regret it, Hildon."

Senator Hildon carried the paper to the entry area desk and sat down. Taking his pen from his shirt pocket, he brandished it over the paper.

Ripping and tearing sounds came next as the common wall of the room and hall corridor exploded with wildly flying bits and pieces of sheetrock and insulation. Hearing no loud reports of gunfire, Hartley and his men were stunned by the extent of damage to the wall. When the body of Hildon slid off the chair and bounced to the floor, they regained their wits.

Pulling their pistols, the two sped out the door and into the hallway, but no one was visible. One of them ran to the elevator and the other to the stairs, but neither feature was in use.

Hartley remained rooted to his spot in the room. Without a weapon it would be extremely foolish for him to enter the corridor. Finally, he regained his senses and checked the still form of Hildon. The senator exhibited no pulse. With three large punctures oozing blood from his heart area, this discovery came as no surprise to Hartley. A light tap at the door signaled the return of his agents.

"Boss, we've let you down, but we had no way to know they were here," one of them said. "I'm absolutely amazed by the type of equipment they used. This was definitely done with a sound gun. In case you're not familiar with this equipment, it's an infrared scanner used with a heartbeat identification unit. A headset is used to identify voices as the scanner screen is being read. The unit is made lethal by an attached and silenced automatic weapon. The gun slightly resembles an old fashioned Tommy-gun,"

"I'm unfamiliar with some of the terms you've used in describing this thing, George. Sound guns are not new to me. Heat scanners have been used for a few years. With heartbeat scanners, I can only relate to an EKG evaluation unit as used in hospitals and clinics. Give me more on this if you can. I could ask a political friend to trace the sources of this highly specialized equipment."

"It's a remote infra-red sensing unit that can identify a heartbeat by its own peculiarities. Similar to fingerprints, one heart will often have a particular cadence not shared by others. Once a voice is associated with that heart pattern, identification is comparatively easy. In less than thirty minutes they probably had us down cold. Welcome to the world of electronic wizards," George said.

One of the cops stated, "I have a friend in the FBI and we've talked about this subject. He said only four special weapons teams across the entire country have access to this equipment. I suppose the CIA and Secret Service people have them, but you can see where this level of accessibility reaches. Well, we're in Washington and anything can be had here for the proper price."

George listened carefully and then he spoke.

"Whatever their level of accessibility, they can't fly and they're not invisible. They didn't use the elevator and you heard no running footsteps on the stairs. With this specialized weapon, they wouldn't go running hell bent all over this hotel. I'm betting that they're in a room on this floor and they're stuck here until dark. Listen to my idea and see if you think it has merit."

After laying the foundation for his scheme, they carefully removed every possible trace of their presence from the room and went to the other suite.

George found a cold drink for Hartley and then picked up the phone to punch in the number of hotel security.

"Yes, hello, I want to report a strange occurrence on the fourth floor. I started to call the cops, but then I decided you should be the one to make that determination. Well, just listen then, I got off on four by mistake and the elevator got away from me. While I was waiting, I heard a hell of a noise and shortly after that, two guys came tearing by me and went into a room down the corridor. It looked to me like one of them was carrying an odd sort of rifle. I went a couple of rooms back the other way and saw a wall full of holes. No, I haven't been drinking. Go check it out if you have doubts."

He gave his name and room number, promising to be present if needed and hung up the phone.

He smiled an evil smile, while knowing full well that this game would unfold into one of large-scale dimension.

He established a cover story and the three men would be enjoying a friendly poker game when security arrived at their room.

Ernie, the security man, quickly called a cop friend at the nearby station. He had no back up on hotel duty and this sounded like a threatening situation. The officer dispatched a pair of plainclothes cops and Ernie led them to the fourth floor.

Startled by the damaged wall, they gave it a speedy examination and listened quietly at the door for a few seconds. Hearing no sounds from within, Ernie inserted a card key and turned the doorknob. Seeing the body of Hildon sprawled on the floor, one cop quickly knelt and felt for life signs. Shaking his head in a negative motion, he rose from the floor and checked the remaining rooms of the suite.

"It's all clear. Your strange caller's story must be true. We should do a room-to-room search and see if the shooters are holed up on this floor."

"I have a master key card," Ernie quietly told the others. "We'll take each door and talk to the occupant. We'll ask if we can come in and look around. If they're agreeable, we'll just thank them and move on. If they get nasty, we'll have a suspect."

Near the elevator, they stopped and began the hunt. The first room was unoccupied and the occupant of the second room was very cooperative. Two successive rooms were not occupied either. The room next in line appeared to be rented, but the occupant was absent. When they neared the next room, Ernie took his turn.

Tapping gently on the door panel, he heard a sound from within. In answer to his tap, a voice was heard from just inside the room.

"What do you want?"

"This is Hotel Security, sir," Ernie said calmly. "There's a report of a prowler on this floor. We'd like to come in and talk."

"I'd like you to go away so I can sleep. Shall I call the desk and ask for the manager?"

The voice sounded neither belligerent nor menacing, but it had a ring of finality in its tone.

Ernie looked toward the cops for guidance and one of them stepped forward.

"This is Detective Stover of the police department. You might as well let us inside for a talk. In less than thirty minutes, the Captain will be here with a search warrant."

There was no answer from inside, causing the cops to move away from the door. Once out of hearing range, Stover voiced an opinion.

"I believe we've found the shooters' nest. You saw what they did to the wall of the dead man's room, I think we'd be wise to move apart and wait until we get some back-up. We don't know what weapons they're using."

Using his radio, he contacted his commander and updated him.

"We have shooting suspects holed up in room four-thirty-three. A shooting took place here and the victim is dead. I didn't try to make an ID on him. Yes, I understand, sir. We won't proceed until you have everyone in position."

During that exact moment, the Defense Secretary and the Speaker were seated in a comfortable booth at the Pentagon coffee shop. The Secretary spoke first.

"My news gets worse as I go along. We've traced the vendor histories as far as we dare without a court order. The Federal Contracts and Procurement Division group was badly misused. We now know that thirty percent of the vendors on our questionable list have the same corporate officers."

"I can see where this is leading," the House Speaker remarked.

"Yes, you called it right. This was a scam from the word go and if we dig deeper, I predict that we'll find that ninety-five percent of their technology was stolen from the remaining honorable vendors. If that news fails to alarm you, I'll give you another angle. The two contracts men turned the tables on us. They sold their services to every vendor that would deal. We've quietly put them out of the way until we can get our indictments."

"Are you free to discuss details, Mr. Secretary?"

"Yes, as long as it remains with us," he replied. "We have to be very careful here if we intend to get a successful indictment. I can guess some of your questions. You're wondering if the companies of Senator Whatley and Bob Hartley withstood the scrutiny. Yes, there was a tense moment with Hartley though. His interests were buried in holding companies, but we found nothing illegal. He was lured into taking one fixed contract and the taste of it burned his throat. What else do you wish to know?"

"You scratched my itch. Where do we go from here? Don't we still need these delivery items?"

"Yes, but we're making a change in our bid procedure. Certain parts of this system were brought out of R and D by Hartley and Whatley before anyone else. They will be the only ones from New Mexico that will be invited to bid these items. Their technology was first and their individual competition will be clean and honorable. After a severe warning, the California connection may get some invitations to bid. However, the Phoenix companies are completely out as they have a direct tie to this conspiracy. The eastern corporations have not been fully cleared at this time, but they have little effect on our future needs."

* * *

At his office, Burt Bancroft was taking an important call relating to his lately published order concerning homicides.

"Mr. Director, this is Inspector Frank Beam of the Albuquerque office. I'm responding to your order that any uncommon event in this state be reported directly to you. We have a homicide here with possible mob ties. I've traced the weapon of the victim to a gun shop in your area, but I have no idea where he got his silencer."

"Thank you for the call, Inspector. I may be able to help with that angle. Why do you suspect a mob connection?"

"He has a record in Detroit for manslaughter. The strange part is he was shot with a small caliber gun and that does not indicate a normal mob hit."

"Good work, Inspector. Send a copy of everything you have and I'll put a man on the gun shop."

The director eased back in his chair and carefully eyed the ceiling. It was beginning to break and he'd be willing to wager a month's salary that the problems of the missing senator had roots in New Mexico. His past experience warned that the evasive actions of the Secretary of Defense could be the key to this whole mess. He must have a face-to-face with that arrogant character and no later than today. Leaning back to the desk, he reached for the telephone. A female voice responded.

"Thank you for calling and how may I help you?"

"This is Director Bancroft and I need the Secretary as soon as possible. It is rather urgent."

"I'm sorry, but he is not in his office. He went to the coffee shop and has not returned."

"Thank you and if I miss him, please ask him to return to the coffee shop."

It was only a short walk and the director planned strategy moves as he plodded along the way. This time he would maintain control over his temper. With a potential mob involvement lurking, the Secretary could no longer stonewall. As he turned into the cafe, he spotted the Secretary sitting with the Speaker and walked directly to their booth.

"I'm pleased that the two of you are together," he said pleasantly. "Can I can get a joint statement from you. It will save me the trouble of seeking you out individually."

The Speaker swiftly questioned the Bureau Director.

"Do you have anything new on the Senator, Burt?"

"It's possible. Our office in Albuquerque suspects mob involvement in a homicide there. With this new development you might want to rethink your position, Mr. Secretary. A mob tie could play hell with the missing senator scenario. Any information you have could aid us in solving this abduction. You would like to have this case solved, wouldn't you?"

"I'll tell you very little, Burt. I'm looking for indictments against several people and the senator may be one of those people."

Quickly he added his reasons. "I'll give no further statements until I've consulted with the Attorney General. In honesty, I *can* say there are no hints of mob implications in our matter."

"If an indictment is near, then you're beyond the basic stage of the investigation. I need a full report though just as soon as you can turn it."

Back at the Washington Arms hotel, Detective Stover heard a rapping noise inside the door of the suspects' room.

He held up a hand to signal the others and moved to within hearing range of the supposed perpetrators.

"What do you want now, mister? Have you finally decided to let us in for a talk?"

"No, there's no reason to hold out any longer," the voice said. "We're coming outside."

"Then come out with your hands high and hit the carpet belly first," Stover barked. "There'll be three guns on you."

"We won't give you any trouble. It's easy to see our hand when the cards are dealt face up. You guys are just too damn lucky."

Hostile faced, the men exited and dropped to the carpet.

With Stover and Ernie looking on, the other cop patted them down for weapons. Finding neither man armed, he put handcuffs on one of the men and motioned Stover to cuff the other one.

"We'll take them down to the crime scene and hold them for questioning," Stover said. "We need to get out of this corridor before it fills with nosey spectators."

"I'll stay with this room until back-up arrives," the other cop said. "I don't want anyone to enter or leave until we get a search warrant on the scene."

Burt Bancroft's phone was hot again.

"This is Captain Blaney of the Parkside police department, Mr. Director. I'm calling in response to your faxed request. We have a possible homicide at the Washington Arms hotel. I don't know if there is anything unusual about it, but we have suspects trapped in one of the fourth floor rooms. We should be making an arrest shortly and I wanted you to know. We might be able to use the Bureau's help in identifying the victim, as well as the suspects."

"Hell! I'm not far from that area. To get first hand information, I'll bring an agent and come over to the scene. We won't interfere with your operation, but we'd like to observe."

Burt Bancroft had tediously worked his way up the chain of command toward the director's job. Along the way he had served with distinction. Though often accused of being too plain spoken, his honesty and integrity had served him well. With the tenacity of a Wolverine, he continually pursued those outside the law.

He missed the excitement of those former years and often found himself hating the politics that stifled the actions of the office that he now held. Suddenly, the thrill of being in the field was filling his blood with new vigor. He wanted to smell and taste the excitement of field involvement one more time. This action might be just the thing to relieve some of his damnable stress build-up. As he was being driven to the hotel, his agent had been silent for some time.

"We're almost there, sir. I'll get you in the delivery zone if you want to go in the front?"

"No, we'll go in by the side entrance. There'll be more than enough official cars at the front. Let's park in one of the loading zones near the side door. This should be a quick once-over and then we'll return to the car."

The elevator ride to fourth floor was quiet and fast. In getting out of the cab, Burt saw men in the corridor to his left and to his right.

Puzzled by this situation, he sent his agent in one direction and he took the other route.

Approaching the room where the shooting had occurred, he was stopped by Detective Stover. Burt immediately flashed his FBI shield and Stover looked at him in puzzlement.

"Mind telling me how and why the FBI got on the scene?"

"I don't mind at all, Detective. We want to know who you have and we were invited here by your Boss."

"We don't know who we have yet," Stover replied. "He has no ID and we can't search the room of the shooters yet. The search warrant is still on its way."

“I promised not to interfere with your investigation, but I would like to see the crime scene. Seeing the wall from this side has me curious to see what happened on the inside,” Burt said.

“I’ll take you in,” Stover said amiably. “The Medical Examiner is on the scene and he’s pretty touchy about having too many people near the body.”

As Burt walked into the room, he saw the two men in custody and then turned left to view the area of the wall where the bullets had wreaked their deadly damage. Bancroft surveyed the scene and eyed the chair that had seated Hildon when the bullets struck.

“This wasn’t guesswork, Detective. These men used very sophisticated equipment.”

“That’s why we didn’t break into their room,” Stover said. “I’ll see if the ME will let you see the body. He caught three in the chest area, but several slugs are in the opposite wall.”

At the medical examiner’s nod, Burt raised the sheet and looked into Hildon’s face.

“Oh crap, Detective. You may not recognize this victim, but I do,” he told Stover excitedly. “I’m sorry, but I’m taking over this investigation as of right now. This victim is Senator Hildon and he’s been missing for nearly two weeks. You are advised and warned to keep this news confidential until further notice. I want everyone out of here and off the premises immediately. I intend to put a seal on this room and another on the room that these men occupied.”

“The hell you say! I don’t know how much weight you swing, but you’re not taking my case until the Captain tells me so.”

“Get your Captain on the horn, Detective, and tell him that FBI Director Burt Bancroft has personally taken over your crime scene. The only other thing I need from you is an exact report of everything that you saw and heard after you reached this scene.”

Burt immediately flipped his cell phone and contacted his aides.

In a matter of minutes, FBI personnel and their own medical investigative team would replace this entire squad of local police.

His next call was to the office of the Secretary of Defense.

When the Secretary was on the line, the voice of Burt became very professional and unbelievably cordial.

“Mr. Secretary, I want to personally inform you that Senator Hildon has been found. He was shot to death in the Washington Arms hotel sometime today and there's not much more that I can tell you at this moment. I'd like you to use extreme discretion about this news. I don't even want his family notified until we learn more about this situation. I'm telling you this since you believe he may be named in an upcoming indictment. I want that action squelched until we get on top of this situation."

"I really appreciate your call, Burt," the Secretary said sadly. "I'm sorry this happened, but I'll keep Hildon's name out of the conspiracy thing for awhile."

Up in the sixth floor suite, Hartley paced nervously and commented to the others.

"Waiting like this is hell, but I can't leave before trying to learn the result of this mess. I could be questioned before I get clear of the elevator. The smart thing is to wait a bit longer."

"Almost an hour has passed," George replied. "It can't be very much longer now."

Another hour passed while Hartley and the other two men waited for someone to come and verify their story. Something had definitely happened to alter the normal flow of events, but Hartley could not afford to wait any longer. It was imperative that he return to his own arena and avoid questions that might arise from this investigation.

After so much time had passed, getting out of the hotel should pose no problem. Failure to get the prized sworn statement caused much regret, but he did destroy the document. He had too much to lose by staying longer in Washington.

In the elevator cab, he pressed the ground floor button and rode the entire six floors without company. On reaching the lobby, he gave sidelong peeks at the few people moving between the desk and the exit. Without incident, he reached the street and hailed a taxi.

Once inside the yellow vehicle, he gave directions to the driver and in a matter of minutes was delivered to the airport. Within an hour from the time he left the hotel, he was on a flight to New Mexico. Though he was depressed over the loss of the affidavit, he knew he was lucky to escape involvement. His rigged abduction of Hildon had cost the man his life and if that act were laid at his door, he would be a loser all the way around the course.

* * *

At Katie's condo, Don finished his task.

"I've opened all three of the devices and they were made in France, by the same electronics company. I don't know what good that can do; we're a long way from France."

"France is not as far away as another planet," she said stubbornly. "When I first arrived here, Alexi hinted strongly that I was from another planet. I think that may be a lie. If his agents are all outfitted with French communicating devices, I'd say that shoots his alien theory pretty full of holes."

"That's no big deal," Don snorted. "We could be from anywhere."

"We'll take one fact at a time. I'm very happy to finally learn something from our background. Now, I can have a showdown with him with less fear of the results. If I fully believed that I was from another world, I'd need his help to return home. Anywhere on planet Earth is reachable without his aid."

"I won't buck Alexi until I know more about him," Don said stubbornly. "He told me this mission was of extreme urgency and getting worse with the passing of each day."

"I'm not your boss, thank God, and you can do as you see fit. I'll be careful to inform him that I'm alone in my thinking. Just do me a favor and see if you can reach him by using Teresa's unit."

Don received no response on his first three attempts to reach Alexi, but connected on the next one. He swiftly passed the device to her.

"Alexi, this is Katie. Yes, we recovered the device that belonged to Teresa. That may be, but I don't know how long you'll remain relieved. I'm tired of your one-sided games and I want to know more about this operation or I'm out. You've continually hand fed bits and pieces of information to me from the day of our first contact. Things are going to change if I continue to help. If you had leveled with Teresa, she might be alive today. Well, you won't find me so easy to die off."

"You better hear me out before you make an error that you could regret," he told her angrily. "I'll tell you this much and no more. Where you came from, you have family and friends. If you entertain the tiniest sliver of hope that you might ever see them again, you will follow orders."

"I won't buy your deal, it's just too one sided," she said. "We could never expect to get much backup from a man who hides in a communicating device. Whatever your mission is, it will have to be pursued without much help from me. If you want my assistance, you can explain the mission in detail. Any plan that you want my help in must be fully detailed. I still won't make any promises though until I hear the reason for this quest."

A long period of silence followed before he spoke again.

"Are you speaking as a solitary individual, or has this become a dual insurrection?"

Don could hear the conversation in its entirety and when she glanced his way, he nodded and spoke.

"Tell him for me that we are speaking as one voice."

"We are in total agreement here," she said firmly. "Why don't you show your face and we can discuss this situation?"

"That is impossible. I will not reveal myself to you. Should the mission die, I still have a solemn duty to perform as long as I remain unidentified. I can tell you of the mission's purpose without fear of reprisal. This hateful country is developing and testing a new weapons system that strikes fear in the heart of every independent nation of the world. If it is successfully developed and deployed, we could become slaves to America's wishes. They must not be allowed to hold exclusive possession of this system. If we cannot stop the development and deployment, we must have a complete set of plans and build our own. If you help me in securing our goal, I will see that you are returned to your loved ones."

"If for no other reason, I thank you for the small enlightenment that you've given. I still make no promises to you, except that I'll continue to search for these plans," she told him doggedly.

"I have other contacts and some are in high places," he continued. "These sources tell me that things are developing rapidly and this fact may impede your search. Only a few days ago, Senator Hildon was found shot to death in a Washington hotel. The two men responsible seem unconnected to any of the known players. The FBI is holding them in custody and they have taken over the present investigation."

"I believe it's time for you to get technical with me, Alexi. I need to know the specific weapon, or weapons, that you are seeking. I might learn a lot from the senator and if necessary, I could try to pull something from Hartley."

In an act of full disclosure, he described the products that comprised the weapons delivery system.

He clearly had some precious inside information, but that source had been unable to secure any further data.

He promised to stay in closer contact and be more open with them if they cooperated. After he closed the communication, she breathed a sigh of relief.

"What caused your change of heart, Don? I thought your mind was set against being a rebel."

"If he had seen dissention between us, he might have set us against each other. Who knows what evil thoughts lurk in his head?"

"We either must work together, or aim for the same goals independently if we're to have any chance of returning to our past. I intend to hunt for these plans that are so important to Alexi, but he'll pay my price if he gets them."

The following day she approached Todd carefully and thoughtfully

"Sir, I have a request to make and I hope you won't let me down. I'm asking for one evening out of your lifetime. If you'll share this special event with me, under my rules, I'm sure you will never regret it."

"We've come a long way together in a very short time. I believe we're safely past the stage of suspicion. Bring on this surprise and we'll see if I can handle it."

"Tonight, I'd like you to have dinner with me. Bob Hartley will be joining us at the Fat Calf. I've already managed to strong arm him into agreement and he promised to play by the rules."

"I can't be less of a man than Hartley," Todd replied slowly. "You play a tough game. I'll show the extent of my faith in you by accepting this dinner date."

She turned her attention back to her work with a face full of smiles. She had plans for these two men and if those plans were successful, everyone would come out winners.

* * *

A noted attorney was visiting the Federal holding cell.

"Mr. Lawton, I have been asked to provide legal representation for you. Your employers want you to have everything that's in their power to provide. Your future needs will be provided for and in return, they expect you to let me do all the talking. I want to know everything that took place in the Washington Arms hotel. If you value your freedom, don't hold anything back."

Ollie took the lawyer, step by step, through the entire incident and he spoke in a barely audible tone of voice.

If the room was bugged, he intended to outfox the feds.

The lawyer gave words of encouragement and more advice and then made a parting promise.

"I intend to visit your partner. The next time we meet, I'll have your stories ready and we'll make absolutely certain that they're identical. I'll advise you as to what will work to your advantage and the things that you must avoid at all costs."

After completing his duties toward his clients, he consulted an address book and pressed the necessary phone numbers. Weiss heard the line noise as the connection was made.

The voice of Valenkov was gruff and questioning. "Yes?"

"Sir, this is Attorney Weiss. I've seen my clients and I want to report that they are in good spirits. They understand the situation and are comfortable in knowing that their future will be secure."

"Have you developed a plan for their defense?"

"Yes, I have and they must do hard time. Now please don't yell at me if you want me to work for you."

Sergai answered carefully. "I apologize, Weiss. You don't understand the difficulty I feel in expecting these two men to stay silent while they're in prison."

"I do understand, sir. However, a stretch in prison for the men is inevitable. They were caught on the victim's floor with the death weapon in their possession. I'm working magic in keeping them off death row."

"I see your point, Weiss. My personal problems of the moment have me on edge. Explain further and I'll keep silent."

"I have them in the hotel, to set up a sale for the exotic weapons. The arms were brought in through the stairwell. They had just entered the corridor when this automatic weapon inadvertently gets triggered. They quickly fled to an empty room without knowing that a man was killed. Senator Hildon was simply a man in the wrong place at the right time. As a worst case scenario, I see a manslaughter charge for them."

Solemnly, he added, "An illegal weapons possession charge also seems inescapable, but it can't be proved that our men stole the guns."

"Excellent, Weiss," Sergai exclaimed. "I understand now why you get the big bucks."

"Thanks for the compliment, sir. I'll try extremely hard to earn my fees and then I'll be going back to Meldor and Associates."

This same company was on the mind of the FBI Director during this very moment. Burt rubbed his right earlobe delicately and sighed with a deep purging of breath. With all the power at the Bureau's disposal, they failed miserably to unearth anything of value to this case. Although Attorney Weiss was traced to Meldor and Associates, this fact came to naught. A list of their employees uncovered the name of Harvey Walton.

He was the uncle of Ollie and had met Weiss on the golf course. Through this golfing connection, Harvey had prevailed on the noted attorney to intervene in his nephew's legal problems.

He studied the accumulation of facts on attorney Weiss for many minutes before finally accepting the theory of coincident. Weiss was a nationally famous criminal lawyer. However, his talents also included the field of corporate law. Meldor and Associates had a perfectly sound reason for keeping him on a yearly retainer.

A few days later, Director Bancroft was seated outside the interrogation room as his best agent worked. He watched and listened with great interest as the speaker system divulged dialogue ranging from mere dullness to hopeful expectation during an intense interrogation.

"Ollie, why don't we recap our little talk? I'll remind you that if you answer two simple little questions, it might keep you off death row. I want to know who you work for and I need to know why the Senator was murdered."

"I don't work for anybody," Ollie told him sullenly. "I've been out of work for quite a while now. As for your other question, the senator was not murdered. It was purely accidental."

"Okay! So we'll work with what we have for the moment. Your name is Ollie Lawton and you have a record. You have long been out of work, but you have several hundred dollars in your pocket. You had absolutely no idea that this man was a senator, but you killed him anyhow. You found these sophisticated weapons in an abandoned house and took possession of them. These weapons are unusual and it takes weeks of training to use them, but you managed real well."

He paused briefly and then continued.

"Ollie, I've had my toilet training and I dutifully completed my elementary education. Those two basic accomplishments are enough to tell me that you are full of it. We've got you and your good buddy nailed to the wall. Watch closely and see what happens. If your boss gets an attorney for you, we'll find out who pays him. He can't possibly get you off the hook. You *will* be executed for this murder. You've assassinated a very important man and it *is* a Federal crime. Have you ever seen a man executed? I've watched the Electric Chair do its job and it's a gruesome sight. Can we try those two questions again, Ollie boy?"

Watching the face of the suspect change along with the thrust of the conversation, Burt smiled in remembrance of a similar role he had played in other times. His forehead wrinkled at the thought of the possible time that might elapse before the suspects caved in.

The time factor might be disagreeable, but the end result would be the same. The suspects were caught at the scene of the crime with the murder weapon in their possession. Their future was bleak in spite of the talent that their defense attorney might possess. As he mulled the situation to this point, Burt's thoughts wandered to another time and place.

He'd spent several years in the spotlight as one of the top agents in the business. But holding down this high office was the toughest duty he'd ever pulled. On the street, he'd known what to expect and stayed prepared. Here on mahogany row, politics played dirty tricks on the best of men. His only consolation came in knowing that he would persevere because of his tenacity. He must always believe only what he could see and nothing that he heard.

CHAPTER NINE

At Katie's condo, the second day of coping with a houseguest passed without incident. The initial irritation at having Don tossed into her life seemed justified, but she gradually realized it was wrong to take it out on him. He could no more alter his role than could she. If he carried out his part in maintaining a civil friendship, she would do no less.

Months had passed since this ordeal began in Socorro and she'd learned nothing of her past life. She sensed that Florida held the key to her puzzle, but this gleaning was a piddling gain. Lately, she was so involved in other matters that it was impossible to concentrate on her past.

Everyone should have a history and her past must include a country that could be called home. Where was her country? Had she been happy in her earlier life? If she had family, were they worried about her? If the quest of Alexi were satisfied before she learned more of herself, would that be a bad or good thing? In her first briefing, he hinted that she was from another world. She was beginning to doubt his integrity and intentions. What about Teresa? From what alien place had she been recruited? The thought of her late friend brought a strange light to her face.

What happened to Teresa's communicator? Alexi must have had some means to reach her. Almost a month had passed since she died. Her apartment rent was due soon and her possessions would likely be sold to offset the payment. Teresa likely had items of value for trading purposes.

When night came, she took Don along to check out Teresa's apartment. Once at Teresa's door, he disappointed her again.

"Hell, I don't know how to pick a lock. I'd never even heard that expression until you mentioned it."

"I'm beginning to wonder what abilities you *do* have," Katie said impatiently. "Stand aside and let me at the thing. I don't know if I've had training either, but I'll at least try. Someone got in here before she went to my place and I doubt if they had a key."

Using several items from her purse, she managed the door lock and they entered cautiously. Don used a flashlight and made sure the shades were drawn before turning on the lights.

The place was still in a mess and Katie felt a sudden flash of remorse. That same old feeling that so often dogged her was returning again. This poor woman had died alone, had no known relatives and no one gave a damn about her departure. How terribly awful that she had no one to care.

"What's wrong? You've been quiet for some time now," he said gently.

"It's not important at the moment," she told him. "We need to sift through her stuff and get the hell out of here."

She paid little attention to the articles scattered about the house, for they were well searched. Her full interest was directed toward the places where the articles had been stored.

In an antique chest she found one of the excellent hiding places that Teresa had used. The top drawer had been tossed and articles removed from the interior of the chest until the bottom was exposed.

When she tried to remove the chest from the storage closet, its unexpected weight surprised her.

With her curiosity suddenly aroused, she began examining the expensive wooden object carefully.

Though it took a few minutes, she discovered that the brass plate surrounding the locking eye would lift.

With the ornamental plate raised, a small pivoting lever was used to trip a spring-loaded false bottom panel.

In pressing this lever, she discovered something the others had failed to find. The chest bottom contained several gold pieces and other valuable items that were similar to the ones that Katie possessed.

There were other things stored inside and these items gave her much more than she expected to find. Teresa's business and personal bankbooks were safely stored in the chest.

With a closer examination, she discovered Teresa's journal, for it lay underneath all the other things. She began reading into the first page before she knew exactly what it was.

At the beginning of her diary, Teresa wrote of approximate dates. This uncertainty of earlier dates seemed to indicate a passage of time before she began keeping a log. The mere fact that she kept a log, gave Katie hope of learning more about this strange adventure.

She learned that the woman's beginning was much the same as her own. She had come out of the hills above Socorro and made her way to

Albuquerque. Once she located here, the first sales and trades of her valuables had put her in the antique business. She did not need to convert many of these articles though, as her store had been successful from the start.

She told of meeting Simpson and although admitting that she loved him, she wrote of having a tremendous fear of him. According to the log, Teresa knew that he was a strange and mysterious man at the onset of their association.

She decided to pursue the reading later. She had good reason to continue her search. Having watched carefully as Teresa packed, only her clothing had gone to Socorro unless the device was in her purse. Though it could have been consumed in the car fire, she still must search for it. Teresa owned many purses and now they were scattered about the room.

As she checked them out, she found one that was as heavy as her own. It contained nothing except a small AM-FM radio. As she moved toward another purse, she paused and returned. Removing the device from the purse, she pressed the on button and nothing happened. Curious now, she pressed the selector button and the back panel dropped to expose control knobs.

"Find the drawer for this chest and bring everything to the car. We don't want to hang around here any longer," she told him hurriedly.

When the pair was safe and back in her condo, she turned to Don with a question.

"Is this communicator like yours?"

"No, mine is much different and I know why. Teresa's unit can be used for short distance transmitting and receiving. She could contact Alexi with her unit anytime he was in range. My communicator has the ability to receive, but I can respond with it."

She looked at him strangely, and then offered another question.

"Do you have any practical thoughts about how much area this device will cover in a transmitting mode?"

"I'm almost certain that ten miles would be its maximum limit," he said confidently.

"We never discussed your training. What do you know about electronics, Don?"

"I should qualify as an expert, if training means anything. I've had more than my share. I can't explain any further. I don't even know where

I got the training. When you asked, I just blurted out my answer," he told her.

"I've been through this before. Don't let it bother you, but things will suddenly come to you and you'll find answers that you didn't expect to know."

"That's about the same message that I got from him," he replied.

"Whoever prepared us for this mission sure played hell with our brains," she said sadly. "We have a tremendous memory of the things they intend for us to know, but we draw a blank on anything of a personal nature. Let your training go to work for us. Tomorrow, check out these devices and try to learn where they were made. Take one apart if necessary and see if we can learn anything from that angle. I'll get some tea going and we'll have a drink before bedtime."

"It'll be a simple chore. Inside the unit, each component will have part numbers and some will involve a language. With luck, a country may be mentioned. It will only take a half hour to completely disassemble the unit."

The next day appeared to be a difficult one for Katie, as Todd was back at work. She approached his desk with apprehension. Earlier, he sounded perturbed and now she was unsure of her ground.

"It is so good to see you back here, Senator. How is Brad progressing?"

"Brad is improving every day and I'm glad to be back. I want to talk about you, though. I'll never find a way to properly repay you for the fine job that you've done in my absence. I've just completed a full status recap and we're in excellent shape. I never worried about things at the plant while I was with Brad. I knew you would keep things running. It's your safety that I'm concerned about. Our friend, Fred Wallace, gave me a license number to check out. A van was spying on your place in Socorro. I asked a friend to get a read out on that license tag. I found that this van is registered to an outfit known as Meldor and Associates. Have you ever heard of them?"

"I've seen their name, Senator. It appears in an orbiting circle of names that constitutes the bulk of your competition. Along with Robert Hartley, you're fighting a battle against a strange alliance. As far as I can see, the two of you have been bidding into a stacked deck. It's a wonder that you've managed to win any federal contracts at all."

"Katie, don't take up Hartley's case. He's guilty as sin in this conspiracy."

"He was involved in an illegal action only one time. It made him sick to his stomach and he asked for an investigation, but nothing came of it. That is why he wrote the message I told you about. I think you should get together and fight this thing as a team. You could at least give it some thought."

"You're trying to change the subject, lady. I called you in here to discuss your safety. You're the one in danger, not me. If we knew why they're so paranoid about you, we might be able to minimize your danger."

"Well, Hartley said they think I'm a federal agent. He supposedly has some kind of information on them, but he refused to explain. In his opinion, I've already dug too deeply into their organization."

"Well, at last Hartley and I finally agree on something. I don't want you digging anymore. I expect to hear from Washington before long. They simply can't sit on this thing very much longer. If I don't get something pretty soon, I intend to call the Secretary of Defense."

At that same moment another caller was phoning the esteemed Secretary.

"Good morning, Mr. Secretary, this is General TreMayne. Yes, it *has* been a long time. You know how it goes during times of peace and prosperity. Golf, fishing, swimming, and occasional travel between our obligations become the itinerary of the times. We seldom ever talk business these days. Golf caused me to make this call, Mr. Secretary. The lack of golfing might be more of an accurate phrase I suppose. Your name has been mentioned several times in talks that I've had with Senator Hildon. I had a golfing date with the senator and he didn't show. I intended to ask him about the status of our New Mexico projects and I phoned his office trying to reschedule. They couldn't give me much, except that he was out of reach. In these days of the new electronic age, I believe none of us are out of reach. What is your take on this, sir?"

It took several seconds for the Secretary to reply. He had long ago learned how information is pursued in Washington. Many important facts are sometimes gleaned through seemingly innocent questions.

The general should not expect to be treated in a manner unlike others seeking information. TreMayne should have called the senatorial staff for answers.

"I believe you should accept their claim as the gospel truth, General. The man could very well be out of the country. He has been off the senate floor now for nearly two weeks."

The general gave a polite reply.

"Well, I'll catch him at some later date. Thanks for your time, Sir."

* * *

As Don dug into his new job, he discovered that his ability had not been overstated. Hartley was so impressed by the young man's talents that he moved him into the new joint venture program. Without any assistance from Katie, the young engineer assembled plan copies and specifications for Hartley's entire system. Using the facilities of a local print shop, he cut copies of all the important paper work and returned the originals to the secured plan room of the Hartley Corporation.

Katie eagerly looked through the plans in hopes of finding the reason Alexi placed such importance upon their acquisition. Despite the lack of an engineering background, she quickly saw enough to convince her that it was a very important project. The possessor of this system could easily discourage any nation from making an aggressive move. Having this system in one's arsenal also made a potential aggressor subject to a first strike possibility. It was capable of delivering warheads to a target within an eighteen hundred mile range. As a potential weapon, it was a huge threat and the added radar deflecting ability made it extremely fearful.

Only those nations willing to live in peace would not fear this weapon. Did Alexi's nation want to live in peace, or did they have warlike ambitions? Now she had another mystery to solve. Before she could offer the plans to him for bargaining purposes, she had to know his nation's intentions. It was hard enough to consider selling out the senator and Hartley for personal reasons, but the possibility of worldwide conflict was making it a real poser. There must be some way to offset the problems that continually flailed her, but the answers wouldn't come from Albuquerque. With grim determination, she decided to return to Socorro for a few days.

All along the way down I-25, she pondered the hard questions. Why was Florida the key, if it truly was? She failed to find concrete answers back there despite her earlier eager search. In the case of Hartley and the Senator's trust, where did her duty lie? Was the remote possibility of returning to her past, worth prostituting her fidelity to her friends? If Alexi's nation got these plans, developed the system, and then attacked America, her Socorro friends would suffer along with everyone else.

The senator had given her a few days off and Don was fending very well for himself. She needed some time to relax and she had other business to tend to as well. She brought many of the objects that belonged to Teresa and meant for Sam to turn them into cash. She would share with Don, but Alexi would never see a dime of the money. The thought of Sam brought memories of Rosalie and her clairvoyant powers. If she could just spend a few hours with her, it might be helpful. Knowing that her mind had been tampered with, Rosalie was powerless to affect any change. Since she no longer believed she'd been brought here from an alien world, the Indian woman might possibly be of help.

Sam was alone in his shop and seemed overjoyed to see her. He talked non-stop about her valuables and the excellent price that Pepper paid for them. The wholesaler was pressing to get more articles to sell and she quickly surprised Sam, by dumping her handbag on the counter. The articles that once belonged to Teresa seemed of equal value to those already sold to Pepper.

"What a priceless assortment you have here," he told her after a speedy appraisal. "Your aunt couldn't possibly have known the real worth of her collection. Is this the last of her valuables?"

"No, there are several left, but I should hold them for a rainy day."

"With the money you'll have left after this sale, you can afford to go where the sun always shines. Pepper tells me the people of Phoenix are worrying him to death trying to locate more items like these."

"I made this trip for reasons other than money. I'd like to visit with Rosalie for a little while."

"Go on over to the house, she'll be pleased to see you. I'll close the shop early and maybe you'll eat dinner with us."

Rosalie beamed at her in motherly fashion and began firing questions. She read that Teresa had died in a car accident, but Katie refused to disclose her darkest suspicion. When their talk lulled, Rosalie turned the conversation to Katie's memory.

"Have you remembered anything?"

"Nothing has come to mind. I can sense it hanging out there, but it won't come on in."

"I'd like to put you under again and try something new. I've given much thought to your problem and I have an idea that's worth a try."

After agreeing to another hypnotic effort, she went under quickly and easily. Rosalie brought her along slowly until she was certain that Katie was ready.

"Were you happy as a child? Can you remember any unhappiness? Can you recall any big events...like your sixteenth birthday for instance?"

"I can't remember ever being a child," Katie said sadly.

"We won't worry about that, we'll just move on to your later life.

Now, you're in a car with the man that took your purse. Tell me the color of his eyes, his hair, and his complexion."

A few moments of silence passed as Katie struggled with the questions.

"I'm trying to see him, but there's no image of him in my mind."

"By what name did you call him?"

Katie again wore a puzzled look and made an odd face.

"I can't remember calling his name."

"Your purse is on the seat beside you. What color is it?"

"I don't know. I can't see it."

"That's okay. Try to think of the last time you opened the purse and looked at the contents. What do you see?"

"I see some cash, credit cards, Social Security card, and other types of identification."

"Good! Now look closely at one of the credit cards and tell me which bank issued it."

"I can't see that at all and I'm looking hard."

Rosalie spoke in an irate tone of voice. "Just give me a small description of any one of the cards. You know darn well that every card has a certain designation."

"I know what you want, but it's not there. I can't see anything, but other than a credit card."

Deciding that Katie had been frustrated long enough, Rosalie quickly brought her out of the trance.

"Well, did you get anything new this time?"

"I got enough to feel certain of at least two things. Supposedly, you left Phoenix with a man and were on your way to Albuquerque. I'm convinced there was no man and there was no purse. Had there been a man, you'd have kept a fragment of his image. If you had no purse, it follows that you had no identification. I asked for a description of your credit card and you gave me none. If a credit card existed, you would have said it was either Visa or Master charge. Someone has altered your mind. You were given certain things to remember, but not the little details. Everything that you've done since you came to Socorro has been to suit someone else's purpose."

"You must think I'm an awful person, but I haven't lied to you or Sam. I'm not in any way trying to use you."

"Nonsense, we think no such thing. You're not to blame for what someone else may have done to you. After the generosity that you've shown us, how could we see you in a bad light? Instead of feeling sorry for yourself, you need to work on your problems and I'll try to help."

"What more can we possibly do until I remember something useful?"

"We can return to our very first hypnotic session. You made a statement that I recall very clearly. You told me you were born in Florida. I took that as a pure fact, since falsifying is extremely rare under hypnosis and you had no reason to lie. You traveled back to Florida shortly after you came here. Why did you go back there, Katie? What were you hunting for in Fort Lauderdale?"

"I went back there trying to find some answers. I had no memory and no roots, but I spoke this language fluently and I can't recall knowing any other language. If I wanted to find decent employment, I needed a background. Since I had already told Sam that I was born there, I hoped to find something that would fill in some of the blanks. I didn't intentionally lie to him. The words just came spilling out of my mouth. For all I know, I may have been born there. I found a name that resembles mine and her age is similar."

"Did you try to find her?"

"She was lost at sea along with her family and some friends. Next year, they're to be legally declared as deceased."

An odd look appeared on the face of the Indian woman. It was only a fleeting expression, but it was followed by a strange question.

"Describe your reaction on learning of her death," she demanded in a calm voice.

"I had very little feeling about the girl. Strangely though, on learning that her parents were probably dead I had strong feelings of sadness. It put me in a bad mood that lasted until I returned here from Florida."

“There is a blockage of your memory here and we may never remove it until you have a partial recall. I wish there was more that I could do, but I can’t pull out something that doesn’t exist.”

“I feel that Florida holds the key, Rosalie. I don’t know where to take it from there, but it’s a strong feeling. I hoped you would be able to help solve this riddle.”

The balance of the Socorro trip was a total waste of her time. Though Rosalie prepared a lovely dinner, the appetite of Katie had already disappeared.

* * *

In a Washington restaurant the Defense Secretary and the House Speaker ordered lunch and were hoisting Martinis. The Secretary looked very pleased with himself.

“We’re all alone now, Ward. You can tell me why you’re so damned happy.”

“Brooks, I have a smile for the first time in months. I think our troubles are about over.”

“You mean those indictments are ready to hand down this soon?”

“No, but I’m speaking of something equally important. I’ve just been notified that we have a new entry in the bidding wars for the delivery system.”

“How the hell can that help, Ward? You already have more than you can handle. That’s what got you into trouble in the first place.”

“Listen to me, you damned old goat. Do the names Whatley, Hartley, and Ryan Enterprises ring any bells for you?”

Two of them do, but I don’t get the Ryan connection.”

“According to the senator, without Ryan there would be no Hartley-Whatley connection. Brooks, these two men have formed a joint venture to produce the complete delivery system. For their other support, they only require a few minor component parts. We can legally sole source them until some other competitor appears.”

He added hastily, “Do you realize how much this will clean up our act?”“If the Senator is involved, we will finally be dealing with a reputable company. That will certainly be a novelty,” Brooks said softly. “Will this change any of your plans toward the indictments?”

"It will greatly accelerate those plans. We were hesitant to act due to the urgency of the ongoing contracts. Now, we can cancel any unfilled contracts and invite this new corporation to join the bidding process."

He would had been even more pleased if could have seen the transformation in Albuquerque.

Three newly decorated offices sparkled in the mid-morning sunlight. The warm golden rays came streaming through the large windows overlooking the interstate and spilled generously across the expensive carpet. Into these luxurious surroundings, fine selections of office furniture had been moved. It was clearly a unique, but still highly efficient office layout. Somewhat resembling a pie wedge, Katie's office was directly in the corner. The two offices belonging to the men, opened on either side. She could quickly respond to either man's request for aid.

This particular building was picked as a neutral site. From here, they would direct the operations of the new corporation. Hartley would handle the private matters of his other operations from this same location. The Senator would eventually turn his main plant operations over to Brad. It was fully understood that Katie would work between the offices of the two men. In a surprise move, they gave her to understand that she would be a very minor partner. If she refused their offer, they informed her firmly, the money would go to some charitable organization.

Even though she was extremely pleased by their generous offer she didn't need the money. To refuse the partnership offer though, might seem highly suspicious. With an air of humbleness and appreciation, she agreed to their wishes. They could not know that her internal organs were on fire from the shame of the detestable role that she was playing. Though lacking memory of her background ethics and morals, she knew it was wrong to betray a trust.

* * *

The elaborate home of Sergai was tastefully and expensively furnished and the surrounding grounds landscaped with an artistic touch. All this finery was launched in the fond hope that he would eventually acquire a circle of important friends to entertain. He failed to reach that sought after plateau, but he had accumulated a good measure of wealth. This home was now quietly for sale and its offering was being handled by an exclusive agency.

On this warm sunny morning, two federal marshals staked out Valenkov's fabulous home. They had subpoenas and search warrants, but the servants did not know the whereabouts of Sergai. After an extensive and useless search of the main house and adjoining buildings, the marshals returned to their car. This man, they decided, was not one to take his work home. No scrap of paper was found that could tie him to the suspect companies. After the marshals reported to their superior, their orders were to stay outside the home of Sergai and wait for his return.

Law enforcement officials were also busy across town. The receptionist at the Phantum Company was visibly upset as she talked with her boss.

"Mr. Simpson, two men in my office that I think you should see. They are federal marshals and they have a search crew with them."

Simpson emitted a string of curses as he closed the intercom button. The dreaded moment had come and as he feared, it came without warning. Moving into the reception room, he saw marshals with papers in hand. Having no previous legal search experience to draw from, he could only guess at their next moves.

"Are you James Simpson, sir?"

He answered meekly in a strained voice with one word. "Yes."

Staring with a hard gaze, the marshal spoke firmly. "Since you are named as Chief Executive Officer of the Phantum Corporation, I am placing you under arrest."

"There must be some mistake here," James said heatedly. "On what charge are you basing my arrest?"

"Suspicion of conspiracy to defraud the federal government and suspicion of federal bid rigging are the charges listed on the warrant. We have a federal indictment pending and I warn you that anything you say may be used against you in a federal court of law. I will read your rights and then you will go with us to the federal building for further investigation."

As Simpson was hustled out of the building, he looked over his shoulder and saw the search crew begin the searching of his files.

At the building that housed the offices of the Blue Horizon Corporation, Arnold Montgomery received essentially the same treatment as that given to Simpson. In a few moments, he too was whisked away to the federal building.

In Phoenix, the Meldor Corporation and the office of Desert Enterprises were suddenly surprised by visits from federal officers. Managers of both organizations were taken into custody and held for further questioning. These investigations were timed to coincide with those in New Mexico, ostensibly to prevent any possible destruction of records. Though the federal noose was tightening around the other corporation officers, Valenkov was still free.

* * *

"Senator, this is Ward Bonding and I need a few moments of your time, if I may."

"Certainly, Mr. Secretary, how may I be of service?"

"It seems we are faced with a small crisis, Todd," he said carefully. "I know that you and Hartley are underway with a joint venture. Just how close are you from an assembled package?"

"We haven't put any sort of rush on our operations. We could put a package together in less than a month, but it would not be indicative of our best effort. We would have to use existing products and the end result would be a far cry from our best."

"Make it happen. We'll even authorize overtime, but please get this mill running at top speed," Ward said firmly.

"Can you enlighten me a bit on this direct order, Ward? I'll meet with Bob and get the wheels turning, but you've certainly juiced my curiosity."

"No one must know this, but you. We have indictments underway for most of your competitors and some of them are holding fat contracts. We need to cancel those contracts, but we lack a legal reason. Until they are convicted, these vendors have every right to pursue their livelihood. If you can get a total package ready to test and then submit those plans, we can legally obsolete their products. With outdated offerings, their legal recourse evaporates," he told Todd.

"Thank you for sharing this information with me. What is their present status? Are you holding them for questioning? How long can you hold them before an attorney rips them out of jail?"

"Three days would normally be the maximum, but there's a kicker. There is a death involved here, possibly a murder, and that allows us to hold them in protective custody."

"I was sorry to learn of Senator Hildon's death. I'm sure you are alluding to him, but I don't figure his role in this affair. Have you been able to apprehend all those involved in the conspiracy?"

"We haven't located Sergai Valenkov. He seems to play a large hand in several of the suspect organizations. We moved to deny passports and visas to all known players in this game. If he's not already out of the country, then he won't make it. Thanks again, Senator, for your cooperation and I wish you much good luck in your new venture."

Todd replaced the phone, while creases began appearing on his forehead. Things were unfolding entirely too fast. He signaled for Katie and she came swiftly to his desk.

"I need to set a conference with Bob and then we need a planning session with our joint engineers. Things are rolling faster than we anticipated. I just had confidential words with the Defense Secretary and he unloaded on me. The three of us can share this news, but it must go no further. Indictments are ready for several of our competitors and most of them are already in custody."

Katie asked a fitting question and waited for Todd's reply.

"Which ones have turned up missing, Senator?"

"Valenkov is unaccounted for at the moment. He could be holed up most any place, but I doubt that he has left town. The feds have kept a tight lid on this, mainly because of Hildon's death. I don't believe Valenkov could have learned of the indictments."

She was patiently quiet for a few moments. Katie knew there was a limit to what she could relate to the senator. How could she successfully place a stop point, once she began to divulge information? Her mind worked swiftly and a decision was reached.

"If a trace could be put on a local phone number, you might find Sergai. I am almost positive that I recognized his voice, but I might be wrong," she told Todd quietly.

She went to her desk and retrieved a Phantum Corporation business card from her purse.

This was the card she took from Gene Evans at her apartment. Handing the item to Todd, she spoke in calm tones.

"I had an intruder, several weeks ago and I took this card from him along with his wallet and pistol. The number that's penciled on the backside probably belongs to Sergai."

Todd looked at her with eyes that clearly reflected astonishment.

"You leave me almost speechless. Are you totally proficient at everything you do? How did you dare face this man if he had a gun?"

"I had no choice, Todd. He was in my condo. I had taken special precautions and I knew someone was inside. It's no big deal, I mean...really."

"Well, I'll call an FBI friend and let him take it from here. This could be a big lead."

"I'll get to work on these new conferences, Senator. I hope the number helps."

In only a few minutes, Todd was on the phone.

"Inspector Beam, please," Todd, said into the mouthpiece. "Yes, I'll hold."

"This is Inspector Frank Beam. "I'm sorry to keep you waiting; how may I help you?"

"Frank, this is Todd Whatley. I came across something that might be of use to you. I realize that I'm treading in privileged waters, but I know your office is seeking Sergai Valenkov. If you can trace this phone number without alerting him, you might get a fix on Valenkov."

"Give me the number, Senator, and then we'll talk some more. I may need to know more about this tip."

After jotting the numbers on his pad, he motioned to a nearby agent.

"Hang on one second, Senator and I'll pass this off to an agent."

Todd was pensive for the few moments that Frank was entrusting the tracing chore to his agent. He had known Frank for several years and was confident that he could be trusted.

"I'm back, Senator. I hope I don't rub you the wrong way, but I need answers. There just has to be a story behind a senator's possession of the unlisted phone number of a suspected felon. I've known you for some time now and I know that you still swing some weight in DC, but the hunt for Valenkov and his associates was top security. I'll bet you've violated a top line trust, but you chose the right man. I have tremendous respect for you, but I may have a strong need to know your source. I won't push for it, unless I'm pushed. If this tip leads us to him, I'll call you. Hell! I may call you anyway," he said with a laugh.

Katie remained at her desk during Todd's phone talk. She had many things fleeting through her mind and none of them were especially gratifying. One of the bigger things that she had hoped fervently to avenge was Teresa's useless death. It would seem that with all the top players in the hands of the FBI, she would never find her murderer. She could not know that in shooting Quince, she had already avenged her friend's death.

Another item that plagued her was the underhanded way she was treating the kindness and generosity of her two employers. She was having terrible attacks of conscience torment and this fact disclosed another puzzle. With the training that Alexi's people provided and because of their brain tampering, she should have been without conscience. Since her training on this point had apparently broken down and since it appeared that she was developing a new set of moral values, she felt extremely guilty in double-dealing her employers. Try as she might, she could not thrust away the feeling of self-indulgence. Somewhere within this perplexing labyrinth, there had to be a moral balance. With all her heart, she wanted to return to her homeland and regain the memories of the past, but where was the fairness to these Americans that had shown such trust and kindness?

CHAPTER TEN

Don worked with intensity at his drafting table. Occasionally, he stepped away to look at the drawing from a different viewpoint. This was an excellent delivery system and there seemed to be little room for improvement if money was not a factor. A populace that stood as sheep, while being fleeced in the name of the national defense, might never question the cost of such weapons.

In Don's keen imagination, he saw a way to drastically pare this cost. Robert Hartley might not appreciate the loss of millions in anticipated revenue, but Don could never approach the senator. He had been hired by Hartley Corporation and would be expected to bring everything to them. Grimly, he turned back to his assigned tasks and decided that he must work on this idea strictly on his own time. Down the road, he would discuss his idea with Katie and get her input.

About that same time in Washington, the renowned lawyer, Weiss, entered the federal building and made his presence known to the proper authorities. Summoned here by an urgent phone message from Sergai Valenkov, he knew that his abilities would be put to the test. After being escorted to the receiving area, he waited patiently until Valenkov was seated behind the glassed partition and then he offered the first question.

"Have you made any type of statement or comment to the feds?"

"I asked what charges were pending against me. They named one, but I made no statement."

"Give me the details, immediately prior to and including your arrest," Weiss demanded.

"I was secluded in a hotel suite and the location was unknown to anyone. The Feds simply knocked on the door, read me my rights and took me away. I asked for an explanation of their actions and they refused to comment," Sergai said wearily.

"They must have tapped your phone," Weiss said thoughtfully. "Had you made or received any calls prior to your arrest?"

"Hell yes! I *am* a businessman, you know. I made several calls and received a few."

"That's it then and we just have to hope that your calls held nothing of incriminating value. Try to remember everyone that you talked with and the content of your conversation. You need not recall these talks now, but use the time between today and your arraignment to remember those talks. I'll make sure they had a court order to tap your phone before my next visit. In the meantime, don't say anything to them. They may hunt a deal of some kind, but it would certainly not be in your best interest," Weiss said tersely.

Sergai spoke in a tight voice, "Don't leave me here an hour longer than necessary. I have no liking for this confinement."

Back in Albuquerque, Todd received a call from the local FBI office.

"Senator, your information was correct and we owe you one," Beam said proudly. "We have Valenkov in custody and a formal arraignment is pending. So far, no demands have been made for me to reveal my source. It appears, as of now, that everyone involved in this activity has been taken down."

"You are mistaken, Inspector. From my experience in DC, I learned that there are certain limitations to information gathering capabilities. Hildon had no committee attachments that could have gained him the inside poop on the DOD contracts. He gained some informational edge as a senator from a state that contracted and constructed these particular systems, but not enough to satisfy all their needs. No, I'm afraid that Mr. Big is still running free and waiting for another opportunity to ply his trade," Todd said sadly.

"If you're correct, Valenkov will know the man. It might be wise to offer him a sweet deal, but that's not my call to make," Beam said dryly.

* * *

Katie watched with gathering interest as Don moved restlessly about the room. Something was on his mind to cause this unrest and she was determined to pry it from him. Direct questioning would accomplish nothing and she had learned this the hard way. When he suspected her of grilling him, he shut up like a clam. She wondered if total trust between them would ever be realized.

"Don a lot of time has passed since I was delivered here for this quest," she said slowly. "I'm not getting used to this strange life and I seriously doubt it will get better unless I get my memory back. I intend to clarify our relationship in a few simple words. I didn't ask for you and I certainly didn't need you. Other than by obtaining the weapons system information, you've done absolutely nothing to benefit our team. Given a little more time, I could have gotten the plans myself. Lately, you're not even a good companion. For some strange reason, you want to live in your own little world. When you first came here, I was strangely attracted to you and sensed that I might want to know you better. With the weird attitude that you've shown for days, I don't really care if I ever know you any better."

"You've been here longer and have a better understanding of this odd situation," he replied angrily. "I have to feel my way along. I'm trying to avoid stepping on the wrong toes until I get more familiar with everyone. Meanwhile, it seems that you're looking for any little chance to burn me down. I felt a sense of familiarity about you when I arrived and I kept waiting for a clue as to what that feeling meant, but none came. Now as I see it, I probably had an association with a witch during my other life. Seriously, you seem to think you have an exclusive on problems."

"Name a problem you feel is your sole property. Put your problem where your big mouth is."

"For one thing, I have a plan that would reduce the overall cost of the weapons delivery system in drastic fashion. Will Hartley resent my plan since it will cut his income by millions? Will he throw me out the door and try to shut me up? Since he's the one who hired me, any attempt to get the plan to Whatley would likely cause more problems," he said in troubled tones.

"Is this plan on the boards, or is it still in your head."

"It's on the plan board. It's a modification of the existing system, but it's an effective one."

"Let me feel the senator out on this. We'll go with what he feels is the best move. He is an honorable man and I believe he and Hartley can come to terms without anger over this supposed loss of income. Hartley would never resent the fact that you brought the idea to me."

He paused for a moment as if groping for direction.

"I'll go with your suggestion. I'm really sorry for blowing off at you earlier. I suppose knowing nothing of our past makes it more difficult to handle the present. We must respect that fact and be more tolerant. In my view, you are one beautiful lady and it would be extremely easy for you to stir my interest. I would never take unfair advantage of you and until we regain our memories, we have no idea of the commitments that we may have behind us. For all I know, you could be married or engaged and I suppose that also holds true for me. We should try to be good friends and remain constant in our efforts to return to our real life, whatever that may be."

"I appreciate the compliment. You are making a lot of sense, I suppose. We're looking at a hang-up with Alexi that greatly overshadows our personal problems. We don't know what country he represents and we have no idea of the use they would make of this weapon if we deliver it to him. I've learned a lot about the people in this country. If the ones that I've come to know are symbolic of the American race, I don't want to see them hurt in any warlike way."

"I can appreciate that view. We still have a right to seek our roots though and we must find some way to do that before committing to Alexi."

"We can't possibly unearth your background, unless there is some type of link. I'm sure you have no idea where you originated, or grew up. In my case, I believe the answer lies in Florida. If those people hadn't perished during that awful storm, I might not have this problem," she said wistfully.

"Maybe the boat didn't sink in Florida. Maybe the mast broke and they drifted toward Cuba, or even beyond. They could have capsized away from the Bahamas."

She looked quickly at him with a strange new light busily spreading across her face. He had innocently given her a new direction in which to seek answers. To properly cover this new lead, she needed the help of a very powerful individual and though Todd quickly came to mind, she dreaded asking for yet another favor. Despite her reluctance to draw from his well of favors, she knew the stakes were too high to allow her pride to interfere. The senator alone held enough power and the potential desire to aid in her search.

* * *

Burt Bancroft scanned his PC with a practiced eye. All the known players were listed, along with their proven connections. It was as clear as a normal Montana day that Hildon's death was entirely due to someone named on this screen. Somewhere within this web of intrigue, conspiracy, and fraud, a link must exist that would lead to the motive for his murder.

Since Ollie Lawton had already been linked to Meldor and Associates, supposedly through his uncle, it came as no surprise to learn that Meldor had ties to Valenkov. All of the conspiracy suspects had ties to Valenkov. Another murder victim, Quince Petersen, had been discovered outside the apartment of James Simpson and Simpson was CEO of Phantum Enterprises. Here again, another link to Valenkov.

Organized crime involvement had been ruled out as a suspect in both of these crimes, but the finger of evidence again pointed toward a conspiracy. What was missing from these assorted facts? The only possible motive for Hildon's death appeared to be for the protection of the conspiracy members. Why had Hildon gone to this hotel suite? Was someone afraid that he would turn them in to the law? How had the unidentified renter of the suite managed to lure him there to meet his death? The renter had used false ID to secure the suite and had paid two weeks rent. This period was about equal to the amount of time that Hildon had been reported as missing.

Common sense dictates that a hotel suite should have an abundance of fingerprints, but this place had been wiped clean. Ollie and his partner had not gone into the suite. They chose to shoot through the wall instead. This was direct proof that someone else was involved. Most likely it was someone not yet been connected to the conspirators activities. Burt shrugged tired shoulders and shut down the PC. He'd wait and get a fresh start tomorrow. Valenkov would be interrogated at that time and he wanted to be well rested for the event.

On the following day, Weiss was plying his trade.

"Mr. Valenkov, I want to repeat the words that I spoke earlier. Either take my advice, or get another attorney. For you, there is no middle ground. I know the questions they will ask and I know the answers that you must give. As you earlier directed, I visited with Simpson and Montgomery. They both agreed to play this out as I ordered, for I saw no alternative. You might wind up with a fine and a suspended sentence if you follow my directions, but you have my word that any other route will lead to a far more severe sentence."

"If the two insiders don't sell out for a better deal, what you suggest could work. I guess I have no choice except to follow your lead," Sergai said dejectedly.

"Look! I know my business, Mr. Valenkov. I can paint a life-like picture of these innocent contractors lured into a trap by money hungry contracts men. I'll depict the Defense Department as being so hell-bent toward securing this product that they were willing to prostitute their positions of trust to accomplish this end. I won't be surprised if the Secretary of Defense loses his job over this incident."

A little later, inside the interrogation room, Sergai and Weiss sat facing the FBI questioner. The table was cleverly arranged to allow all three faces to be seen from the viewing window. Inside the viewing room, Burt waited patiently for the questioning to begin. Weiss was boldly laying out the ground rules that must be followed, if the agent wanted full cooperation from Sergai.

Burt looked anxiously at his watch and swore softly. The prosecuting attorney had not arrived and his absence threatened to delay the questioning of Sergai. Nervously pacing the small room, Burt considered suspending the whole show. Seeing his agent suddenly go to the door and admit the long awaited attorney brought a sigh of relief from the Director.

Following brief introductions, the federal attorney offered a startling piece of information. Whatever his reasons for elucidating, his speech came as a surprise and his audacity shocked the entire audience.

"After examining the available facts of this affair, I felt it necessary to attend and offer my services in case the circumstances warrant plea bargaining. Mr. Valenkov, I'm sure you realize that the other members of this alleged conspiracy will point a finger at you. We've sifted through the business arrangements and holding companies and determined that these men are essentially working for you. They are nothing more than figureheads and helpful officers. I can offer you protection from taking the entire blast of heat, but only concerning the conspiracy angle. I understand that two murders have been committed and could possibly be connected to this case. If you are found to be connected to those deaths, that will be a separate charge and would be set aside from any plea bargain that we might execute. If I seem blunt, you must try to understand that I see several similar cases every year. Those that do go to trial are dragged out, delayed, and costly, but the defendant still bites the big one in nearly every incident. I'm telling you this because quite often, the defendant's attorney won't give his client the full story."

Weiss quickly spoke then, in a highly indignant manner.

"This is not only highly irregular and unwarranted, but I also find it to be extremely offensive. You are conducting yourself in a very unprofessional and slanderous way. My client has retained me for the express purpose of protecting him from people like you. This shameful action will definitely be brought to the attention of the Bar Association."

Weiss turned hate filled eyes toward the agent.

"We came in here with a spirit of cooperation, but you've allowed this man to blunt that spirit quite well. I'll advise my client to give you nothing but clear blue sky throughout the rest of this session. I have one parting shot before your questioning begins. I sincerely hope that the resumes of everyone on your side of this case have been updated. When this thing goes to trial and the press gets into their work, some big time heads will roll. This is not a threat, it's a solemn promise."

"I believe the show and tell portion of this show is over, gentlemen," the FBI agent said patiently. "I think both of you are in the wrong and the true victim of your outbursts, Mr. Valenkov, has yet to be heard. We are neither your judge nor your jury, sir. It is my job to ask questions of you and hope to reach the truth through the making of that effort. I will ask nothing that might be construed as entrapment. I will ask no questions that violate your rights. Mr. Valenkov, these simple forthright questions deserve to be answered. If I follow these guidelines, are you willing to proceed with the interrogation?"

"Your guidelines seem fair and reasonable," Sergai said with a glance toward Weiss.

"Are you upset at being brought to the national capitol, from your home state?"

"Not really. Since it's a federal charge that I face, I expected it to happen. I don't relish being held in custody wherever it takes place," Sergai said.

"Well, lets move on to the issues. I don't need you to explain bid procedures, but I do wish to know the approximate percentage of the bids you've won this year."

"Do you want the Meldor and Associates ratio of wins compared to the number of bids submitted, or the ratio as compared to total offerings from DOD?"

"I was referring to the combined bid wins from all of your assorted companies, sir."

"I'm sorry, but I can't answer that question. It has not yet been established that I'm anything more than an officer in these other companies and as such, I'm not privileged to know those answers," Sergai made this statement without aid from Weiss.

"Were you acquainted with Senator Hildon?"

"Yes, as a Senator from New Mexico he was invited to many social gatherings and I attended many of these same functions. He was especially well known at the charity benefits. I was also privileged to share several hours of conversation with the Senator and I found him to be extremely interested in the field of electronics," Valenkov offered.

"Did you ever have an occasion to ask him to intercede on your behalf, with the Department of Defense?"

"No sir! Although he expressed interest in my defense contract work, he made a point of mentioning that he pulled no weight with the DOD."

Weiss sat quietly through this portion of the questioning. He had been in complete awe of the masterful way that Sergai was conducting himself. Up to this point, Weiss was not pulling his weight. Even in his silence though, he remained alert for some slip from the FBI.

"I have another name for you to consider, Mr. Valenkov. Do you recall a man by the name of Quince Petersen?"

"I hire and fire many men each year, sir. It would place a terrible strain on my memory to try and remember each of them. To be perfectly honest, I've never tried to remember anyone except my immediate staff."

"Someone must have known him quite well, Mr. Valenkov. He received payroll checks from three of your four companies."

"I must again remind you that it is not a proven fact that these are my companies. Several names appear on the lists of corporate officers and the only requirement is that these officers must hold the minimum amount of interest in that particular corporation. I have complied with these requirements and I'm well within the law that governs corporations," Sergai asserted strongly.

The FBI questioner hated to cut short this interrogation, but it had gotten off on a bad footing and continued on a downhill skid. There was little need to prolong this agony.

"Why don't we just call it a day, guys? We're getting absolutely nowhere and we're just burning up good daylight. The next time we get together, we'll have a more productive meeting and that's a promise."

Tapping at the door brought an agent into the room to return Sergai to his cell and the federal attorney was left alone with the FBI agent, but not for long.

Burt burst into the room as angry as a bull elephant.

"Son, I'm going to have a talk with your boss. You really screwed up this questioning session. You were so damn bad that I began to have sympathy for the defendant. Whatever possessed you to fire on them in the way that you did?"

"When I came in and saw that smug face of Weiss, I wanted to explode. He is an arrogant legal bully and as crooked as they come. He's sitting on something that will blow this case wide open and I can't figure out what it can be."

"Well, you blew any chance of our putting a deal out for them," Burt said heatedly. "I agree with you on one point though. They definitely believe they have an edge. Whatever hole cards they are holding will be kept for the last play of the game and you can bank on that. My advice is to start with the Secretary of Defense and work your way down. Someone in that group holds the key to Weiss' hole cards. Tell them that, in our view, Weiss looks like the cat that ate the bird and whatever he's got may damn well blow up in their face. If the DOD wants to play it cool, their skirts had better be pretty damn clean."

* * *

Todd was occupied with a small stack of communications when Katie approached his desk. Glancing quickly in her direction, he knew something was amiss. He wanted to right this wrong in rapid order. He loved this young lady very much and he detested the thought of anything that might cause her even momentary grief. Seeing her in this brief turmoil, he raised the first question.

"How may I help you, young lady? I see by your eyes that something is troubling you."

"Is there no end to my problems, Senator? I would dearly love to come to your desk one day and have nothing to whine about. I hate a whiner and I expect everyone else to do the same."

"Please don't let those thoughts enter your mind. You're much too dear to me for anything except a pleasant view of you. Whatever bothers you can only be of someone else's doing and I can only help if you ask. What is this problem young lady?"

"It has to do with the disappearance of my relatives. I am bothered day and night by thoughts of their disappearance. I don't believe an adequate search was made in the effort to find them, or at least some sign of them. I was away and of absolutely no help to them. I feel extremely guilty because no other relatives were there to press the search."

"Give me more detail," Todd demanded eagerly as his interest perked.

"On the twenty-ninth day of June, in nineteen-ninety-two, they were with friends and near Fort Lauderdale in the sailboat *Star Princess,* when a mid-day storm evidently drove them out to sea. They were never heard from again, but no debris or bodies ever surfaced and to my way of thinking some sign should have remained of those seven who perished. I've finally accumulated enough money to search for some indication of their death. This summer they are to be declared legally dead and if I do anything at all, it has to be done soon."

"If you intended to search, what would you be seeking and where would you begin the search? In what possible way can I be of service to you?"

"In the short space of time that is left, I can't possibly get all the answers that I need. I would like an expert maritime coastal flow plotter to chart the route that a drifting sailboat might follow if it were blown into the ocean currents. I would like to learn the identity of every seafaring ship that was off the coast on that day. I would attempt to correspond with any of those ships' Captains that might have intersected the route of my family's sailboat. If none of these ships logged sightings of debris or lifejackets, then I will have done my best," she told him softly.

"I don't consider those requests to be much of a challenge," Todd said quickly. "I'll call the Democratic Senator from Florida and let him handle the details. People down there are usually eager to help George in any way they can. If you want to follow up and double-check the information that will be forthcoming, that's your call. I would expect faxed information or a telephone call within thirty-six hours. I thought you had a difficult problem of some kind, girl," he teased.

"I also need your advice on another matter, but it's only a problem if Bob allows it to be one. He hired my friend, Don Brim and put him to work on our joint venture. Don tells me he can modify this system in such a way that it may save millions of dollars in costs to DOD. He is hesitant to offer the idea because the company would lose much income. He can't come to you because Bob hired him. I think you should make the call and we'll go with your decision."

"Darling, there is a huge amount of income involved in this program under any circumstance. If we can cut governmental costs, we owe it to the DOD to notify them immediately. We have no competition as things stand today and none on the immediate horizon. Have Don put his ideas on the drawing board as soon as possible. I'll simply explain this to Bob in the same manner that you gave it to me. I'm certain that Bob will be extremely pleased and he will probably be as eager to see Don's mod plan as I am. When it's ready for presentation, let me know and I'll set up a meet. Now get out of here and let me go to work on your personal problems."

He placed his call to Florida and gave the information to his friend George. The Florida senator seemed confident that he could draw competent information within twenty-four hours.

A day later, in the conference room, Don was readying his presentation. It was a joint decision that none of the other engineers would be present during this meeting. Bob and Todd wanted a chance to fully analyze the modification scheme, before any type of premature word could leak out that might jeopardize the plan. This was only a preliminary look at Don's idea with just the four of them present.

Bob spoke to reassure him. "When you are ready to begin, I want to take notes. I won't trouble you with immediate questions; we can do the fine points after you're done with your presentation."

Todd chimed in cheerfully, "The same applies here. I want your total vocal layout before any questions are raised."

"I'm ready now," Don said confidently. "I could have reduced copies of the mod plans and shown slides, but I don't feel that will be necessary. Mr. Hartley, you are very familiar with the engines and airframe, but there are no changes in that area. Senator Whatley, this guidance system has been your pet baby for a long time and between your technical staff and Mr. Hartley's, it has been fine-tuned to perfection. I could do nothing to improve on that great work. My modification plan only eliminates the need for much of the expensive guidance brainwork. With redundant circuitry and costly electronic gear, you have made each unit wholly self-standing. My mod plan uses circuitry that delivers three of these similar units as drones. They are designed and styled to follow the leader. They are complete slaves to the master and as a safeguard against jamming they will continue onward to the last target position indicated by the master. Their inexpensive brain will reduce the overall cost, but will maintain the integrity of the weapon. Gentlemen, the plans are on the table."

"I have no questions," Hartley said in a stunned voice.

The senator was almost speechless.

"I may have a few questions after a plan study, but I'm in shock at the moment. You make it seem so simple that I feel foolish for not seeing it earlier."

"Don what I think is happening is that they are extremely pleased with you. Sooner or later, they'll get around to telling you of this fact," Katie said with a melodious laugh.

Don looked at her as if for the first time and saw what he believed was pride in her eyes. Was this show of pride strictly due to her role in placing him in the employ of Hartley, or was it because he had finally become a productive member of the Ryan-Brim team?"

"This is fine work, Don. Having worked and sweated over our original guidance system, I have no trouble at all in reading your schematic. It must have taken considerable time to provide the sophisticated circuitry for the target lock. I don't recall any mention of your having had previous missile experience, but something very similar was used in the old Patriot missile. I see that you have target override and alternate target choices during the first four minutes of the mission. Yes Don, I'd say this is excellent work."

"I'm sorry that I'm unable to add my voice here," Hartley said sadly. "I'm proud for you and for us, but my expertise in the guidance system is very trivial. I always try to avoid making statements at an important time if my knowledge of the subject is lacking."

"That is why we will make a great team, Bob. I don't know beans about the airframe and damned little about the engine. I must learn to lean heavily on you if a problem arises in these areas. Why don't we go into my office and call the Secretary? This could really put a rosy glow on his day."

Later in the day, Todd received a phone call from Florida.

"Todd, this is George. I have a little news to report on your request. Although it would be unwise to get your hopes too high, we've had a little piece of extraordinary luck."

"I certainly appreciate your call. I didn't expect you to get personal with this investigation. I felt at the start that we were chasing a wild goose, but I'm doing it for someone that I like."

"You're getting ahead of my story, Todd. There is something very strange about this matter. One of the best ocean currents men in Florida worked this case for me. Based on the time of day and by using his excellent plotting ability, only two ships could have intersected the course of the *Star Princess*. A vessel of Iranian registry, the *Eastern Pearl*, was reportedly outbound for the Persian Gulf. Below the southern tip of the Great Abaco Island they should have sighted the *Princess* just about sundown. The *Pearl's* log failed to report a sighting or signs of debris. Fifteen minutes after the Iranian vessel intersected this course; a Dutch freighter bound for Luanda, after earlier making a course correction, crossed this same area and logged a sighting of debris. Because of the amount of visible debris, the *Holland Lady* circled the area extensively and found further signs. The Captain's log reports spotting a raft, a broken mast, and five lifejackets awash, but no survivors. Though the skipper tried to radio news of the finding, he was unable to make contact with ship or shore."

"I see your point, George. The Skipper of the Iranian vessel was probably aware of the nearby presence of the Dutch freighter, but didn't anticipate their course correction. Either the Iranian vessel rammed the *Star Princess* or scuttled it. In either case if there were any survivors, their fate was up to the Captain of the Iranian vessel. I know you haven't had much time to consider the alternatives, but what's your feel for this?"

"I hate to raise this problem, but I can do it for your ears only. CIA reports have increasingly warned that missing Americans may have been captured by mid-eastern nations. In the past few years there have been a number of unexplained disappearances. Since the gender of these missing people has not favored male or female, the possibility of slave labor is dismissible. The intelligence group strongly believes that future terrorism or espionage is the reason for these disappearances. If these Americans could somehow be controlled and furnished with false papers, they could be used in an extremely formidable manner."

"What course do we take here, George? Could money buy more information? Is this strictly a matter for the state department? Would our foreign embassy be any source of help?"

"It's a touchy situation, Todd. You know how brittle our relations are with some of these mid-eastern nations. Iran and Iraq have long considered us the big Satan. Neither of them seems inclined to do favors for us and money would not affect their decision. Any State department effort would only consume time and it might hurt future clandestine operations that could be raised to learn more about this peculiar situation. Without the Dutch Captain, we could have easily written off the Ryan party. As it stands today, the circumstances definitely point toward them being held somewhere against their will."

"You vaguely hinted at some type of possible covert operation. Can you be a little more specific about this?"

"Not at the moment and it's not a matter of trust. It's just that a plan is brewing, but not shaped well enough to discuss. According to the CIA, they need an insider and there's none available. The Iranians are suspicious of the agents that we have in their country. They are watching our people so closely that it would be imprudent to use them in any plan of action."

"Is there any way that you can intercede in this matter and prevent the Ryan party from being declared legally dead? My source says this action is due sometime this summer. She is afraid that if they are legally deceased, all interest in them will end."

"I can handle that in a quiet, but effective way. Tell your source that should anything else arise out of this matter, I'll notify you immediately."

With the click of George's disconnected line, Todd began plotting how to tell Katie what he had just learned. She would have to find inner strength and bear this burden a while longer. Having been without those relatives so long, her concern should be able to withstand a few more months. How much should he tell her about the possibility that they had fallen into foreign hands? In a shrug of frustration, he decided to withhold nothing from her. She already had his heart, why not give her his full confidence and then live wholly on trust?

"I want to speak with you about the Florida thing," the senator told Katie at a later time. "I hope you are mentally prepared to accept another long delay. I'm going to tell you something in confidence and it should be treated as top secret. There is a slight possibility that your family might be held hostage for some devious purpose."

He watched carefully as this information permeated her brain and saw worry lines spread across her forehead. Katie's lightly rouged lips parted slightly before expelling a short breath of air. A slight moistening of perspiration appeared on the bridge of her nose. Almost alarmed, he saw her regroup and then her facial features settled into a display of grim determination. Her eyes began burning with intensity before she gave voice to her thoughts.

"What possible reason could anyone have to hold an innocent family away from their normal lives and friends? How could anyone become so damned desperate as to separate families? Do you have any clue as to the perpetrator of this terrible action?"

Taking both her hands in his own, he carefully and slowly briefed her on much of what he had learned. Though reluctant to cry, her eyes grew moist and her shoulders shook for a moment. Then, as though drawing on a reserve tank of grit, she pulled out of the blue funk and grew strong. Smiling as he noticed her rekindled spirit, he began retracing the probable path of the *Star Princess*.

"I've read up on this subject, sweetheart. The *Princess* probably had her sails gutted and blown away by the intensity of the storm. The boat was likely drawn into the current quickly and drifted away from the mainland, but parallel to Cuba. It is possible that some sailcloth hung onto the mast and helped propel them on that course. We know the mast was not lost off the Florida coast, since the Dutch Captain reported it in his log. For some reason, the Iranian Captain decided to scuttle the boat or earlier collided with it."

"So the Iranian gathered in the crew of the *Princess* and sailed away," she said angrily.

"Don't leap to conclusions, honey. If the Iranian vessel accidentally rammed the *Princess*, he may have let them all drown to escape reparation. There is no existing proof that any of them survived," he told her sternly.

"Yes, but there certainly is," she exclaimed harshly. "If the Captain knew for certain that they were dead, he would have simply entered the sighting of debris and then he would have been forever legally clear of any maritime offense."

"That makes a lot of sense, and you may be right. All the same, you should face reality head on. Your relatives will probably never be seen again."

"Don't just close the door on me, Senator," she yelped. "We need to talk more about this. What haven't you told me? I'm a rather big girl, in case you haven't noticed."

He pondered her question and her state of mind. His earlier decision to bare it all to her now seemed the wise move.

"This disappearance is not an isolated incident, honey. The CIA firmly believes in the theory that several Americans have been taken captive for the purposes of future terrorism and espionage. If they find some means of controlling these hostages, they would have a tremendous opportunity to infiltrate an American installation. The Agency wants to mount some type of covert action inside Iran, but they have no reliable insiders to aid in this effort. George wanted you to know that any new developments will immediately be reported back to me. I thought he did a fine job by unearthing this much evidence. It's been a long time since that storm, you know."

"I'm sorry if I sounded ungrateful, Todd," she told him softly. "You'll never know how much I appreciate your efforts on my behalf. One day soon I'll need to talk to you again about this subject and on that day I may become a whole woman. Until then, I suppose we must wait until the CIA decides to take some form of action."

Her sudden departure left a very puzzled senator scratching his head in frustration. He was clueless to the direction her last remarks were pointing. If he had ever met a whole woman other than his late wife, he would have guessed it was Katie. He shrugged ever so slightly and returned to his work. Katie was a mature and capable person in many different ways. Whatever was happening within her closed world would eventually be revealed to him if her communicative record remained consistent.

Katie was frustrated as she walked back to her desk. With grim determination, she buzzed the receptionist.

"Helen unless the call is from the senator or Bob, I don't want my phone to ring for the balance of this day. I need time to clear my mind."

Sinking into the soft folds of her chair, she let her mind float through the time that had elapsed since her arrival at Socorro. The attitude of Alexi was completely different from the personalities of the people she met following her arrival. He carried an arrogant and haughty air and seemed to insult her with every word that he spoke. She began to sense that the reason she fit so well in this world of Americans was not from her training program, as he had stated on more than one occasion. It was becoming clearer with each passing day and every unfolding event, that she *was* an American.

This latest important discovery made through the efforts of the Florida senator was cementing some of the fragmented clues that orbited her path since her arrival. With the relief that flooded her mind knowing that she might not be an alien, came an added burden. If she *was* Katie Ryan and had survived that terrible storm, there was a possibility that her parents were also alive. If it were at all possible, any surviving member of that party would have reported their location. Without a doubt, they were being held captive and Alexi must know where they were being kept.

Pleased at piecing these parts together, though nothing was yet proven, she concentrated on Alexi. Why was he afraid to show his face? Earlier, he stated that he had much important work to do and it would be impossible, if recognized. Was his face so well known that exposure to his own agents might cause recognition? He had lied before and might be telling another lie.

Where was he located and how did he maintain communication with his agents unless he was within range of their units? He was aware of her movements as she did her thing in Albuquerque and to accomplish that feat, he must be locally established. The kink in this reasoning was that as a local he could hardly be important internationally. Such feats as bringing agents to Socorro took tremendous power. Furnishing an agent with a vast amount of collectibles to bankroll operations was no small thing either. It all reeked of power, riches, and foreign intrigue.

If the senator's information was correct and the Iranian government had a hand in this plot, she needed to find some way to tie Alexi to Iran. Washington would be the logical place for him to headquarter if he had international ties. In desperation, she racked her brain to find some clue to his ability to stay in range of his agents. Logic told her that if he maintained a local home and commuted with some regularity to DC, he could satisfy both demands of his time.

Pleased with her reasoning, she decided to do some detective work. If he had a home in Albuquerque, she must learn its location and the time element was growing short. It would not be long before he began pressing for the plans to the weapon and any delaying excuses would seem suspect. Suddenly she recalled one of his threats and mentally reconsidered his words.

"You have family and friends where you came from. If you have a sliver of hope that you will ever see them again, you will follow my orders."

This ominous threat seemed directed at her, but now she knew he was threatening her family and friends. By Alexi's failure to pursue his veiled warning with further clarification, she missed his true meaning. The safety of those people was now her first priority.

There was little doubt about the proper way of dealing with this tyrant. She must identify him, isolate him, and execute him before he could warn his cohorts. But before this scheming monster could be executed, he must be made to reveal the location of her family. Torturing him to extract this information was a distinct possibility if she ever got him in her grasp.

She considered working with Don on this plan, but questioned his ability to be of any real help. Temporarily, she vetoed any idea of his involvement. Though he seemed pleasant and owned a smooth personality, he was severely lacking in aggressiveness.

CHAPTER ELEVEN

The Attorney General eyed the young man and attempted to conceal his anger. The Director had been very upset by the young assistant's actions. Now the AG was demanding a reason for his unprofessional display.

"I've been involved in other cases that were more important, but they were nothing like this one. This man is being hauled up on extremely serious charges and he has absolutely no fear. His attorney is the most arrogant individual that I've ever faced during what should have been a very grave moment. The Director was right on with his observation. He said these men held some very high-class cards and only someone in the Defense department could give us a clue to what these cards are. I didn't help much at the time, but my unprofessional outburst may have prevented a shameful scene in court. Can you put pressure on the Secretary to air his dirty linen?"

"I can only try, Norvell. You haven't entirely escaped my wrath for your actions, but my anger is somewhat blunted. It is time to meet with the Secretary and see what we can learn."

Undaunted by the summons from the Attorney General, Ward Bonding was still curious. He decided to do more listening than talking.

"Ward, it's good to see you again. I've been looking forward to a full recap of events leading up to your request for an arraignment. I have sources, as I know you do, and they told me there was trouble in the old Contract Barn. If I'm to proceed with this arraignment issue, I think I had better know everything that you know. I'm saying that the events leading up to this conspiracy charge could be terribly important and I don't want to learn of those events on our first day in court. Several sources have already warned me that the attorney for the accused is the most brazen puppy to ever come down the road. I want you to know that he's been thoroughly checked out and he *is* good. Never before has he exhibited such pre-trial confidence though and it worries the hell out of me. What does he have on you, Ward? Please don't stonewall me now. It would be extremely bad for both of us, if we let him diddle us out of our britches."

"I'll hold nothing back, Henry. We must be prepared for a rough and tough fight. I let this country's need for a superior weapons system override my better judgment."

Bonding told the full details to the Attorney General and he responded swiftly and with glowing promise.

"With what I know now, we can squash that little bug. Weiss will be in for a huge surprise. He won't be prepared for the turn of this case since he's so sure of himself. I'll have charges filed immediately on the men from contracts. I want their trial dates to coincide with those of the conspirators. I want nothing made public until the opening of court and then I want a prepared statement handed to the judge. I want it read in open court…if the judge will allow it. The whole world is sick to its guts with constant cover-ups. It will be so vitally refreshing to finally see someone who brings it all out into the open. I'll be greatly surprised if you don't get a medal."

* * *

"You're very quiet tonight, Katie. Do you want to talk about what's on your mind, or is it something that you need to work out by yourself?"

"I don't mind talking about it. I'm just not sure that you could help me on this one."

"Since we're in this mess together, I think you owe me a shot at it. No matter what your problem might be, another person's viewpoint can only help," he said in an aggravated tone.

She was irked by his persistence, but obstinately refused to portray her feelings. She needed no help from this man. Still, he was present and his dilemma certainly equaled hers. She decided to give him one chance, but she certainly didn't intend to give him a full briefing.

"I think Alexi is a part time resident of Albuquerque. I see no other way for him to communicate with me and still take part in international affairs."

"What causes you to believe that he has an international role to play? I've never heard him mention a clue to that direction."

"See! You're giving me negative input with your first words. I need to concentrate with all the positive thoughts that I can muster and you're jamming my brain."

Don quickly apologized.

"I'm sorry, Katie. I had no reason to question your conclusion, but it surprised me. Supposing he really is a local, how can we discover his hideaway?"

"That's the problem that I'm fighting. He will be a very private person. His phone number will be unlisted. His name is obviously not Alexi, that's just another lie he's told us. I really don't know where to begin a search, but I'm certain that he is here."

"It costs a good deal of money to fly across the country on such a regular basis. He must have servants to maintain his estate while he's away and he needs a driver for the airport runs."

"Wait just a minute," she said pensively. "These servants are probably from his home country. If they're from the eastern part of the world, American food won't satisfy their daily diet. To get native fare, they must find a place that imports foreign food products. The average store won't stock the items favored by these people because they would be a slow mover. I'll look for a specialty shop that carries food from the mid-east. Since the arrival of computer related products to this area, people from the mid-eastern countries have located here. These new people may change their lifestyle in some ways, but their food and religion preferences seldom change."

"What do you know about mid-eastern food? What type of food will you seek?"

"According to my latest information, Alexi may be from Iran. I'll go to the Internet and find the latest fads in Iranian gourmet cooking, along with some of the old standards. I'll be able to ask questions at the local deli. With persistence and a bit of good luck, I might even come up with a residential location for him."

The *Bazaar of the Genie* was bare of customers when Katie entered. She strolled from one display case to another to make her indecision known to the shopkeeper. The shop was easy enough to find, but her moves must be made carefully now that she was here. The proprietor must not become suspicious if she hoped to learn anything of value. After patiently watching her move about the shop for several minutes, the man made an offer to help.

"Is there something in particular you are seeking that you haven't found, Madam? Might I be of some small service in helping you to make a selection?"

Taking the proper amount of time to respond, she adopted a shy attitude and then seemed resigned to his offer of assistance.

"I met this gentleman and invited him to dinner. I now believe I made a mistake. I planned American food and he is Iranian. I'm sure he'll be unimpressed him by our local food."

"You have come to the right place, Madam," he said with a toothy smile. "I have all the ingredients for a meal that will steal the heart of any Iranian male. I might, if allowed, also furnish the recipes that would assure the success of that meal. Is this man a local individual, or has he just lately arrived?"

"He's been in town for a while. I'm almost certain that he's been in your shop. He did mention the name of this place. I'm afraid to try just any old recipe on him. He is a very important man and I want everything to be right. This could be terribly important to me and my future."

"I have had a surge of customers in the last year. The more important ones do not come to my Bazaar though. I have a man that delivers these orders to their residences. If I knew the name of this man, I might be able to reveal his most favorite dish to you."

She replied in a seemingly shy voice.

"I appreciate your offer, but I must not disclose his name. He's having some temporary personal problems and it might bring harm to him if word got out that he is seeing me."

"I know of the mysterious ways of the heart," he said sadly. "Though I refuse to personally involve myself in any type of impropriety, I have always been discreet in my dealings with those who do. Your secrets would certainly be safe with me, but I realize you can't take that chance."

Being an egotistical little man on this slow business day, he was determined to make a sale. Very few important Iranians lived in the area. If he were to pick up his order book, he would likely find the name of this man that she seemed so anxious to please. Smugly, he decided to show this snobby woman that he could identify her man of mystery.

"Just one moment, I beg of you," he told her in cheeky tones. "I have a regular customer that could set a model for any man you hope to impress. I will give you a list of the food he favors. If your man is half the gourmet that Amahd seems, he will be most thrilled with your cooking. Amahd Rashooti is local, is rich, and he is supposedly single. He orders food to be delivered weekly to his place at Number Five, Mountain Road."

"Would you do that for me, please? I'd love to have that list of food. Even if my man can't find a favorite among this selection, he can't doubt my attempt in trying to please him."

With a face that clearly displayed his disappointment, the proprietor ran the list through the copy machine and handed it to her with an anguished look. He had failed miserably in his attempt to impress her. His smug attitude had been shot down in flames.

"I'd like everything on this list boxed and loaded into my car, but double the order. I have a hunch that my man will want to make a return engagement."

With a smile of satisfaction she drove on toward her condo. There was a huge question troubling her mind.

How much of her success was due to her training background? Might there not be just a smidgen of natural talent and ability residing in Katie Ryan? She was amazed by the ease she found in acting and laying down a web of lies. Certain that her conscience was not flawed, she told herself that most lies were usually told because of desperate times. Today's lies were no exception. Finding the address of Amahd was simply the product of those lies.

Thinking back to earlier days with Teresa at the Charity affairs, the chance encounter with the ill-mannered Rashooti became a vivid recollection. Teresa believed him to have Washington connections and so did Simpson. This was not conclusive proof that Alexi and Rashooti were the same man. Still, it gave her a good lead that needed checking out. She fully intended to push this finding to a conclusion.

Taking Don along, she drove the winding road toward the address given her by the Deli man. It was a very good road and wide enough to support four lanes, but the development had not yet warranted the extra lanes. As they rode, she noted that mailboxes were alongside the highway and that all of the estates were some distance away from road. She slowed her powerful import to allow time to read the names and addresses and suddenly braked and pulled to the shoulder.

"What's wrong? Why are you stopping?"

He asked these questions as she backed the car slowly toward the last mailbox. Without speaking, she halted beside the metal mail receptacle to read the name.

She recited in stunned amazement. "Sergai Valenkov. Number Two, Mountain Road. What a small damned world we live in and we haven't seen half of it yet. I'd bet my next month salary that Alexi doesn't know his neighbor."

Continuing up the mountainside and slightly beyond her destination, she pulled to the shoulder of the road. From this point she could see various parts of two estates, including the one that she suspected was the home of Rashooti. With binoculars from the storage compartment, she focused on the nearest of two elegant homes. Only one other estate was above them and the rest of the upper mountain was undeveloped. The place that was drew her full focus was that of Amahd Rashooti.

Several times she swept a view of the length and breadth of the grounds. Between tree branches, she could see parts of the pool and the patio serving area, but saw no human movement. Swinging the glasses back toward the side of the house, she could see parts of the garage and driveway. A black Mercedes was parked on the concrete slab and she assumed that someone was preparing to use it.

"We'll sit here and see if the car goes away. If this is really his place I'm not ready to face him. He might recognize us immediately, but we have no idea what he looks like. If the car does go away, we'll drive down there and ask a few questions."

"I hope we aren't lessening our chances of returning to our own world. You say there's a chance that he lives here, but you're not sure. I know you haven't told me all you know about this place and how you came to find it, but you're risking my future along with your own. I doubt if I would have the gall to do you this way."

"I'm sure that you wouldn't act in this same manner. A lack of aggressive behavior is one of your biggest faults. The fact is, one of us has to show some aggressive action and I've given up hope on you. I don't mean to sound callous and I don't mean this as a put down, but you seem terribly short on guts. This lack can sometimes be a good thing, but this is not one of those times. If we don't make something happen, we may never get back home."

Movement from the asphalt driveway interrupted her little tirade. With a small burst of exhaust, the car moved out the estate road and entered the highway.

"We'll get down there quickly and nose around, but please let me do the talking," she said.

The estate lacked the expected amount of security and this omission surprised her. She had anticipated a locked estate gate with intercom devices controlling access to the property. With some apprehension, she drove on up the driveway and entered the side yard. When no guard dogs appeared to challenge their arrival, she grew nervier. Easing the pistol into her coat pocket, she exited the car and with Don following, she moved up the sidewalk to press the bell button.

After the third sounding of the interior chimes, she grew impatient. The door suddenly opened and the unsmiling face of an olive skinned woman looked sternly at her. Katie then played her first dramatic card.

"Please tell Amahd that his pregnant concubine is here to see him," she demanded in agitated tones.

The shocked look on the servants face was one of utter consternation and surprise. The Iranian lost all of her impenetrable facade and became a spectator in the question and answer scene that followed.

Katie griped loudly.

"Get him woman. My brother-in-law here can wait, Amahd can wait, but a pregnant woman can wait only so long and then the fruit must be plucked from the tree. I have waited fourteen weeks now and my skirts are getting tight."

The woman was rooted to her spot, but it was obvious that she wanted to run away. With each passing moment, it grew harder for her to face Katie. With downcast eyes, she began to speak.

"He is not here, Madam, and I do not expect his return before the passing of three days."

"Are you telling me that he is still in Washington? That liar promised faithfully to return early. I want you to get him on the phone immediately," demanded Katie turbulently.

"Madam, that I cannot do," she said near to tears. "I have instructions that he is never to be bothered when he is at work in the embassy. To disobey his instructions, would be bad for me."

"Then I have an alternative for you. When he returns here from the embassy, tell him that I was here. Tell him that I'll expect to meet him at the Albuquerque airport ticketing area, Sunday afternoon at six. Remind him that should he not make an appearance there, I will be at the embassy waiting for him on Monday afternoon," Katie said heatedly.

The woman stared uncertainly for a moment before inquiring.

"Madam, who shall I tell him to meet?"

"Don't be ridiculous. How many other women do you think this stud has gotten pregnant?"

This last repartee was made as Katie turned and headed for her car. When Don crawled in and buckled up, he was as dazed as the Iranian woman had been. It was silent in the car as she motored carefully and thoughtfully down the highway. After a few miles, Don cleared his throat in preparation to speak.

"Katie, you are really something. It's like, sometimes you are totally unbelievable. That poor woman will have nightmares for days."

"How much pacifying are you capable of, Don? Some of these people would chew us up, spit us out and never flinch. They have little regard for human life. There is a total lacking of moral values within some of these foreigners as we know them. If they have a goal, any means of reaching that goal is justifiable in their eyes."

"You've admitted having no prior memory and since I've been here, I don't recall your mention of any Iranian acquaintances. So please tell me, my dear, how have you suddenly managed to become an authority on Iran?"

She bit her lip to prevent firing back at Don. Despite sharing the condo and working through a few minor problems together, she really didn't know him. With the latest developments threatening to explode her present world before she could recapture her past, she could take no chances with him. He seemed entirely too flighty and passive to allow him full knowledge of her latest news. If he knew what she had learned from the senator and then failed to handle that information properly, he could place all her hopes in jeopardy.

* * *

The grand jury was assembled in a room with a very high ceiling. Expensive chandeliers hung from this cathedral styled ceiling and furnished softly sufficient lighting.

Although the setting for this legal exploration was one of good taste in the choice of decorating trappings, the very serious people assembling here had not come as critics of the existing decor. At exactly the appointed time, the presiding judge opened the session.

Once the opening formalities were complete, he tapped his gavel lightly.

"I want to remind everyone present that this is not a trial. We are here to investigate some very serious accusations and to see if the evidence warrants an indictment. If both sides are ready, we will proceed."

The prosecutor stood and in his opening statement, read the accusations that had been made against the alleged conspirators. It was a short reading, but direct and to the point.

Rising, Weiss turned and faced the jury members, before returning his eyes to the judge.

"Your Honor and members of this Grand Jury, I sincerely believe this entire judicial effort is a waste of your time and the taxpayers' money. I have no doubt that it will be summarily dismissed in favor of the accused. There is an old saying that you can lead a horse to water, but you can't make him drink. I will reverse that old saw and use it to exonerate my clients. If you do not wish this horse to drink, you must not lead him too many times to the water. The Department of Defense, with the full knowledge of the Secretary, led these men to the water until their moral judgment became impaired. The contracts people requested and received payment from these contractors for information that helped them in winning bids. In your eyes, you must see this entire scene as entrapment. Members of the jury, I take the definition of entrapment to mean...luring others into an illegal act which normally would not have been contemplated."

Before his chair could crease the expensive pants of Weiss, the prosecutor was on his feet.

"May I approach the bench, Your Honor?"

Receiving an affirmative nod from the judge, he proceeded to the bench and handed him two prepared pages. The judge adjusted his glasses and began scanning the material. As he read, his facial expression changed several times. It was an unexpectedly anxious moment for Weiss. Until the judge was finished reading this document, he must not be interrupted. Weiss swore softly under his breath, he was not prepared for new developments.

The judge leaned forward and prepared to speak.

"The information just handed me, puts a new face on these accusations. I will not read a portion of this document aloud, as it might have a bearing on our national security. It will be sufficient just to read the portions that describe our Defense Secretary trying precariously to hold a network of contractors together in a valiant effort to produce a much needed weapon for America's arsenal. In the doing of this, he could not know that the majority of these contractors were in bed together. They are accused of conspiring to enter the federal bidding process with intend to defraud the government. Members of the jury, these five accused men have been identified as corporate officers on all four of these supposedly competing corporations. Our Defense Secretary freely admits to some unethical actions, but I don't believe he has committed a crime. In his sworn statement, he was trying to prevent the downfall of a critical corporation. He had earlier failed to get emergency appropriations from the Senate. I believe the attorney for the defense has erred. I certainly don't believe the jury's time will be wasted."

With this new groundwork laid, Weiss had little chance to prevent the predictable outcome of the grand jury deliberation. The panel of twenty men and three women, overwhelming voted for indictment. Weiss would follow these men to federal court on charges of conspiracy and he would stoutheartedly attempt to defend them, but he would certainly lose.

A few days later, the killers of Senator Hildon were quickly given short sentences on charges of manslaughter. Murder charges were considered, but dropped due to lack of evidence. If Weiss needed the comforting warmth of praise, he received very little from them. They heard about Valenkov's indictment and began to doubt his promises. They meekly accepted their sentences and decided to wait for the outcome of Sergai's trial before making long-term decisions.

* * *

"Todd, did you know that an employee of the Iranian embassy lived in this city?"

"Yes, but I can't imagine why. That fact had escaped me until you mentioned it. We have an arid local atmosphere much of the time. The health of this man may require time away from the humidity of Washington. Does this conversation relate in any way to your missing relatives?"

"Yes, it certainly does. His position gives him the opportunity to know about captive Americans and I don't believe he's here for health reasons. I think he's trying to get information about our weapons systems. I feel certain that if our final tests prove the value of this delivery system, his country will have second thoughts about terrorism and their threats of war against their neighbors. It could totally dull their appetite for adventurism. Do you know how long he's been living here?"

"I know what you're driving at and you have a point. He arrived shortly after the first invitations for bids. No open bidding was allowed. The DOD wanted to furnish several competent contractors with an opportunity to compete. It was their idea to break the system into segments and see who came up with the best products. They knew the end product they wanted, but for security reasons they wouldn't expose the fully designed system requirements. We had just won a first bid for the engines and were awaiting the bid results on the guidance contract when I learned the Iranian was coming here. In case you're wondering how I can remember so well, the embassy called and asked me to recommend a piece of property for them to view. They mentioned that one of their top aides wanted to locate a second residence here."

"I'll bet this man could tell us if any American captives are in Iran," she said grimly. "I wish there was some way to force him to talk."

"This man has diplomatic immunity. He's free to go almost anywhere with few questions asked of him. Our state employees are not granted the same privileges in other countries, but we try to set a good example."

"We're turning into a nation of pacifiers. The foreign world does not respect a pacifier. Pacification has never won a war, nor prevented one. It seems that America is adopting an attitude of rolling over and playing dead to avoid any type of confrontation."

"Katie, your tutors have burned hard lessons into your brain. Much of your belief may be true, but a vast gap exists between pacification and diplomacy. A war definitely *could* be won or prevented through diplomatic efforts," Todd said stubbornly.

"If a potential foe is morally adequate, diplomacy might have a weak opportunity of success. If you find yourself at odds with an amoral brute with tunnel vision toward his own desires, diplomacy winds up in the same pocket with pacification and Senator, that pocket begets nothing more than a stalling of time. I should be ashamed at this war of words with you. I am from nowhere, while you've been an honored and beloved senator of the people. You have probably forgotten more wisdom than I'll ever gain. Please accept my apologies, Todd."

He sat silently for several moments and looked steadily at this strong willed woman. Because she had surprised him in so many ways already, he should not be shocked by her strong stand on governmental views. She had also touched a very tender spot. Todd had never been fully satisfied with the role that he played on the senate floor. He had acquiesced many times on important stands to help achieve a partial victory. Though he accomplished more than the average senator during his tenure, his successes had often been watered down through compromises. Had he been more like her, Todd could have brought life to many wonderful ideas. Bravely, he beamed a smile at Katie.

"If you think you need forgiving, consider yourself pardoned. I personally feel that your strong stand is pointing toward a need for political involvement. During the last few moments, I've been contemplating your making a run for the state senate. It's just the first step on a road that leads to the national capitol. I would be thrilled to endorse you as a candidate in the next election. You could win this position so easily that you should give it serious thought," he said warmly.

"I can't even dream of that possibility until I know more about my family. I would have to clarify my background a great deal before climbing into the political arena," she said firmly.

For her, any idea of holding public office was an unreachable goal. Simpson was aware that she shot Quince and may have told others. Though that death came about in an act of self-defense, she was guilty of withholding evidence of a crime and the proving of self-defense grew more difficult with each passing day. Even if there were no background skeletons, the immediate future clearly indicated further illegal activity on her part. Sunday, she would be waiting at the airport for Alexi or Amahd. If these two men proved to be one and the same, the next moves could endanger her very existence.

"Senator, I need a vacation. Grant me a week. I'll shorten it some if you find sudden need of me. I've decided that I must learn something of value about my relatives. If I haven't phoned by Thursday, open the office safe and read my letter. I don't expect trouble, but I'm taking no chances. You might need to correct any mistake that I might make along the way."

"You're speaking in riddles, honey," he said anxiously. "I can probably help fix anything that's bothering you, but you have to level with me. I don't like the sound of this at all. You must not endanger yourself needlessly by trying to find answers that will eventually come out."

"Todd I am taking the only course open to me. I've worried with this situation like a dog with a bone. My mind is set now and my plans are made. In the end you will understand what I'm trying to do."

On returning to her office desk, Katie waited a few thoughtful moments and then she punched the intercom key.

"For the next hour, I'm unavailable to everyone except Robert Hartley and the senator," she informed the receptionist.

She found the work phone number of Justin Wade. This would be a difficult conversation for each of them. She knew it was mandatory to control her emotion. He answered on the second ring.

"Justin, I've really missed you and there's nothing we can do about it at this time. Some important things are coming together and if the details work out I'll be calling you again. I'll be out of reach for several weeks, but it's for a good cause. I hope you'll try to understand."

"After being away from you for so long, I know you're definitely worth waiting for. I may not like this damnable wait, but I know it must be very important. Just take good care of yourself and hurry back," he said with feeling.

CHAPTER TWELVE

The flow of people inside the airport ticketing area was maddening. She was early, but she was still planning the details of her plot. She scanned the surrounding area looking for possible set-up men. If Amahd was conceiving a plan of action to be used against her, it had to be in place before her scheduled arrival. Seeing no suspicious types hanging in the area, she returned to the main entrance. If possible, she wanted him to enter first and then follow him to the ticket area. If he was escorted, or had a plant inside the airport, she might prevent an attempt to trap her.

On the appointed hour, she watched his black Mercedes draw alongside the curb and saw the stylishly dressed Iranian step from the car. He marched directly to the main entry, while his driver pulled away to find proper parking. With obvious signs of worry spread across his brow, his gait brought him past her and then continued toward ticketing. She positioned herself behind Amahd and trailed him throughout the short walk to his destination.

No thought of personal safety crossed her mind during this small window of time. She had a goal that far outweighed any peril that might befall her. She hoped with all her being that he was truly Amahd. It would make her task much simpler if she could deal with the Iranian and crush the sinister plans of Alexi at the same time. Her only known contact with Alexi was through voice communication and she was unsure if recognizing his voice would be an easy task. The voice of Ahmad Rashooti and that of Alexi had speech similarities, but that fact proved nothing.

Reaching the ticketing area, he turned and surveyed the crowd. It was now obvious that no ambush was set and none planned, at least on airport property. The driver could be waiting for him to exit the terminal with a security force to back him up. She had plans ready for a possible intervention by his aide, but hoped that no moves would be made against her.

With quickening steps she moved to the side of Amahd and touched him lightly on the shoulder.

She spoke in a low and firm voice.

"Mr. Rashooti, I have a small pistol in my pocket. It would be beneficial to us both, if you'd come along with me. I have no reason to shrink from killing you at the slightest wrong move. Do not speak; do not even open your mouth, until I tell you. If you understand the seriousness of this situation, give me a confirming nod."

His face paled slightly, but he nodded with understanding.

"We'll move quickly toward the gift shop now and I want your attention directed toward that destination. Do not look in any direction except that of the gift shop."

The Iranian nodded and obeyed. On reaching the shop, she selected a gray sweatshirt with orange letters that spelled out the name of the city. Next, she chose a dark major league baseball cap. She paid for these items and they again moved in a direction that she requested.

"We'll go over to the telephone area and stop for a moment. I want you to remove your coat and pull on this nice sweatshirt. I believe you'll look much nicer in your new outfit. Do you understand what I'm asking you to do?"

Again he nodded silently. When he had donned the new things, she folded his coat in a neat bundle and placed it inside the plastic bag furnished by the gift shop. Handing the package to the Iranian, she looked him over carefully.

"Carrying the sack will keep one of your hands busy and I'll be watching the other one very carefully. If I even suspect you of signaling, this gun will forever explode your hopes and dreams. In case you're wondering, Amahd, you look like a new man. I'd be willing to bet that your mother wouldn't know you."

They walked unchallenged to her car and drove away from the airport. He looked as if he wanted to kill, but remained quiet as she drove the interstate. She did not intend to divulge information or request any, until she arrived at Socorro.

After ushering him into her house, she began following a strict plan. He was ordered to sit and he obliged. Opening the conversation with a key question, she immediately put him on the defense.

"Are you thinking that you might overpower me and get away, Amahd? I certainly hope you don't try. I once considered shooting you in the leg just as a precaution. I haven't tossed out that idea, but you can prevent that ugliness from coming to pass. I may decide to bind your hands with duct tape. I'm forced to consider these options for one reason. We may be here for a long time. It's up to you to determine the duration of your stay. There are questions to which I need answers and you have those answers. If you cooperate, we will reassess the situation," she said coldly.

Almost pathetically he looked helplessly at her.

"May I speak freely now?"

She answered hatefully. "Yes, you certainly may. I brought you to this place for that specific purpose."

"I'm unsure why you have brought me here, but I have no money with me. Still, I have means of obtaining money if you tell what amount you expect to receive from this abduction."

"Money is of no interest to me," she replied coldly. "I see that you don't recognize my voice. You are unsure of my identity. We'll keep it that way for a little while. I want you to tell me about the American captives that your country has stashed away. Where are they being kept and how many are in captivity?"

"I should have guessed you to be an agent of the CIA. Only a shrewd organization could have hatched such an effective plan. My housekeeper was convinced of your truthfulness. You have wasted your precious time with me. I have no information that you want. I am an employee of the Embassy. I am not privileged to know important secrets. I do not know if your suspicions are true about prisoners. You need facts to back your wild and false claim."

"Mr. Rashooti, we do have certain facts and this information comes from very reliable sources. I see that I've made an error in bringing you here. My group is somewhat similar to your secret police. They simply refuse to tolerate mistakes and I must take steps to avoid my error coming to light. Since you're no longer of value to me and have become a liability, you must be terminated."

Pulling the pistol from her pocket, she leveled it at the Iranian.

She spoke in crisp tones, "Nothing personal toward you. We all do what we have to do."

"Wait a moment, please. There must be some other way," he yelped. "I might learn the whereabouts of these captives, if they truly exist. I have certain contacts and they are in powerful positions. I would make an effort to learn this information from them. I practice my religion, but I am not a fanatic. I am in no particular rush to meet Allah."

In a voice filled with cold threat, she spoke.

"I have no time to wait while you try to acquire information. I also refuse to give you any opportunity to weasel out of this predicament. I know you, Amahd and I know the webs of mystery that you have spun. If nothing else, I will make certain that you never do these things again."

"You can't win this issue even if you are correct about the captives, woman. If I give you the information that you seek, you cannot allow me to go free. If I disappear, the captives will be moved. There is little point in killing me when nothing can be gained from my death?"

She decided to bluff in dangerous fashion.

"There is no reason for me to continue hiding my identity from you. We both know there are captives, because I have been there and I was one of them. I am certain they were moved shortly after I left."

"That's impossible," he shouted. "We can account for every captive that we have held. You are simply using falsehoods to gain leverage."

She pressed her bluff further, "In addition to being Amahd, you are also known as Alexi. You've been communicating with me since my arrival. I have no need to use falsehoods. The brainwashing technique is wearing off. How else could I have found you? All your dirty little schemes are coming unwound. You and your country will pay dearly for these inhuman deeds."

Anger filled the face of the tyrant until his eyes almost protruded from their sockets. He searched for some way to vent his venom, but he was quite helpless. Her training for this mission had surely established her ability to kill. With a feeling of despair, he suddenly understood her entire dilemma. Without the information that she sought, she couldn't turn him loose and if he gave up that information, she would be forced to kill him. He quickly decided to delay his death as long as possible and hope for a miracle.

"So you are Katie, the stubborn wench of an agent. I did not know your face, but I should have recognized your voice and name. This is a deadlock," he shouted at her in angry tones. "From this sorry stalemate, neither of us can win. I absolutely refuse to tell you what you want to know. I reminded you several times earlier of the dire consequences that would occur unless you followed orders. I will give you one last chance to drop this foolishness and get on with your mission."

"No, that will not happen," she said determinedly. "I am my family's only hope. While I am under your control nothing can be done to free them. What we're discussing here is not just a matter of their survival. When their usefulness to your stinking country is over they will be killed anyway. If I am there, I will die along with my loved ones and my death will be for nothing. I'll continue to hold you until I find a workable plan and you should start hoping that you get better treatment from me than my family receives."

She began to devise a plan that would allow her to rest and sleep without fear of an escape attempt by the tyrant. She needed to fashion some means to restrain him and yet leave him freedom to use the bathroom when bodily functions required it. Using several nylon articles of clothing from her wardrobe, she created hobbles for his legs and then connected them to the restraints that she fashioned for his arms. By securing him to the center post of her closet, she felt safe enough to sleep.

Amahd tried in vain to free himself, but her knots failed to loosen. If he tried to remove the center post, the noise would awaken her. The nylon material would not tear and his struggles only served to tighten the knots. Nothing was within his reach that could be used to sever his bonds. He ceased to struggle and decided to wait until morning for further hopes of escape.

* * *

"George, I won't take much of your time. I just couldn't wait any longer to hear if there was any news of the captives. I know you are deeply involved in the committee that interacts with the CIA. It's important for me to learn whether there are any late developing plans regarding the recovery of these unfortunate Americans."

"Todd, it goes without saying that this is important to all of us," George replied. "Why has it suddenly become so all important to you?"

"Because a family member of the captives is digging into their disappearance," he said gently. "If she gets the press involved, the publicity might endanger the CIA efforts. We must not let that happen. If you have something of consequence that I can give her, it might hold her long enough for the agency to act."

"I know everything is stalled for the moment. They still need the same information that has not been forthcoming. The location of the captives is still unknown and they are unable to recruit an insider. We must have more time and you are certainly correct about the press. They must be kept out of this matter if we're to have any chance of success. Tell your friend that I was able to stall the legal declaration of their death. No further action will be taken without word from the State Department."

"I'll get back to you if anything develops here. Continue your fine work, George," Todd told him sincerely.

* * *

Katie arose from her bed fully clothed. She was refreshed and her mind was clear. Following her morning shower, she meant to try a plan of action that might accomplish her combined hopes. Glancing at the glaring Amahd as she passed, she saw that he was still securely bound.

"Let me know if you have need of the bathroom. There are no windows in there and you can't possibly escape. Your hobbles will allow you enough freedom for sanitary purposes."

"I need to go now," he replied.

She freed him from the center post and he spent a while in the bathroom. She had no fear of an escape attempt. Even if he were not fettered, she felt confident that she could physically handle him.

When he returned, she again secured him to the closet post. After gathering certain items of clothing, she hummed a popular tune as she made her way to the bathroom. This day looked like it might hold great promise.

Following a refreshing shower, she placed a call.

"Rosalie, can you come over for a short while? I have something of great importance to ask of you."

Hearing the Indian woman agree, her pulse grew to a more rapid beat. This would be the turning point of her plan. In a few minutes, Rosalie would arrive and her coming could possibly break this thing wide open. Everything was dependent on how Rosalie viewed this situation.

The captive had neither eaten, nor had he been given liquids and Katie went to remedy that fact. She did not intend to mistreat him in that way, but she was not reluctant to shoot him. Placing a plastic glass of water beside him and a bowl of trail mix nearby, she stared intently at the Iranian.

"In a few hours, a decision may be made about your fate. What you see in front of you will help keep you alive until this decision is reached. If you're still here later in the day, I'll furnish better provisions," she promised.

With the sounding of her doorbell, she closed the bedroom door and went to admit Rosalie. The Indian wore a puzzled look and quietly followed her to the kitchen. The act of making a pot of coffee allowed Katie a few moments to set her plans.

"Rosalie, I've got a lot of news for you. Some of this news may not set well with your conscience and should that be the case, I want you to feel free to refuse any further involvement. I've just committed a felony, but there are reasons why this act had to be. If you fully understand what I'm saying and wish to hear no more, I'll not hold it against you."

"My poor Darling, what on earth has happened? I know you wouldn't have acted without good reason," Rosalie said sympathetically. "Please fill in the details and if I can help, I will."

"First, let me tell you that I have not regained my memory. I do have some information concerning my family and why I'm in this mess."

She carefully explained the storm and the kidnapping of her family and friends. With some detail, she described the role that had been assigned to her and the mission that had brought her back to America. When it came time to name the man who controlled her movements, Katie hesitated for a moment before speaking.

"Rosalie, I have captured an Iranian man who is aware of this operation. He's tied up in my bedroom. By kidnapping this evil man and bringing him here, I've committed a felony. You don't have to help me, but please don't turn me in for a while. I'm in desperate need of information from him and you could be my only chance," she said tearfully.

"Tell me how you expect me to help and then I'll determine whether I can morally act on your behalf," Rosalie said carefully.

"I'd like you to use your hypnotic powers on this man. He refuses to give me the location of the captives and advised me that if he's not freed by a certain time, they'll be moved to another site. Without word from the embassy, they'll assume that the location of the captives is at risk. It's just the way they operate and I'm sure he's being truthful on this point. If you put him under against his will, I'm not sure that hypnotism will work on him. I'm just hoping that you will try."

"I will try my very best," Rosalie said. "I must go home and get something before I make this effort. I won't be gone long."

Puzzled, Katie watched her leave and wondered if she would truly return.

She had volunteered that quick promise to help and surely she would not break her word. It seemed an eternity before Rosalie's car tires pressed sand on the driveway.

"I'll describe what I went after. In the old days, medicine men found that certain roots had strange effects on the warriors. The use of this potion causes men to be easily swayed by repeated commands. There are other uses for this concoction and I always keep some of the roots available. I can only use my power in an effective way, if the subject is willing to be hypnotized. With this potion, his will to resist becomes weakened and if that proves sufficient, I can successfully put him under. Are you ready to bring him out, or shall we go into the bedroom?"

"I believe we should go in the bedroom for this ordeal. I want to leave him bound as long as possible. I must not let him escape. The lives of my parents depend on keeping him quiet for several days. Even if they move the captives, they won't kill them unless they hear from him."

The captive turned angry eyes on the two women as they entered. It didn't take him long to begin spewing his hatred.

"I see you have recruited a confederate. When the authorities learn of this abduction, we shall see if the system works for a foreigner. If justice is to be found in this country, you will pay for this unnecessary mistreatment."

They ignored him while Rosalie prepared a spoonful of the mixture. When the concoction was ready, she turned strong eyes onto those of Amahd.

"If you do not willingly take this potion, I'll be forced to use a squirt bottle. I promise that the prepared dosage will leave no harming effects. If I have to use the bottle, I can't make that same guarantee. Since you will be taking it either way, we'll let you make the choice."

With that stern warning, he accepted the spoon and swallowed the potion. He knew full well that the common American had no access to mind altering drugs. These women were hoping to scare him into some type of confession, or thought might he offer information about the captives. They would be surprised and disappointed when he outwitted their pitiful efforts. Even as his tongue began to grow thick, he knew there was no way they could gain information from him. What was this silly woman with the olive skin chanting about? If he didn't know better, he might think of her as a paranormal being and then his mind faded away.

Rosalie nodded, "He's as ready as he'll ever get. If you quietly tell me the questions, we'll see if he cooperates. First, I want to ask him about something that has bothered me for a long time."

Turning toward the Iranian, she began a firm and positive list of commands.

"Amahd, can you hear and understand my voice?"

The one word answer came from the captive. "Yes."

"I will ask questions of you and you wish to oblige me by giving me full and complete answers."

He answered in a robotic voice. "I understand. I want to oblige you."

"You are familiar with this woman by the name of Katie. Is this a correct statement?"

"Yes, I know a great deal about Katie."

"Do you also understand the term, brainwashing?"

"Yes, I do," he said in a cooperative way.

"In what way were you able to accomplish the brainwashing of Katie?"

"A mind altering agent was used to put her in a deep coma. While in this condition, her mind was modified to remove prior memory. She was given certain data to remember and part of her conditioning included the rejection of any attempt to probe her mind. Is this the information that you were seeking?"

"Yes, it is. One other question about this subject and we'll move onward. Is this modified state of mind reversible by any other mind altering drug, or does it require this specific one?"

"I am unable to answer that question. We only have one mind-altering drug that has been fully effective. It has also proved effective in restoring the full memory of the subject."

"Is it true that your country is holding captives, especially Americans?"

"Yes, it has become an accepted practice. This is but one of the many ways in which we will defeat the great Satan," he told her proudly. Rosalie looked carefully at Katie and listened to her soft voice detailing the next question. Then, after nodding agreement, she again questioned Amahd.

"Do you know the present location of the captives? If you do, you will want to tell me and let me understand your need for captives," she said carefully.

Rashooti spoke strangely, "Of course I'll share this with you. They are being held in a training camp, twenty miles east of Ahvaz. We need captives to train for the infiltration of factories of the great Satan who is constructing a powerful weapon that could bring great harm to our country.

"What else do you wish to know from this man? The evilness within this tyrant is causing my stomach to go sour."

After consultation with Katie, Rosalie again questioned Amahd.

"Are these captives moved regularly? Where were some of their other holding sites?"

"They have been relocated only once. They were moved a short distance to the present site because of its strategic location and because the base is two miles in length. Security camps are at both ends of the site and the captives are in between. The captives are separated in barracks. They will not be moved from this site, unless the location is compromised."

They moved away from the Iranian and summarized the results of Rosalie's hypnotic efforts.

"There are two things that I would still like to know, but I'm sure we can't get it from him," Katie said.

"What is it? What haven't you learned from this evil being?"

"I'm wondering if it's possible to make him believe that he went to the airport and couldn't find me. I wonder if you could make him forget the last eighteen hours of his life."

"The danger is too great to consider that angle. Your family could possibly die if he recalls what happened here. What's the other thing that's bothering you?"

"Having learned all these new facts behind my brain altering, what chance does your potion have of bringing back my memory," Katie asked softly.

"I won't attempt such a risky move. I'm not skilled enough to accept that load. The process is reversible by using the right drug, according to Amahd. You must be satisfied with that until we learn more."

"Wait just a minute! There's a small chance this drug may be in their embassy as backup protection. If one of their captives managed to recover his memory, they'd need some way to control him," she said with rising excitement.

"We can ask him," replied Rosalie. "My drug has worked so well that he just can't do enough for us. My hypnotic power has held longer and is more effective than ever before."

"Amahd," she said sharply. "Can you hear me clearly?"

He replied in slurred tones. "Yes, I hear you very well."

"This mind altering drug that your people use, would you recognize it. Would it be in a container that you could carry with you?"

He answered, "I know it quite well. We keep some in the embassy for emergency purposes. The containers are small and easy to transport. We bring this drug from our country in diplomatic pouches."

"How can an embassy aide have easy access to such an important drug? I would expect the ambassador to maintain better control," Rosalie said quickly.

"The ambassador is old and senile," he said coldly. "I should already have his position and power. I have outwitted him in many ways. When I have need of the drug, it is mine for the taking."

"You can't know how to administer this drug, Amahd. Why do you have a need for it?"

"I know much about the drug," he said stubbornly. "I have studied the intelligence reports carefully and I have learned that it helps me with the stubborn ladies."

Rosalie did not want to pursue this startling and sordid bit of information, but she did need other information. She questioned him sharply.

"I don't believe you are being truthful about the drug. Only if you could you bring some of it to us and show us the correct dosage, would I believe that you're not a liar."

"I will show you," he replied strangely. "I can bring some and show you."

"That can't be done, Amahd. We don't have time to go to Washington and visit the embassy."

"There is no need to go to the embassy. I keep some at my home for personal reasons."

This startling revelation brought shocked looks to the faces of both women. This odd turn had been totally unexpected and presented an entirely new road to travel. They again withdrew from the hearing of the captive to ponder this new development.

"We must take advantage of this situation," Katie said quickly. "I want that drug and I want my memory back. At this moment, I'd be willing to kill for it."

"You don't really mean that. Think what we've accomplished during the last hour and be careful."

"I'm sure you're right, Rosalie. I'll control my desires for a while longer. My first priority is to phone the senator. He needs to pass this information on to the CIA and quickly."

"Go make your call, honey. I don't intend to bring this beast back for a little while. I'll watch him until you return."

With eager fingers, Katie punched in the numbers of Whatley's telephone.

"Senator, I've learned where the captives are and I'm certain they'll be there for quite some time. The difficult part of their location is that the site covers a two mile area. The captives are in a common barracks. They can't escape, because of an electrified fence that surrounds the entire base. Two armed camps are in place at this base, one at either end. The area where the captives are held is almost dead center between the camps. I hope you can pass this news on to the agency."

"I'm worried about your safety, honey. You've done a fine job in getting this news, but pull back now. Don't get into deeper involvement with this action. We have people that are more knowledgeable in these matters. Give me all you know about the site and I'll call George. He should know how to handle this news. Please come back to work. We miss you and we need you."

She gave the information to the senator, but she didn't give him any promises. Too many loose ends were hanging. Until they were wrapped up, she refused to commit to anything.

Todd pushed the numbers of the Florida senator and waited. He wasn't sure how to explain the source of his news. He hadn't even asked her how she came by this new information. George must act on this news as though it was pure fact, even though no proof would be forthcoming.

Todd gave the latest information to the senator. As George put this latest news on paper, his mind sped toward the possibilities. The agency would order copies of satellite photographs. On each orbit, there would be additional data. By pulling previous photos, they could quickly prove or disprove this claim.

"We'll talk more about this later. I must get this info to the agency and let them get cracking."

On receiving this news, the agency chief seemed unconvinced.

"Senator Bushnell is this all you've got for us? Can't you give background on the source of this news? I find this new disclosure highly suspicious. We've checked with the Israelis, the French and the Brits. None of them report anything of interest coming from their informers. The timing of your information is extremely coincidental. That one factor casts a lot of suspicion on your story."

"If you want your agency's last request for additional funding to get serious consideration, my advice is to move with this news," George said heatedly. "I'm a busy man and there are more productive things I can do with my time besides bringing an asinine story to your agency. Just pull the damned satellite photos and do your job. If I've made an error in judgment, I'll send you twenty pounds of marlin and my deepest apologies."

"Please accept my honest apology, Senator. I was way out of line and you can count on me to do my job. I'll keep you informed of any new developments," he said.

George spent a few more minutes contemplating this extreme situation in which he had become embroiled. He had confidence in Todd Whatley that almost knew no bounds, but he was finding himself in deep water. He needed more grasp on where Todd's information was coming to convince the CIA. If a way existed to explain his source, Todd would have told him. He must convince Todd how difficult it was to draw help from the CIA without solid sources.

Back in Socorro, Amahd was in a partially dazed condition, but he was alert enough to cooperate and respond to questions. During the previous questioning period he appeared to have a need for boasting. Rosalie determined that even in his altered state, his ego was dominating his subconscious. She used his ego to get answers that would never be obtained under normal circumstances. Having already pulled so much information from the tyrant, they pushed their luck with reckless daring. Since a chance of obtaining the Iranian's drug stash existed, Katie intended to make the trip. She voiced her objection to Rosalie's decision to go along.

"If anything goes wrong and you're found with me, you'll become an accessory. You've already helped me tremendously and I can't allow you to get more deeply involved in this thing."

"I don't believe you have the power to make me stay out of it," the Indian said firmly. "I must be there to make sure that Amahd stays under. He may face questions from his housekeeping staff. They can suspect whatever they wish, but this philandering little beast has probably been AWOL before tonight. When he returns to us from the house, the hypnotic spell may have been weakened by the familiar surroundings. If we are to effectively control this monster, I need to keep him sedated and under the spell."

The matter seemed beyond the control of Katie and she reluctantly agreed. At the direction of Rosalie, Amahd followed them meekly to the import. Seating the Iranian in the passenger seat alongside Katie, Rosalie took a seat behind him and they began the drive to Albuquerque.

As they sped up the interstate, the Indian woman occasionally asked questions of Amahd. In most of these instances, it was simply to check on his state of mind. One question though, brought an unexpected bonus.

"Have you personally visited the site of the hostages?"

He replied boastfully. "Yes, I was at the camp on two occasions."

"Why were you authorized to be there? What need arose that called for an embassy aide's presence?"

"It was after the senseless invasion by the forces of Iraq. The ambassador wanted a report on the military fortifications that needed to be installed."

"What qualifications do you have as a garrison strengthening specialist?"

"I had extensive military training before accepting diplomatic service," he replied with obvious self-satisfaction.

"Were you able to provide the necessary data to make the garrison more secure?"

"Certainly, even a fool could see the need for tank traps, missile launchers, and proper mortar emplacements," he bragged importantly. "It was my idea for deploying security forces at each end of the site and separating the captives. This action won important medals for me."

"I'm puzzled," she told him frankly. "What purpose was there to strengthen the garrisons after the failure of the Iraqis?"

Amahd spoke without feeling.

"We expect a military force to hit this site and attempt to free the captives. They will fail to penetrate our perimeters, of course, but they could not possibly win if they did. If the camp is ever overrun, the standing order is to execute the captives."

A dark gloom descended over Katie, on hearing this news. The CIA must be informed about this and as soon as possible. If they should mount any kind of attack, it could spell the death of the captives.

They arrived at the outskirts of their destination and the sun was sinking behind a bank of purple clouds. It would soon be dark and the time was ripe for them to deliver Amahd to his home. With increasing darkness partially hiding the car's interior, she drove carefully up the winding mountain road and entered the driveway. It had been almost twenty-four hours since Amahd's driver had dropped him at the airport, but there were no visible signs of concern near the house. Only the black Mercedes, protruded slightly from the garage and no other vehicles could be seen. It was time to make their move and Rosalie quietly questioned him.

"Do you understand what you are supposed to do?"

"I am to get the drug and return to the car."

"If you are questioned by the staff, what will you tell them?"

"I will tell them that I have a woman waiting in the car and we intend to return to her place," he said indifferently.

After hearing this, Rosalie stepped out of the vehicle and opened Amahd's door. The courtesy light came on immediately and flooded the car's interior.

Rosalie hissed at him.

"Go quickly and return with all possible speed. We need to be on our way home."

Closing the car door in haste, they watched as he moved across the yard. He was barely illuminated by the low landscape lighting, but they saw his backsides disappear through the side door.

The time hung heavily inside the car and each minute became a lifetime. This became that special time when one's courage is tested to the very edge and nerves are strained to the breaking point. No way could they determine what was occurring inside his place.

It was impossible to know that a security force would not come boiling out at any moment.

After a period elapsed that aged them both, the door opened and the Iranian stepped outside.

Without a falter, he strode to their car and opened the door himself. Dropping carefully into the seat, he turned toward Rosalie.

"I came back as you ordered."

His statement was direct and his subservience quite evident. He was still under the control of Rosalie.

"Do you have the drug?"

Her question was framed in a manner that did not expose the degree of importance that would be attached to the answer. It was not meant to sound like a life or death situation.

"Yes, I have it. I told you I was not a liar," he said resolutely.

The car sped on toward Socorro, with only the hum of the powerful engine to disturb the quiet that prevailed inside the car. Rosalie leaned forward toward Amahd and listened to the sounds of his breathing.

"How far are we from Socorro?"

"Fifteen minutes should put us in my driveway."

"The timing will be very close," Rosalie warned. "The spell and the potion are both wearing off. He will be very difficult to handle when he comes out from under the effects of the potion."

Katie spoke in a low voice. "In that case, get the drug from him now. He might try to destroy it, if he's alert. He has no way to tell if my memory has returned, but he'd like to see that it never happens."

"Amahd, pass the drug over the back of the seat and give it to me," Rosalie commanded.

Meekly, the Iranian did as ordered and Rosalie placed the container inside her purse.

"At least we know now that you told the truth about the drug. In some ways though, we still consider you as a liar."

With a concerned look, she posed one last question to the Iranian. "You did not say whether this drug must be injected or if it could be swallowed. Which of these methods do you prefer?"

"It does not matter," he said impatiently. "One half of a teaspoon is sufficient quantity in either manner."

Cruising slowly into her driveway, she began to get more optimistic about the future. If this drug worked, what would be her first reaction to the recovery of her memory? Her reactions and many other details simply could not be anticipated. They must be dealt with as they arose.

As they made their exit from the car, an angry question from Amahd broke the silence of the night.

"Where have we been and why have you brought me here? Katie, I will eventually regain control over you and when that time arrives, you will die a thousand deaths. You will cry out for the angel of darkness to take you away and save you from me."

"I believe the beast has finally regained his senses," Rosalie said dryly. "If you wish, I'll be glad to gag him after we get inside."

"It may become necessary," Katie agreed.

"First, I must call Sam. I left a message to let him know I was over here, but if he called and got no answer, he's probably gone wild by now," she said with a smile.

After leading the Iranian back to the bedroom, she retied him securely to the closet post. She remained impassive to his speech, even when it got profane, and made only one statement to him.

"I'll fix some food and you will have an opportunity to eat. You won't starve, but I can't offer you any other accommodations. You would never understand the inner battle I'm fighting to prevent shooting you. The Iranian training taught me to kill, but it didn't teach me to like it. In your case though, I might find killing quite enjoyable. So, do not push me too far."

Rosalie returned from using the phone.

"I managed to pacify Sam," she told Katie. "I told him we were working out some of your problems and he said to take as long as we need."

"We must fix something to eat. I'm starved and I'm sure you need food. I also need to call the senator and let him know what we've learned."

Call the man," Rosalie ordered. "I haven't forgotten how to prepare food and I know where you keep everything. After we've eaten, there is something else that we must talk about."

She placed the call and waited patiently until he answered.

"I know it's late and I hate to bother you, but I have more information. The CIA needs as many details as possible before they stage any sort of operation. My family's life depends on them getting the facts. Senator, there are two detachments of Iranian troops at that site. One garrison at each end, with tank traps, missile launchers, and mortar emplacements. This is bad, but it gets worse. If the site seems destined to be overrun, the standing order is to execute the captives. Can you get this information to the agency?"

"I can and I will, but I have to ask how you are getting this information. I know of only one way and that would be through the embassy. Has this something to do with Amahd Rashooti?"

"Yes it has, but please don't ask any more questions. Things are going on that you must not become involved with or know about. When the proper time comes, I intend to give you a full briefing about this matter."

Todd immediately punched in the numbers for Senator Bushnell.

"George, it's late here and you're two hours ahead of us."

"Never mind the hour, Todd. You must have more news to deliver."

"I do. My source must be using the old water torture method to extract her information."

Todd related the information he had received from Katie.

"They evidently expect trouble and have made damned solid plans to resist."

"They have indeed made plans," George said with a low whistle. "I've heard nothing from the agency since our last contact, but it takes time to study the photos. If they've seen anything worthwhile, they'll want the latest releases before making a judgment. I'll pass this on tonight, Todd. If anything else arises, feel free to call day or night."

CHAPTER THIRTEEN

Back in Socorro, the women finished eating and Amahd had been fed. His bonds were slack enough that he could eat from a plate and he had been quite hungry. As they were resting in the kitchen, enjoying a cup of hot coffee, Rosalie made a bold statement.

"You should have your memory back before you make any more decisions. In your present condition, you can view only one side of this situation. You know where you are now, but you don't have enough facts about where you've been. In my opinion, you should try this drug of Amahd's. I can put you under and try to bring you back to the present in a controlled manner."

Though apprehensive about the process, Katie knew the search for her lost memory could possibly end here...tonight. With this thought goading her, she agreed to the trial.

The Indian woman's calming voice quickly put her under a hypnotic spell and nothing was left except to try the drug.

As she carefully poured the nearly clear liquid into a spoon, Rosalie had time to reflect on the seriousness of this undertaking. As a mind altering drug to blunt the will of a stubborn romantic partner, its use was not particularly sophisticated and Amahd's use of it was sufficient proof of that fact. It was a wholly different circumstance when this powerful drug was used in mind altering situations. The mind and memory are as one and the initial separation of Katie's mental ability may have left her extremely vulnerable. Rosalie was aware that for a few moments during the process the mental future of this young woman was in her hands and this realization was very frightening.

"Open your mouth and swallow this potion," Rosalie commanded.

During a period of fourteen minutes, Rosalie watched the clock hands crawl agonizingly slow. Suddenly, with all her heart, she wished she hadn't become involved with this risky venture and because she was so deeply involved, she began to pray earnestly for divine guidance. If things went badly and she was forced to call 911, it would likely be the end for both women.

"I know you can hear me, but I doubt if you can answer. Let me assure you that you are in no physical danger. Your name is Katie

Ryan and you're an American. Please don't be afraid, for you are not alone."

She talked in low tones hoping that her voice would penetrate the void that lay between them. She talked of how impressed she was during their first meeting. Though sensing a deep mystery about Katie, she never challenged her integrity. She named other people that had found her to be a trusted friend. It took a tremendous personality to acquire so many friends in such a short time.

"Don't let this all be a waste, God," she prayed. "This young lady has already borne more than her share of troubles. Please give her some room for happiness and joy."

Katie suddenly began speaking, though in an odd voice.

"Are you talking to someone? I keep hearing this voice, but there's no one here but you."

"Oh honey, I was so scared for you. You seemed so far away. Do you know who I am?"

"I feel like I ought to know you," she replied.

"Your voice sounds a bit strange. Are you feeling alright?"

"I feel like I've had a shot of Novocain. I don't remember having any dental work done. Have I missed something?"

"Do you know where you are?"

Katie looked around the kitchen carefully before returning her gaze to Rosalie. Then, with eyes wide with bewilderment, she answered.

"I'm in a kitchen, with you," she said simply.

"Listen carefully, Katie. You've been away for a while, but you're going to return when you hear me clap my hands. During the moment that you hear this clap of noise, everything will be as it should be and you'll still be in the kitchen. Do you understand me?"

"Yes, I understand. I will listen for the noise," she said as though far away.

With a strong handclap, Rosalie watched as a major change took place on the face of Katie. First in coming was a look of confusion and then came several stages of understanding. Last and finally, a sense of happiness and relief began filling her face with the complete joy that she felt. Rosalie knew the girl's present mental fabric was being interlaced with the past and that most, if not all, of her memories would be restored. It was an extremely happy moment for each of them, but Katie suddenly stiffened in their embrace.

"I have no right to be this happy."

"Why do you say this, honey? You *do* have a right to be happy."

"Not until my family and friends are safe and away from that monstrous place," she replied angrily. "Every single day is one of degradation and terror. The guards constantly search to find new ways to humiliate the captives. Thing are coming to my mind now and that memory hurts."

"During this moment, try to count your blessings. You're in America with a chance to help them. You have friends who will use their voice and influence to help you. The senator has been given much information. He was once a very powerful man and Fred assures us that his influence is still very strong. Please take each day as it comes and deal with problems as they arise. One thing that you must face is the disposal of Amahd. What can you possibly do with him?"

"I have not forgotten about him, but I really don't have an answer. I need more time to think about him. It's a difficult problem to tackle. If he is freed, he'll inform the embassy and the captives will be moved or killed. While I have him in my possession, I'm a kidnapper and a felon. Until I have word that action is underway to free the captives, I guess I'm stuck with the beast. You should go home and get some rest, Rosalie. I can't do anything more about this before morning."

For nearly two hours, she agonized in full remembrance of the events leading her to Socorro. For the first leg of her trip from Iran, she was not drugged. She followed orders because of the threats to her parents. The flight from the Iranian airport was uneventful until she and her escort reached Mexico. On arrival there she was drugged and loaded into a helicopter for the flight into New Mexico. Just before she passed out, she heard one of her escorts communicate a short radio message to someone. Without a doubt, it was Rashooti with whom he spoke. When her tired eyes finally closed for the night, she gave silent thanks to the many friends that had given her the opportunity to fight for her freedom and that of the other captives.

* * *

A heated debate raged in Virginia and Florida. A teleconference had been arranged between the CIA Agency Director and his agents in Florida. The subjects under discussion were the American captives.

"Granted, the photos show very suspicious activity at the alleged site and I'm aware of the presence of Caucasians, but there is no discernable proof that they are being forcibly detained. We simply can't stage an operation, based on unproven allegations. When I called the Secretary of Defense and asked for a meeting with the Joint Chiefs, he refused. What I'm about to tell you is top secret, but hear this...he said an urgent investigation was underway regarding our esteemed Air Force Chief. Any type of operation that we might undertake would be without the support of our Air Force."

"Bullshit sir," an agent replied angrily. "The Navy has all the tools we need and we would need them in any instance. Anything that we stage will originate off the coast of Kuwait. It's the most strategic point to reach the Ahvaz area and our operation would face the smallest chance of being observed by Iranian radar. We can't wait forever to pull this thing off."

"Wilson, you're a damned fine agent. I respect your opinions, but you fail to hear me. My words were that, based on these allegations, we're unable to stage anything. This is a difficult undertaking because of Iran's military preparedness. We must never again fail in an attempted covert operation. We need to get some people inside Iran and confirm the fact that these are indeed American captives. Get back to the Senator and tell him to try prodding more information from his source."

* * *

"Todd, I am making this call because I'm in deep trouble and I don't know where to turn, except to you. My needs seem to be filling nearly every day of your life and again, I apologize. Is there possibly any extra compassion left in your spare tank?"

"Honey, for you there will always be a compassionate ear to hear any problem that you have. I can't bear the idea of seeing you in any kind of trouble and I know this must be serious. Brief me on this matter before it gets out of hand."

"For several months now, I've had no memory of my past life. Sir, I lied to you about my past because I was desperate for employment. I've never lied to you about anything else and I've never done you any wrong. Before I continue with this story, I must know that you believe me."

"At this particular moment, I don't believe it would be possible for you to lie to me. I have more faith in you than you do in yourself."

"Todd, my memory was taken from me by the Iranians and I was sent here as a spy. They could do this in complete confidence because my parents are there as captives. If I ever wanted to see them again, I was told to do their bidding. Arriving here and having no memory, I was without conscience. Thankfully, I began to develop an active conscience and with it, I began to regain some of my self-respect. You know most of my activities beyond this point."

After a slight pause, she continued.

"Now, I find myself back here in Socorro with one of the most hated men in my new memory. I'm holding Rashooti here as my prisoner. Though I certainly should have a right to abduct him, technically I'm a kidnapper. If I turn him loose, my parents and friends will surely die. Todd, what can I possibly do about this mess?"

"Stay put and don't leave the house," he ordered. "Is Rashooti secured? Are you safe with him in your house?"

"Yes, he's securely bound and I'm physically strong enough to do combat with him if it should come to that. I suppose I'm as safe as I could be under these circumstances."

"Just sit tight then, honey, and give me some time to work on this problem. I don't come face to face with this type of hardship every day you know."

Many gaps were evident in the story she imparted to Todd. He had lots of questions that needed answers, but not at this time. Now it was time to act in some sane way to preserve the relationship that he so enjoyed with this young lady. She was in a very delicate situation and even his powerful influence with the local police and the FBI could not help her. She had broken a law and one that involved a man with diplomatic immunity.

His mind reeled with the magnitude of her problem. Damn it all, though she did not deserve to be in this mess there appeared to be no legal way to save her. Although stalling for time with knowledge of a felony would make him an accomplice, he knew that she held information beneficial to the CIA. If these captives were ever to be freed, the agency needed to debrief her. Without a thought for his own accountability, he reached for the phone and punched up the number of his friend from Florida. When George responded promptly, Todd breathed a breath of relief.

"My friend, I need quick action from you and the Agency. Do you have enough influence to get fast action from them if it includes one of their private jets to the Albuquerque airport?"

"My God, what has happened there? I can tell from your voice that it is very serious, Todd. I can get an Agency plane there, but there are hard questions that will be asked before and after the trip. Can you brief me on the urgency? I do have a need to know."

"George, I will have a former captive of the Ahvaz site with me and she will need to be fully debriefed. I will not allow her to come alone, so expect me to accompany her. There will be another passenger with us, but do not ask questions about this man. Whatever the Agency decides to do with this man is strictly their personal business. Neither of us will have a right to know."

"I'll get back to you with an ETA and a receiving area. Airport Security will probably furnish transportation to the Agency jet. Hang tough Senator, I'm sure this is taking a toll on your nerves," George said politely.

Todd leaned back in his chair and eyed the ceiling thoughtfully. Due to these new plans, he had several calls to make. Hartley needed to know of his departure. Todd's many responsibilities would need to be sufficiently covered. Calmly, he walked into Hartley's office.

"Bob, I'll be gone several days and when I return, I'll owe you a pile of favors. I'm asking several of my appointments to try and fit in with your scheduling. When I get where I'm going, I'll contact you."

"First Katie, and now you...everyone seems to be pulling out on me. It must be important and I won't pry. You *will* tell me when you're able. Take care of yourself."

As he called his housekeeper, he wondered about Brad. What should he tell him about this sudden trip? He had almost fully recovered from the accident and Todd was eager to get him back in the business.

"I'm leaving on a short business trip. Will you please pack some things for me and get them delivered to my office. I need enough items for a three-day stay. Is Bradford nearby, Jessica? Well, when he returns please tell him that I'll talk to him later in the week."

He began gathering a few things for his briefcase. Having a slight modification problem with the guidance system that needed attention, he pulled plans from a drawer and stowed them in the case. The sudden ringing of his phone got immediate attention.

"Todd, there will be a modified Lear waiting at Three-thirty, your time, today. Any time after three, approach Security gate two and ask for Milton. Your car will be allowed access and the security people will handle its storage. Your group will be flown to Florida and you will be taken directly to Agency offices. They have accommodations to keep you from leaving the facility until debriefing is completed. At some time in the late evening, I will meet with you. I am looking forward to that moment; it's been a long time."

The senator lost no time in calling Katie and she answered on the second ring.

"Honey, I've made some productive plans. Pack lightly, but enough for at least three days and get your friend ready to travel. We're going to take a little trip down to Florida. I intend to leave my car at your condo, so meet me there and we'll take your vehicle to the airport. We won't be using airport parking; we're going through a security gate. We must be at the terminal by three this afternoon. I don't know how you intend to persuade your friend to come with you. It is a rather long drive from Socorro. You'll simply have to work out some kind of plan," he said lightly.

She answered quickly.

"I've got that covered, Todd. If you can handle enormous problems in such a speedy fashion, I ought to manage a short drive up the interstate."

She immediately punched off the phone and began gathering a few things. Several times, she passed by the Iranian while packing and he finally glared at her menacingly.

"Are you going somewhere, Wench? Are the authorities nearby? I knew it was only a matter of time until the Ambassador got them on your trail. You will pay dearly for the ill treatment that you have shown me. You will get no mercy from me, or from the Ambassador."

She paid little attention to him and went on with her packing chores. When finished, she telephoned Rosalie.

"I need one more favor," she told her friend. "I need Amahd drugged and hypnotized. I'm flying out of Albuquerque around three, this afternoon. Will you do this for me, please?"

"I'll be there, honey. We'll wait until the last minute before putting him under. I'm sure the spell will hold until you're airborne, but he'll get very dangerous when he comes out."

Todd was there when she reached her condo and he peered nervously at Amahd. The Iranian seemed tame enough, but that didn't mean he would stay that way. As she motored swiftly toward the airport, Todd leaned across the seat toward Katie.

"We can't afford to have a scene at the airport gate. Can we keep him under control? Why is he so quiet and submissive?"

"He's drugged and hypnotized, Senator," she replied simply.

"You are a lady of many talents. I'm simply stunned."

"Please don't give me the credit, Senator. I have no such ability, but I have a talented friend.""I hope this friend can be trusted, honey. Until we reach our destination, we're in a very delicate position. It will be bad enough for us when we finally get there."

Amahd remained in a half-dazed state and stared straight ahead. As they drew closer to their destination, she made a suggestion to the senator.

"When we leave the car, take his arm as if he were an old friend. This way, you can control his movements. Anyone observing us will believe that we're a friendly traveling party."

"Good thinking, honey, I'll do it just that way. As I told you earlier, we are to use security gate two and I believe it's located on the near side of the terminal. The guard will be on your side of the car. When he approaches, ask for Milton."

In rapid fashion, Security took command of the car and drove it to a waiting jet that was parked on the tarmac.

"When you return, just ask for Milton and we'll bring your car to you," he told them politely.

Only the pilot was aboard the Lear jet, but he helped stow the luggage and in less than five minutes, they were airborne.

The Iranian was seated where he could be watched by either of them and he remained very passive. During this quiet time with only the low whine of the jet engine noise, she gave voice to her thoughts.

"It's very reassuring to have you with me, Todd. I fully understand the seriousness of this situation and having you to lean on may be more than I deserve."

"You deserve as much assistance as I can deliver. I fully intend to be by your side throughout this whole issue. I intend to be present even during your debriefing."

Met by agents at a private area of Miami airport, they were swiftly whisked away to the Agency stronghold. According to the CIA agents, their base was a combined structure that housed offices, living quarters, and a cafeteria.

They were swiftly escorted to the living quarters where they stowed their luggage and were then taken to the cafeteria, where they could refresh themselves from the effects of the long flight. They were allowed easy access to these accommodations, but other doors were equipped with the punch code type locks.

The agents seemed extremely wary of Amahd and his angry face, but asked no questions. The Iranian kept his mouth shut and this helped to hold their curiosity to a minimum. These men were not the agents that formulated the flight arrangements and they were without a need to know.

The pair had barely finished their refreshments when another agent appeared and introduced himself.

"I'm Agent Wilson," he said politely. "If you're rested from your trip, I'd like you to follow me."

He led them into a suite of offices and waved them into seats. Amahd was developing a look of increasing belligerence that threatened to explode. The senator noticed the Iranian's change in attitude and decided to act.

"Agent Wilson, I have a request for you to consider. For the benefit of all of us, I would like this man placed in a secured holding room. After he is secured, I'll gladly explain my reasons."

"We can accommodate your request, sir," he replied and pressed a button on his desk. Another agent appeared immediately and Wilson pointed to Amahd.

"Take this man to medium security and sit on him," he directed.

"Now, let's have some introductions," he smiled as the room cleared. "You already know who I am."

"My name is Todd Whatley," the senator offered. "This young lady is Katie Ryan and her parents are captives of the Iranian Government. The man that you have just taken away is an aide to the Iranian Ambassador. Most of the information that you have came from him. Please don't interpret my statement to mean that he is cooperating. He never has and I doubt if he ever will cooperate freely. Acting out of sheer desperation and impulse, Miss Ryan captured this Iranian and began questioning him."

Before the senator could continue, Wilson interrupted him and questioned her.

"Is this man your attorney? It sounds like you should have a good lawyer present."

Katie spoke with a fierce light burning from her eyes. "No, Agent Wilson, he is not my attorney. What I need is some action that might help to recover my parents from their Iranian prison. I believe that is the reason we came here. Do you want to help me or do you just want to jail me for an illegal act. Time is an important factor now. Either help me or get your superior down here."

"Take it easy, Miss. I'm still feeling my way through this thing. I had no warning about this diplomatic snarl. I'm not trying to incarcerate you. Believe that one fact and let's get to the bottom of this mess. We can move to a better location where I'll be able to tape a statement from you. We won't be too long, Mr. Whatley. Just make yourself comfortable in here."

"I don't think so, Mr. Wilson," replied the senator. "Where she goes, I go and that's only the first rule. I may think of other rules as we go along. Miss Ryan is very special to me."

Wilson rubbed at his chin thoughtfully.

"I see nothing wrong with that, at least not at the moment."

The entrance of another agent caused a delay in the plans of Wilson.

"The Florida Senator is here, sir. He insists on becoming involved in the interrogation."

"Escort him to the sound room, Jacob," Wilson said with resignation. "It looks like the whole world may want to set in on this debriefing."

When George entered the room, he went directly to Todd and greeted him in a manner of total familiarity.

"Senator, it's very good to see you after all this time. I'm glad you decided to accompany your source. Wilson, I can see by your face that you don't know this man. He was never one to trade on his name."

Wilson listened with great interest to the explanation of Todd's past involvement in Washington circles and began viewing the man in a new light. When the conversation ended about Todd's past credentials, Wilson sighed with relief. With the backing of these two powerful men, he might finally see this mission get off the ground.

"I want to deal with Miss Ryan's abduction, first. Let me completely debrief her and after we've sorted those details, we can work on the Iranian diplomat's entanglement."

With her memory restored, Katie had very little trouble narrating the sequence of events that stemmed from that stormy day off Fort Lauderdale. Tears filled her eyes as she recounted the despair they all felt on discovering that the badly damaged sailboat was drifting into the seagoing trade currents.

With sails almost totally gone, they desperately tried to turn away from the oceangoing current. Helpless after failing to maneuver, they spent hour after hour scouring the horizon for signs of other ships. Their eyes were glazed from searching for a sighting of land. Their hoarded rations of water and food were almost fully depleted when the Iranian vessel loomed from out of the distance.

With elated hopes, they eagerly boarded the foreign craft and then saw their hopes crushed as the Iranians unceremoniously scuttled their sailboat. After allowing the rescued party to view the sinking of their vessel, they were taken below deck and placed under guard.

The Americans were so exhausted from exposure and the lack of food and water that resistance was completely out of the question. In the coming days, they learned that these foreigners were totally without mercy. Katie and her party were fed little more food than was necessary to keep them alive and their mental treatment equaled that usually given to animals.

After reaching port at Bushehr, they were dragged into an army truck and transported to a desert camp between Ahvaz and Susa. One of the captives had traveled through this area during the Iranian war with Iraq and was quite familiar with the territory. During the few times when they were allowed to talk, this man tried to let the others know exactly where they were. Shortly before they reached the base camp they could still see the lights from the oil refinery burn-off stacks at Ahvaz. They saw these huge flames of light through the holes in the dirty, brown-colored canvas of their military vehicle.

This secluded camp had been converted into a training center. In this place, the captives saw others who had suffered similar fates. They were not allowed to fraternize with the other captives. Katie and her parents were even separated from the friends with whom they had shared this experience. The first part of their indoctrination highlighted the fact that each of the captives stood alone against the world. No one would be coming to assist them and after a short passage of time, no one would be concerned about their disappearance.

Wilson was very curious about her mental treatment and the specific charge that she made regarding brainwashing. He wanted full details and seemed disappointed that she had never heard the drug referred to by its name.

Wilson sighed, "It could be vitally important to know the altering agent that they used."

"I brought some of it with me," she told him quickly. "I took it from Amahd and that's how I regained my memory. I was saving some of the drug for Don."

After saying this, the face of Katie reddened with embarrassment. She had completely forgotten about Don Brim. In her desperate attempts to deal effectively with Amahd, she had lost sight of everything else.

Quickly, she began recounting the entrance of this man into the scheme that the Iranian had plotted. She explained to Todd that none of their actions had been detrimental to his interests and that no information was given to Amahd.

"You can do more explaining of the details at a later date, but I want to get that drug to the lab. We need to identify it and duplicate it," Wilson said swiftly.

He departed with the bottle and headed for a lab, leaving them with some time for discussion.

"Please don't apologize for your actions," Todd told her. "I can understand the extreme position you held in this situation. To my knowledge, there is absolutely nothing in existence for comparison.

George, have you heard of anything similar in your dealings with the Agency?"

"As far as I know, this is the first case of an American hostage being used against his homeland."

Wilson deposited the drug with the lab and set in motion a call to the CIA Director.

"Mr. Director, I have one of the former captives here. I presently have Senator Bushnell here and I also have a former senator in attendance," Wilson told the agency director. "We now have absolute proof of the captives and we know their location. We have a good handle on their defenses and we have a damned good motive. Now do we have a mission, sir?"

"Wilson, we've got a burr in the mix. There is damned little we can do until this mess is cleared up about the Air Chief and the Army Chief. I'd give an immediate green on staging a mission except for this lousy snag. Let me expound upon this matter."

He paused for only a few seconds, "If we used the Navy and some of its equipment, we could stage the job without Air Force help. We could use navy choppers to successfully recover the captives, but taking out the missile sites to weaken their defense force is entirely another matter. To hold down our losses and prevent the execution of the captives, their defenses must be rendered incapable of functioning. To do that important job we need missiles. To get the needed missiles, the President must sign off on the mission and he can hardly do that without a conference with the joint chiefs. No American servicemen can be used in this mission and all missiles will have to be accountable. Under those circumstances, do you see any chance of our mounting a mission?"

"I can see the wisdom of your decision, sir. I'll do my best to pacify the young lady that waits in my office," Wilson said dejectedly.

Returning to the sound room, he anticipated the frustration that would explode upon hearing his news. The woman and the former senator might be shrugged off, but George would be furious. His heart pumped patriotic American blood of the first order through his veins and an attack directed on any American, was an attack on George himself.

"The lab has begun work on the drug. I asked them to reserve some for your friend, Don. It would be wise to convince your friend to come here, Miss Ryan. We have experts on hand that can assist him in recovering his memory. You were lucky enough to get through the ordeal unscathed, but it is a very serious undertaking."

"I'll place the call whenever you are ready," she replied.

"You were gone long enough to have made a report to the director," George guessed. "I'm anxious to see action taken on this matter. How long do you think it will be before definite plans are under way?"

Wilson pondered the moment. If developments in the Capitol didn't flow faster than the usual rate of speed, the senator's term could be over before he saw any resolution of this matter. Wilson's problem consisted of what he could tell George, in the presence of the others.

"Sir, let me remind you that a matter of extreme secrecy is involved here and it may hold up all action for a considerable length of time."

"Wilson, I don't have my usual amount of patience. I see this as a situation where you're dealing with a responsible working senator and an extremely honorable ex-senator. I shouldn't have to mention how the fate of the parents of this young woman depends on her secrecy. Given this set of facts, why in the hell can't you tell us about this hang-up?"

"I'll try to do that, sir. I won't mention names or ranks and I won't cite the exact reason, but we are unable to get a sign-off from the President. The details are classified and the Director probably went out on a limb by telling me."

"I know full well that the President must sign off on any action involving the lives of servicemen or the use of certain specified weapons. I know that the agency can mount an operation that consists of its own manpower with nothing more than a verbal authorization. You need to do a better job of explaining than this, Wilson. The director will be damned mad if I call him."

"I'll try to explain one more time and then you can either keep threatening me, or call my boss. Unless we want to lose the captives, and risk taking a huge loss of our attacking force, their defenses must be eradicated. To effectively silence this defense we need missiles. If you are with me to this point you'll know that the President must authorize all missile use. You can understand that following news of a foreign missile strike, a demand for a missile audit would be raised. If the President authorizes a strike against a foreign country without consultation from those duly designated, he will be in serious trouble," Wilson concluded with a frown.

"I'll just have to sort out the wheat from the chaff. You are essentially telling me that without missiles, the mission is off. For some mysterious reason all the heads can't agree to the use of our missiles. I guess we really do have a problem, Wilson," George said sorrowfully.

Todd posed a question. "What if there is an alternate source for missiles?"

"Damn! I never even thought of that," admitted Wilson. "The Israelis owe us several favors."

"I'm not considering the weapons of another country," Todd said quietly. "How many units would you need for this operation? What if I could furnish the missiles?"

"We would need a minimum of ten, but you've totally lost me. What source of missiles can you have?"

"I manufacture them, Wilson. We've worked a lot of overtime to get them off our line and into the hands of the defense department. We'll have a dozen crated and ready to go in only a few days. I want the origin of these missiles kept secret. They are not yet foolproof, but it is the best missile on the horizon. They have shown better performance than the Tomahawk and the Patriot. These birds have a range of eighteen hundred miles with a payload of one ton."

Wilson emitted a low whistle. "Sounds like an interesting possibility. It'll take time to get checked out with their technology though."

Katie quickly included a thought. "When Don gets here, he can help check you out. He's a brain when it comes to electronics.

"I want to update the Director, right away. This new idea could turn things around."

"I have two calls to make," Todd told him. "Do you have another phone that I can use?"

The Director was ecstatic at the news. "Why didn't you tell me that the ex-senator was Todd Whatley? I knew he was into defense contracts and I heard that he had formed a union with another contractor to produce missiles. If he wants the source of these missiles kept secret, we'll accommodate him. The cost factor can be addressed later and we'll see that he is reimbursed. That old geezer knows this business real well. The Agency has used him in the past for many things that appeared unobtainable. He never failed to come through for us. I don't know him personally, but I know his history. A square shooter in every way, he's as tough as they come. Deal confidently with him, Wilson. You will be breaking no confidence to discuss anything with him. Start staging this mission and code-name it *Thorn Bud*."

"Consider it underway, sir. I'll keep you briefed until we have a rough scenario for your approval."

"I need time to prepare the President, so I must see your proposal as quickly as you can turn it."

Todd was at this moment talking to Bob Hartley.

"Bob, there are some new curves in our road of destiny. Since I haven't been fully briefed, I can't give you complete details and you don't even want to know them, but plans for our missiles have changed. Due to problems that include the CIA, I need twelve of our missiles crated and delivered to the airport. Have the driver ask for Milton, at security gate number two. The guard will take it from there and return the truck. We're giving up a lot of money for the Agency project and we may never see a dime of it back. I'll stand good for the whole amount, but I need your support."

"Unless you've broken our agreement, this was and still is a joint venture. If this project is worthy of your support, you can damn sure have mine," he said in an impassioned voice. "I can't possibly ship them in less than two days though. Is that soon enough?"

"That'll do beautifully, Bob. I want to tell you how thankful I am that Katie brought us together. Our future will get even brighter because of her doings," he said. "I'll brief you in full at our next meeting. Right now, I have another call to make and you know damn well that I'm calling the Secretary. He must be told immediately that he'll not be receiving those missiles."

For a period of several moments he considered what he could possibly tell the Secretary.

"Sir, you may not welcome this call and I hope that won't be the case. I'll drop all formality and talk in man-to-man fashion. Ward, I need more of a favor from you than you may be able to deliver. These missiles that we've been assembling won't be delivered. We intend to run three daily shifts of technicians to reproduce the contracted number. I'll not dwell on the reason for this plan change except to say that you don't want these units. When you receive these new units, I guarantee they will meet with your approval."

"The in-plant DOD inspectors found them in excellent condition, Senator. We weren't attempting to buy a pig-in-a-poke. I won't bandy words with you. If you have something to say, spit it out. If you've suffered a loss of some kind that affects the units, I have a right to know. The Speaker has spoken glowingly of your integrity and devotion to our country. Todd, our country needs these units and I expected more from you than you have given."

"If Brooks Everett told you all this, you should know there is a good reason for my action. It is possible that in a few days, you'll be sitting in a meeting of importance. If this happens, you may be the most informed man at the table. As things are, I'm not asking for the moon. What I need from you is simply a little time."

There was a long period of silence and Todd patiently waited.

"I will ride blindly in the direction that you've pointed me," he told Todd petulantly. "I solemnly promise that we will speak of this later. I hope we can share a laugh at that time. I had meetings set with the Joint Chiefs and looked forward to a formal missile testing date."

Returning to the sound room, Todd found Wilson and Katie deeply engaged in discussion. He listened for awhile before making a disclosure to the agent.

"I took the liberty of using your contact man at Albuquerque airport, Wilson. My truck driver will be told to ask for Milton when he arrives with the missiles. Within three days from today they will be crated and shipped to the airport. I suppose you will have them flown to an arms depot for arming."

"You catch on fast, Mr. Whatley. I'll make the final arrangements with Milton. Yes, the units will be taken to a certain place and loaded with an explosive. The final arming and computerized targeting will be done aboard ship. Will your man, Don, have the necessary expertise to detail this technically important phase?"

"He is a very competent young man. My partner seems to think he can do anything if it involves electronics," Todd replied.

CHAPTER FOURTEEN

Inside the Map room of the White House, the quiet hum of the air conditioner was the prevailing sound. It was a sweltering hot Washington day and tempers were on edge, but contained. In addition to the President, those present were the Secretary of Defense, the Secretary of State, the House Speaker, the Senate Majority Leader and Admiral Wentzel, the Naval Chief of Staff. They were waiting for the Director of the CIA, Thomas Burns, whose extended absence was causing a slow burn among some of those present. A gentle rap at the door suddenly drew their attention and a uniformed officer admitted the tardy director.

He smiled hopefully at those gathered and waiting, but received no returning looks of support.

"It was a bad commute," he said simply. "There seems to be a tremendous amount of road rage out there today."

"Are you about ready, Mr. Director?" the President suggested. "Personally, I'm not in a rush and I'm sure you aren't, but there are others who feel that time is an essential quality."

Burns carried his briefcase to a hastily arranged lectern and spoke politely.

"I extend my deepest apologies to all of you."

Without opening the briefcase, he began weaving the fabric of the captive situation into a careful pattern. Explaining that the practice of taking captives was becoming more frequent, he pounded home the fact that one known group had been confined for almost six years. In their best estimation the number of captives totaled sixteen, but two of them were now in American hands.

He carefully explained the plot of intrigue that caused the planned taking and confinement of these prisoners. Looks of disgust and anger emerged as he described the drugging and brainwashing. Having set the stage for further elaboration, he moved to the large world map and used a pointer.

"This is the target of a mission code named *Thorn Bud.* The captives are in a converted staging camp outside of Ahvaz. It was a base camp during their war with Iraq and is now used as a training ground for terrorists and infiltrators. Their defenses have been bolstered, but we have learned the extent of their fortifications. According to the latest satellite photos, there are less than sixty men stationed at the base and they appear to be equally dispersed at each end of the base. This is area A, to the left of the target area. Toward the right edge, you can see area B. The captives are being held between these points at a spot that we have designated as area C. We can stage and successfully perform a mission to rescue these captives, Sir. *Thorn Bud* will not fail," he said looking intently at the President.

"It is a serious and hazardous step to take, Mr. Director," the Chief Executive stated grimly. "Are you suggesting that we mount such a mission with American Servicemen?"

"No Sir, I had no such intent. We will gladly form a party from within the ranks of the Agency for this operation. We've searched our files and found twenty men that will handle this volunteer assignment. We will need the services of an aircraft carrier, four HUEYs loaded with ammo, and sufficient fuel for a return flight. We know American servicemen cannot be involved in this covert operation. The world will think this strike was carried out by a band of Mercenaries."

The Naval Chief raised his hand and voice.

"From your basic prelims, you cannot carry this raid to success without missile strikes. We have cruise missiles that could neutralize their defenses and cut your estimated losses."

"Excuse me, Chief, but we have considered that angle and dropped it. All of our missiles are serialized and must be accountable to an audit. If we use Tomahawks, the Presidential sign-off becomes a necessity and we know what that entails. I can assure you that missiles will indeed be used, but not the Tomahawks that belong to the Carrier. There will be no embarrassing points left for the President to cover up," the Director said with finality.

Most of the small group immediately identified the source of these missiles as Israel.

It was an ingenious plan and would certainly afford the President the chance to vow that the missiles had not come from the arsenals of their Carriers.

Only one man in attendance knew that the Israelis were not the source. He could only wonder how this had all come about and by whose risky strategy these unproven missiles had been selected as the weapon of choice. His thoughts were interrupted by the sound of the president's voice.

"As Secretary of Defense, you have a big role to play in this decision. The other man that holds a major responsibility is the Naval Chief. Without knowing any further procedural logistics, is this thing a go?"

Of the two, the Naval Chief spoke swiftly.

"It appears to be fully doable and in view of the fact that the target area is well within striking distance, I'll give it a green."

"It would be much easier for me to acquiesce to this, if I had sufficient confidence in these mysterious missiles. I'll reluctantly give the mission a go. And I'll simply pray that whoever chose these substitute missiles, knows what the hell he's doing," the Secretary stated resolutely.

The president turned to the Speaker and Senate leader. It might come to pass that he would vitally need the full support of the Congress.

"You have heard the basic reasons that raise a need for this drastic action. If in your best judgment you find this action acceptable to you and your constituents, I want your support. If you feel this action is not fully warranted, I want your views made known now. We are a team and we will act accordingly," he said with finality.

"There's not a voter in my district that would not burn with anger at this affront to all Americans," the Majority leader said angrily. "Godspeed with this mission and you can count on us to pray for its total success."

"Be assured that I'll fight to the death for the right to pursue this mission," the Speaker stated positively. "The time has come for us to take a strong stand in that area of the world. They must learn how passionately our country views freedom and life. To Americans, these assets are far from being cheap items."

"We'll close this meeting then and let our mission planning group huddle. Gentlemen, when the particulars have been worked out and you're ready for my sign-off, give me a call."

The room cleared, leaving only the President, Secretary Bonding, and the Speaker. They knew the peril involved in this mission.

Of the Joint Chiefs and their Chairman, only the Naval Chief had been asked to attend.

The President was taking full responsibility, but there was still much need to discuss the issue.

"No one really wants to speculate about this matter," the Speaker said gently. "It is a sad fact, but someone is a turncoat and a chance existed that the mission might be jeopardized if all members were present. Do you have any real feel for the full extent of this conspiracy, Mr. President?"

"Not at the moment," he replied gravely. "The FBI and the Agency are tracking every lead and as quietly as possible. We know that a few months ago information was passed to men later convicted in the conspiracy case. We know this information came from one of the highest levels in the system. During our search of these individuals' premises, we recovered copies of blueprint plans and specifications for our new missile system that had been stamped off by the DOD. The conspiracy members were given a hefty leg up in the race to compete with the more honest contractors. Admiral Wentzel was quickly absolved of any connection to the conspiracy, but that leaves the Chairman and General TreMayne hanging in the wind."

"Mr. President, neither of these men are lacking in supportive power. Several members of Congress think highly of both men and they'll probably be looking for scalps when word of this secret meeting leaks out," the Secretary spoke in solemn tones.

"Whatever support I can muster in the House will be at your command until this is resolved. I feel it's important for you to know that up front, sir," the Speaker cut in quickly.

"I thank you for your confidence and backing. This period of unknowing cannot possibly last much longer. The FBI team is deeply into the finances of both men and they are sure to find a money connection that will trap the guilty one. It is a sad day indeed when one so high falls so low," the President said.

* * *

Two days later, in the Florida complex, Admiral Wentzel, Agency Director Burns, and Agent Wilson were huddled at the map board. Their planning was almost complete and full details of the mission would soon be disclosed to the strike force. The Admiral was planning a trip to a Carrier to personally brief the Naval Commander on the upcoming raid and stay until mission completion. The fact that the *USS Houston* was presently in the Gulf was a bonus blessing. Any sudden flurry of incoming ships might have created suspicion.

"I believe we have a very workable plan," said Admiral Wentzel. "With only four men going into area C to secure the captives, you still have sixteen men mopping up areas A and B. If the missile strikes are accurate, the enemy based at A and B, should be pretty well neutralized."

"Wilson has personally volunteered to lead the four men into area C. I have complete confidence in his ability to secure the situation," Director Burns offered in assurance.

Admiral Wentzel spoke again. "If the Navy can be of further service, you have only to ask."

"It's good to know that the Navy is backing us. Even though you can't physically go in with us, I feel sure you will keep your shipboard eyes and ears on the mission," Wilson spoke hopefully.

"I will arrange for an AWAC unit to sweep the area. If enemy radar picks up your activity, the airwaves will be full of messaging. It matters little if their chatter is coded, as any sudden outbreak of radio transmission will be all the warning we need," the Admiral replied.

* * *

Todd moved to a chair near Katie and spoke softly.

"I called Don and told him things were moving so swiftly that you had no time to talk. I asked him to catch the next flight here and wait for the luggage carousel's white courtesy phone to ring. The feds will pick him up when he arrives. They will know his flight number and the arrival time. I told him that we will need his expertise for a new project that would be a go in a matter of hours and for him to pack lightly and travel fast."

"How did he take the news?"

"Like a pro is expected to react," Todd replied. "He said he would act immediately."

"Does Bob Hartley believe he can deliver the missiles on time?"

"He assured me they would be ready for shipping in two days. We have no way to know where they will be taken to be loaded with explosives. We will all connect on the Carrier *Houston*, but I don't know the routing details at the moment."

Senator Bushnell had been listening intently to their talk and he entered the conversation.

"I wish I were staying here with you two, but there is much I need to do. There will be hell to pay in Washington over this deal. We have always had and likely will continue to have more than our fair share of hawks and doves. If the President signs off on this action he'll need all the support he can get. After we say goodbye, I intend to head for DC."

"I'm going on that carrier, George. These are my missiles and I have faith in them. I refuse to sit and wait here like an expectant father. Katie and I will stay with the *Houston* and wait for the return of the crews. We want to be there when the prisoners are brought back. There are many details that must be worked out by Wilson and the rest of the feds, but they still have enough time," Todd said thoughtfully.

Senator Bushnell returned to Washington and Don soon arrived from Albuquerque. He was now involved in a deep discussion with Katie. Admiral Wentzel had flown to make connections with the *U.S.S. Houston*. Director Burns, Wilson, and the rest of the strike force huddled in the ready room. They pored over the maps and plotted courses for the future action.

Todd was on the phone with Hartley and when he cradled the phone his face was full of smiles.

"The missiles are on their way. The truck drivers reported to Hartley that the feds relieved them of their loads. He still refuses to ask questions about this mystery. Bob Hartley is an exceptional man and I'm proud to know him."

"You are both exceptional men and I realize how fortunate I've been to become involved with you."

Don didn't talk much as he was looking at Todd's blueprint and his mind was on his work.

Earlier he had discussed the guidance problem with Todd and believed it could be corrected with minor wiring changes. He looked up expectantly as Wilson entered the room.

"Hey, is anyone ready for a trip? I'm selling tickets for a flight to the Persian Gulf. You will land at Soha, Qatar and take a chopper ride to the *Houston*. My group will fly to an Island nation and board a cruiser there for a rendezvous with the *Houston*. Another ship will receive the missiles and they will be taken aboard the Carrier. This looks like some unnecessary movement on our part, but one never knows who is observing our actions and I don't want any apparent connection made with the three of you. Don, when we arrive at the Carrier there will be plenty of time for arming the missiles. You've assured me that you are experienced and capable. We'll leave within the hour, so I'll say goodbye and I'll see you aboard the Carrier."

The three remaining occupants searched each other's face for reactions.

"It's really coming together isn't it? I'm so impatient that my heart is jumping," Katie told them with excitement shining from her face.

"I'm happy for you, but I have no memory of what I've lost. Will someone be there for me? I'm sorry, Katie. You are so hot for this rescue and you know who is waiting," Don said.

"The feds think it best to not alter your memory at this time, Don. You have a vital role to play in the upcoming raid. There is simply too much at risk. Without these missiles being properly armed and guided, many of our people might be lost in the raid," Todd said patiently.

"I'm sorry sir; it was childish of me to whine. I guess I'm just a little envious of Katie. I've waited this long, a little longer won't hurt," he said with a grin.

The day was one of dazzling sunshine in the national capitol, but Army General Otis Brown was in a sour mood. He really didn't want to meet with General TreMayne, but he had no ready excuse and the General wanted to golf. His day started badly when his aide asked how the meeting turned out. He had tried his best to act nonchalant.

"If you are referring to the meeting with Senator Smith, it went very well."

"No sir, I was inquiring about the one with the Brass. If it requires a need to know only, I'll understand."

"It was rather sensitive, Scotty. I can fill you in on it later."

Now at the clubhouse, awaiting General TreMayne, and with his GI stomach making more gas than usual, he knew something was wrong.

Aides seem to have a better pipeline to the latest information than the President.

He must be cautious with TreMayne. He'd never liked him, but they were on the same team. He laid some plans and watched as he neared.

"Good morning Les, is this a nice day or what? I hope you brought money. I always win in the sunshine."

"Otis, you've been lucky enough to win a couple of rounds. Don't get your hopes high today though."

On the second hole, Otis decided the timing was right to quiz TreMayne in sly fashion.

"Les, I was expecting to see you at the meeting yesterday. Were you ill or otherwise tied up? It is not like you to miss a major meeting."

"I just couldn't make it. Stuff happens, you know. Who was there, Otis?

"Well if you were a regular GI or an Aide, you would refer to them as the Brass. You should have at least sent an aide to update you."

Les lit a cigar with a slight tremble in his fingers. Unless one was extremely observant, the nervous tic under his eye would never be noticed. Otis knew he had struck a nerve in Les and now he knew they both had been shut out of that meeting. Something big was definitely happening on mahogany row.

Otis spoke with importance.

"Well, Les, I can't fill you in on the meeting because it was not supposed to leave the room. Something big is coming down though and I expect it to become very visible within a matter of hours."

Their drives had landed in mid-fairway and within yards of each other. They walked in silence to their lies and selected the proper irons. Les suddenly strode to his ball without waiting for Otis to make his shot. Otis waited until Les reached his lie and then struck the ball with a clean hit to the green. As he looked to TreMayne's position he saw Les with his cell phone to his ear. Slowly he made his way to where Les stood.

"I'm sorry Otis, but I have to go. I have a small emergency that needs my presence. The next time we play, I'll give you two strokes to excuse my breaking off this way."

"Well, like you said...stuff happens. Take care of yourself and we'll have another day."

He slung his bag nonchalantly over his shoulder and headed for the clubhouse behind a rapidly departing Les TreMayne. It had not been a good day, but it seemed an even worse one for old Les. Otis wondered what could be happening that closed them out of that meeting. Thank God for good aides, he thought with a smile.

As General TreMayne motored to his expensive condominium he knew his military life was almost over. This chance golf meeting with Otis should give him time to set plans in motion. With enough lead-time, he would be out of the country and safe from prosecution. As an Air Force General, TreMayne would vanish without a trace. Under a previously established identity, he would be in England in a matter of hours. Another few hours and he would be in another country. He smiled as he thought of the Swiss bank accounts and if the others failed to win their freedom, he would not have to share his spoils. His attorney had been authorized to hold money for the trials and appeals of the other conspirators. The feds could not touch nor freeze those items because they were joint accounts, with the attorney as prime depositor. On the way to Dulles National Airport, he smiled thinking how nice it would to spend his last years in the comfort and splendor of his estate near the Alps.

* * *

Director Burns drummed his fingers absently as he listened to an agents report. He was impatient to reach a hot trail. This man was a treacherous traitor that had sold out his countrymen for money. His position in the armed forces gave him a reach into the very soft underbelly of this country and he must be found and rendered harmless.

"I find it very hard to believe that TreMayne has such a small bank account, Lewis. He has been paid well for services rendered to someone that wants our missile system squelched. What about General Otis Brown? We can get back to TreMayne later."

"General Brown squeaks when he walks...he is that clean. He has money in the bank, he has some real estate and he owns some stock in Electronics. This indicates nothing except that he spends money wisely, invests wisely and is hiding nothing. I checked his entire family out for finances and they are all okay from where I stand."

"Good job Lewis and keep up the good work. How would you like to take an assignment overseas?"

"It's a good time of the year for touring Europe. Exactly what part of the overseas area did you have in mind, sir? "

"The FBI says Switzerland. TreMayne sounds French, but his background shows no French connection. Still, big money goes to the

Swiss bank accounts and I'm sure that it took big money to turn the Air Force Chief of Staff. When you get to Heathrow contact me and we'll chart some plans. In fact, I want you to have a lady partner. Select one from the staff pool and you can act like a couple of sightseeing lovers."

"The lady may have some say about how we act, sir. It's a good idea though and I'll contact you from Heathrow."

* * *

The strike force of CIA agents, Director Burns, Admiral Wentzel, and Captain Gary, the commander of the *Houston,* assembled in a mid-sized room. Joining them within minutes were Agent Wilson, Don, and Todd. This would be the final pre-strike meeting between the participants. This session was for informational and instructional purposes. Meant to be an informal meeting, it was being held in the Officer's Mess. Refreshments were distributed and the chatter was less than expected. Admiral Wentzel took the floor and the hall grew quiet with anticipation.

"I'm sure that everyone here knows the seriousness of this mission and I won't bore you with repetitive words. I only want to inform you that the missiles were brought aboard last night and due to their unique design; the owner's technician will make final arming procedures. Mr. Brim will program their destination coordinates as plotted and verified by our Chief Navigational Officer. Our staging team will have the HUEYs ready and waiting. If any doubts or questions remain in your minds, raise them now."

After a short pause with no hands up for questions, he spoke again.

"Agent Wilson will give you a dry run through the timing, routing, and some of the probabilities of the mission. Our expectations are extremely high as weather and seaboard activity are favoring us."

"Thank you for the introduction and your very welcome backing, sir. We will make this a total nighttime mission. This means we travel by the clock. Our departure time from the *Houston* will come at exactly one hour before dark. The HUEYs will fly in an extremely tight cluster until we reach location X. This desert area has been scouted and is suitable for landing. We'll be flying as low to the ground as is deemed safe by the pilots. On arrival at X, we'll have a waiting period to allow the missiles to be launched from the *Houston*. When the missiles are fully launched, the *Houston's* radioman will transmit three words, 'Hello, Uncle Martin' and then we'll get underway. It's a five-minute flight at top speed from X to our final objective and then the cleanup operation can get underway. Forces will deploy to their A and B objectives, while I take three men and enter C area. I will go in shouting for the Ryan family to come to me and that Katie is looking for them. I hope they'll respond to this plea as they can help assemble all the captives with greater speed. If you have questions, ask them now. I have much gear to check and pack."

No one questioned Wilson and he quickly departed the hall with his men. Admiral Wentzel and Captain Gary drifted away, leaving only Todd and Don in the mess hall. Todd opened with a query.

"What do you expect from these missiles, Don? I have no experience with explosives."

"My training says the payload of this launch will pretty well erase the fortifications at the camps. I do not doubt the effectiveness of your missiles. I do think we were very fortunate that the *Houston's* launchers were adaptable. I only wish that I could have modified some of these as drones. It could have assured us of full saturation explosive effects. I'm certain you'll be extremely proud of your missiles in the future," Don said with a grin.

"It boggles the mind to review the things that have happened in the last few months. With you and Katie on my team and with Hartley backing every move we made, we have taken some great strides. The four of us should take a long week off and enjoy a quiet vacation when this thing is done."

"I sure hope that will be possible, but it seems wrong to make plans until the return of my memory."

"We are dealing with responsible people here. They have an ability to do things that once was considered only fantasy. Katie is living proof that your memory can be recalled. If your morals are as good as hers, there won't be any skeletons in your closet. Nothing that has happened due to the Iranian detainment can be held against you. Keep that in mind for the next few days," Todd said.

The strike force was at location X and it was quiet on the desert. In the distance and on both sides of the choppers, mountains seemed to reach toward the sky. A lonesome stretch of desert trailed between the medium sized peaks. A soft warm breeze wafted through the doorway of the Huey and as Wilson dangled his legs outside the chopper, he listened to low static from the radio. The starry night was without a moon, but it would be rising in less than ten minutes and it would be in a three-quarter phase. Though the mission had night vision equipment, the moonlight was preferable. Waiting for the strike was turning into an eternity. His stomach was growling and he took a pull from his canteen.

"Anybody got any high blood pressure medicine? I believe I can understand some of the tension that a late stages pregnant woman might feel," he told the others.

A volley of nervous laughs erupted following his attempt at humor. Wilson grinned in relief; none of them were scared. But they all realized the serious nature of their work. They were elated at this opportunity to free the hostages and haul them out to safety. He ordered a time check and each of them complied. Wilson was sure that the team leader in another chopper was following the same procedures. The other two choppers were to carry out the hostages and they were to simply follow the leaders.

Glancing again at the night sky, he saw the rim of the moon topping the horizon. He took a deep breath of desert air and swallowed hard. The weather was certainly favoring this mission. As a rule, the desert winds howled with fury and the air was filled with fine grains of sand. Silently he thanked the powers that be for the favors they were bestowing on the mission.

With an eruption of sound that shocked the nerve endings of the men in the chopper, the awaited words, "Hello, Uncle Martin" came from the radio and the chopper engines came to full vibrating life. One by one they rose to move into perfect formation and then began their flight across the desert floor. They flew extremely low to avoid radar detection until the last moment.

Two minutes from zero hour, the desert ahead of them exploded into rising fireballs and bursting mushrooms of black smoke. It seemed to be a concentrated mass of chain explosions, but the roar from the choppers muted the noise. The fires still burned from the strikes as the choppers descended into area C. In full battle gear, the strike teams streamed at double time into their assigned areas to begin a search and destroy mission. It had been decided beforehand they would take no prisoners. Anyone found in this foul hellhole deserved to die.

At area C, Wilson ran into the compound dormitory screaming for the Ryan's as his men deployed into defensive positions. Hearing sounds of muffled weeping down the hall, Wilson headed in that direction. In a calm voice he spoke loudly.

"I am looking for the Ryan family and I know you are here. If you can hear me please come out and I'll take you to Katie. She is very anxious to see you."

They came out then; all of them came from the doorways to meet Wilson and he spoke again.

"Mr. Ryan, I am sure you know all the hostages. Take a head count and quickly follow me to the helicopters? We need to buzz out of here and fast. Do not go back to your rooms for anything. We have no way to know if the enemy has sent reinforcements."

The Ryan team herded the people out of the building and onto the parade grounds. Wilson's squad accompanied them to the choppers and at this point, Wilson queried Mr. Ryan.

"Do we have everyone, sir?"

Mr. Ryan only gave an affirmative nod. He seemed in a daze.

"Sir, you'll be seeing your daughter before morning."

He turned to one of his men and designated him to stay with the hostages in that chopper, while he assigned another of his men to the remaining hostages.

"Take them to Red's chopper and fly back with them," he ordered.

With the hostage chore complete, he spoke softly into the communicator.

"Brownie, this is Red Dog leader. Are you securing there?"

"Yes, Red Dog. We just now mopped up and are moving to C."

"We're ready to leave, Brownie. We have a long way to travel and time is short."

The words were hardly spoken when Wilson saw them crossing the parade ground from both sites. Both teams were back and Brownie reported at once.

"Mission accomplished, sir. What is the status of the hostages?"

"They're loaded and ready to travel. I have one last chore to do," he said.

He knelt to the floor and lifted a blanketed figure to his feet. With a knife, he cut the hobble ropes and wrist ties. When he removed the blanket, a stream of curses erupted from the figure.

"I promise that you will pay dearly for this treatment. The guards will be here soon and I shall have you shot."

"Now just cool it, Rashooti. This is where you get off."

He escorted Amahd to the chopper doorway and roughly shoved him down to the parade ground before moving deeper into the crew compartment.

"Okay, Smitty, our work here is done. Take us home."

Airborne for several minutes and still miles from safety, the intercom blared.

"Smitty, I'm seeing ghosts or worse at two o'clock port side. Please confirm."

This urgent plea came from the chopper pilot on the starboard side of Smitty and got a confirming reply.

"I see two, maybe more. They're closing fast so take evasive action now. We'll spread out to keep from being like sitting ducks. Confirm all moves with the man on your right."

Wilson put on his headset quickly and pushed the mike button.

"Don't worry about radio silence now, guys. Each pilot must know what the hell he is doing and the direction to move for cover. Above all stay as close to the deck as you can."

The pilots immediately put everything on the air and the radio messages were clearly heard through the intercom system. With them spread out on the deck it was not going to be easy for the Iranian MIGS. Suddenly the booming of static introduced a new player as a nonchalant voice drawled out on the airwaves.

"Hello, Uncle Martin, this is your Aunt Martha here. It looks like we're gonna have a little show and tell on the desert tonight. Just stay cool, be dedicated young men and keep your nose pointed home. This is Aunt Martha, signing out."

Wilson knew this scene very well. AWACS had their eyes and ears open and these carrier jet jockeys were on the job in a matter of seconds. He moved to the doorway and partially opened it for a better view. The MIGS had closed dangerously close before one of them exploded in a flaming ball and cart wheeled across the desert floor. Three others pulled up sharply and nosed up into the night sky with afterburners blazing. Their wing lights quickly disappeared.

"We'll trail you on home now, Uncle Martin. It looks like this party is over. If you don't need us again, have a good night."

The fact that this jet pilot seemed so calm and at ease was nothing short of amazing. One might believe this to be a routine thing with this young man. Wilson silently thanked the Navy for its protection as the strike force was cheering boisterously.

Touchdown on the deck of the *Houston* was a glorious moment for all concerned.

The strike force went immediately to the debriefing room. Director Burns; Admiral Wentzel; and Captain Gary gathered to greet them. Very soon, Todd was escorted to the room by the Director's order. Due to the role he played in the recovery, it was the least they could do. The Admiral spoke first.

"First, I want to welcome this team home. I am expressing my warmest congratulations. I will now turn the stage over to Agent Wilson."

"Before the debriefing begins, Admiral, I want to extend my thanks and those of the strike crew to the Navy for watching over us in our moments of need. If the pilot of that jet were a woman, I would marry her tomorrow. We were dead meat out on the desert without his coverage. As you know, I was into the C area and I have no idea what took place in A and B. Those unit leaders are the ones to be debriefed. In C area, with help from the Ryan pair, we herded all the hostages out to the choppers."

During questioning of the unit leaders it was learned that the only injury suffered during the mission was a leg stab wound from an upturned piece of reinforcing bar and there were no Iranian survivors left at the site.

Todd stood for a question. All eyes were on him.

"I have a need to know. Were our missiles on target? Were they effective as is, or do I need to make adjustments?"

One unit leader answered promptly. "Senator, if I might be allowed to answer that question in one sentence. Don't change anything, just make more of them."

Many tears were shed, but they were tears of joy on being liberated. The Ryan family was reunited and reliving memories. The Iranians had done mind altering only on the ones sent out on missions.

Don was unclaimed by any of those in the group of hostages. He would be returned to Florida and the people from CIA would help him regain his memory. At this stage he was still very depressed and a non-person.

Later, Wilson, the Senator, and Katie were together in the mess area when she broke down. She was crying softly and Todd was frantically trying to console her. The agent looked on in apparent embarrassment.

"Katie, I have told you many times that I am no help to you if I don't know the problem," Todd said sadly.

She began weeping again, before replying.

"All you have done for me is priceless. What I have done for you has put you in criminal jeopardy along with me. I am a kidnapper and you are an accomplice."

"I think I better get some input into this conversation," Wilson said hurriedly. "Neither of you are guilty of anything, nor do you have to explain the disappearance of Rashooti. He is no longer a threat to anyone."

Noting the look of shock on Todd's face, Wilson hastened to explain.

"No, Senator, we did not execute him. However, his people may decide to do that job. Once they reach the ruined camp and find that Amahd is the only living survivor, what do you think they will do to him? I believe we can all agree they won't be handing him a medal."

* * *

A young man and woman walked down the street holding hands and laughing. It was a beautiful day and their breakfast had been fabulous. They were in a small sized town almost in the shadow of the Alps. Renting an automobile in Geneva and by leaving early, they arrived in time for their midmorning meal.

They walked along for several blocks in no apparent hurry. Sightseeing takes many forms for different folks. Passing into an area of setback estates that screamed for privacy, the woman pointed toward one in particular. Taking a camera from around his neck, he trespassed toward the building that she had indicated. Hurriedly, he snapped a few pictures before retreating to the safety of the street.

Laughing in a manner that indicated total bliss, she led him hurriedly to a large tree and threw her arms about him, as most young lovers often do. He gave her a quick kiss in open view. As they left, they were observed from the veranda of the estate.

Two blocks later toward town and nearer to their car, he spoke to the woman.

"Well, Kathy, I believe we have what we need. Next, we go to the bank."

Entering a small branch of a well-known Swiss Bank, they went immediately to the manager's station.

"Sir, may we speak to you for a moment please? We need some information."

The man looked at the couple haughtily and immediately recognized them as visitors from America. *Tourist are nothing but trouble*, he thought silently.

"Certainly, sir, how may I help you?"

"A nice elderly man dropped his wallet outside his home and near the street. We could not get his attention before he disappeared into the house. We are sure he dropped it at his mailbox, but there is no name on the box."

He described the location of the house and the eyes of the banker widened.

"Yes, of course I know him. He is often here in season. I'll be happy to see that he gets it."

Lewis answered hastily, "I don't think so. It may be valuable enough for a reward. That would help in paying our expenses. We will take it to him or send him a note if you'll tell us his name. Otherwise we will wait outside his home until he comes out."

"I don't believe that would be a wise thing to do, sir. Mr. Jean-Pierre is a powerful man. He has influence with the authorities. He might have you hauled away if you loiter next to his home."

"Thank you for your advice sir, but we must take that risk. It *is* a heavy wallet," said Lewis.

They left the bank and went to a phone.

"This is Lewis, sir. We found our man less than fifty miles from Geneva. According to airline information, a Mr. Jean-Pierre left Heathrow several days ago. He arrived in Geneva and according to our sources, paid a driver to bring him to this resort area. He has a tremendous home here. The local banker swears that he pulls much weight with the local fuzz. Without a doubt, he is burrowed in here like a mole. If you think we should, we'll stay here and keep an eye out until you send someone big enough to flush his bank account and put the irons on him. Thank you, sir, and a good day to you also."

Three days later Jean-Pierre was doing some small item shopping in town. Quickly two men appeared with one on either side of him and blocked his path.

"Mr. Jean-Pierre, will you please come with us? We have business to discuss with you."

"I don't think we have any business to discuss," Jean-Pierre replied.

"Then I will be plainer with my language," the man retorted. "Come with me *now,* General, or you will be handcuffed and dragged away."

The face of TreMayne blanched and then turned a deep red color. It could not be happening this way. It was never meant to end this way. How could they have trailed him so swiftly?

"You could be making a tragic mistake. The authorities here know me and trust me. I might have them lock you up, until I can go someplace else."

"General, we visited the locals before we came to you. I offered them an opportunity to be in on the arrest. They are ashamed of being taken in by you and told us to handle it alone. We have a date with a military tribunal, or worse, so let's get on the road."

* * *

Before leaving the Florida CIA Complex, the former hostages put their signature on a document. This legal paper swore total secrecy about the rescue mission for five years. State Department felt that the less said about the matter, the fewer repercussions would follow the incident. It was the official belief that the Iranians could not make a formal protest without facing full international disclosure of their shameful activities.

Katie begged some time away from the others. She had a very happy phone call to make and she found Justin at his office desk.

"Talk to me, Justin. Tell me how much you'd like to see me and multiply that amount by one hundred. That's about how strong my wish is to see you."

"Where are you? Can I come to you? I'm having a fit to see you."

"Within two days, I'll be home. I'm in Florida at the moment and things are working out. I'll be catching a plane soon and if it seems slow, I'll get out and run home. I have no schedule to follow, so you need not make plans. I'll call you when I arrive."

She was awash with emotion. Her future mate was waiting and seemed as eager as she felt.

No longer must she doubt her future. All of her hopes and dreams would begin to come true very soon in Albuquerque.

With a happy face, she walked swiftly to the cafeteria and joined the others. They were discussing the plight of the former captives and she posed a question to Todd.

"What will happen to these people now? How can they pick up the pieces of their lives?"

"They'll melt back into society with the help of a Federal Assistance program. The exception is your family. They came out of this mess better than the others. Their home was paid for and the utilities and taxes were being deducted from their bank account. Once they learned that you were alive and responsible for their freedom, their mental state has improved immensely. They seem as tough and resilient as you have proved to be."

Todd was very vocal about the future.

As he gathered with the entire Ryan family in the Florida complex, he paced the floor and talked to them earnestly.

"We'll create something in the Albuquerque area that will hold your interest. You can live where you choose, but Katie is a part of my life now and I'll do whatever is needed to keep her. We have more need for close association now than even before. We have missiles to build and we need to diversify. It'll take the minds of Katie and Don, along with Hartley's help, if we want to keep our name in the National spotlight."

"My parents and I owe you more than we can ever repay, Todd.

"You owe me nothing, Honey. It is so rewarding for me to see this thing come together."

Quickly he added words that caught the attention of everyone.

"Katie has a fabulous young man to introduce to us and I've made big plans for them. When we get back to Albuquerque, I intend to cater the finest party you can imagine. Not a pompous affair, but one with excellent food, top entertainment, and good relaxing conversation. We'll have it in a park area with lots of shade and space. Don will likely be back by then and we can hear his story. If it's as full of twists and wild adventure as Katie's amazing episode, we may decide to go joint venture and write a book about it."

The End

ABOUT THE AUTHOR

Born in Garvin County, Oklahoma, Bob spent the first years of his life in a farm/ranch environment. After marriage to an Oklahoma girl, he relocated to the area of California that became known as Silicon Valley. After a stint at San Jose City College, he became a Journeyman Electrician and later gained his Electrical Contracting license. In the midst of raising a family and plying his trade, he felt something was missing. Having been an avid reader since grade school, he began to wonder if he might be able to become an author and relate some of his favorite experiences. He now leaves it up to the readers to decide if he has reached a decent level of writing. Whatever their decision might be, Bob feels that his efforts have given him a nice reward and a sense of satisfaction.

www.ingramcontent.com/pod-product-compliance
Lightning Source LLC
Chambersburg PA
CBHW072224170626
46813CB00003B/1079

* 9 7 8 0 6 1 5 5 0 1 0 2 4 *